国内独家授权，全球热销上亿册

双语 精华版

心灵鸡汤

[女性系列]

U0133164

挥洒四季的芬芳

许炳坤 主译

Sprinkling Fragrance of Four Seasons

Jack Canfield & Mark Victor Hansen 等 著

Chicken Soup for the Soul

安徽科学技术出版社
Health Communications, Inc.

图书在版编目(CIP)数据

心灵鸡汤:双语精华版.挥洒四季的芬芳/(美)坎费尔德(Canfield, J.)等著;许炳坤主译. —合肥:安徽科学技术出版社,2007.9
ISBN 978-7-5337-3881-5

Ⅰ.心… Ⅱ.①坎…②许… Ⅲ.①英语-汉语-对照读物②故事-作品集-美国-现代 Ⅳ.H319.4:I

中国版本图书馆 CIP 数据核字(2007)第 129497 号

心灵鸡汤:双语精华版.挥洒四季的芬芳
(美)坎费尔德(Canfield, J.)等著　许炳坤主译

出 版 人:朱智润
责任编辑:付　莉
封面设计:王国亮
出版发行:安徽科学技术出版社(合肥市政务文化新区圣泉路 1118 号
　　　　　出版传媒广场,邮编:230071)
电　　话:(0551)3533330
网　　址:www. ahstp. com. cn
E－mail: yougoubu@sina. com
经　　销:新华书店
排　　版:安徽事达科技贸易有限公司
印　　刷:合肥晓星印务有限责任公司
开　　本:889×1100　1/24
印　　张:10
字　　数:202 千
版　　次:2007 年 9 月第 1 版　2007 年 9 月第 1 次印刷
印　　数:10 000
定　　价:25.00 元

作为原生于美国的大众心理自助与人生励志类的闪亮品牌,《心灵鸡汤》语言地道新颖,优美流畅,极富时代感。书中一个个叩人心扉的故事,充分挖掘平凡小事所蕴藏的精神力量和人性之美,真率倾诉对生命的全新体验和深层感悟,字里行间洋溢着爱心、感恩、信念、鼓励和希望。因其内涵哲思深邃,豁朗释然,央视"百家讲坛"曾引用其作为解读援例。

文本适读性与亲和力、故事的吸引力和感召力、内涵的人文性和震撼力,煲出了鲜香润泽的《心灵鸡汤》——发行40多个国家和地区,总销量达一亿多册的全球超级畅销书!

安徽科学技术出版社独家引进的该系列英文版,深得广大读者的推崇与青睐,频登各大书店及"开卷市场零售监测系统"的畅销书排行榜,多次荣获全国出版发行业的各类奖项。

就学英语而言,本系列读物的功效已获广大读者乃至英语教学界的充分肯定。由于书中文章的信度和效度完全符合大规模标准化考试对考题的质量要求,全国大学英语四级考试、全国成人高考的阅读理解真题曾采用其中的文章。大学英语通用教材曾采用其中的文章作为精读课文。

为了让更多读者受惠于这一品牌,我社又获国内独家授权,隆重推出双语精华版《心灵鸡汤》系列:英汉美文并蓄、双语同一视面对照——广大读者既能在轻松阅读中提高英语水平,又能从中感悟人生的真谛,激发你搏击风雨、奋发向上的生命激情!

CONTENTS

目 录

目录

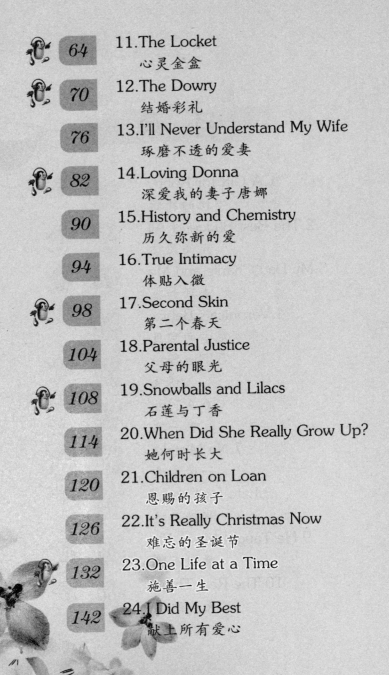

A Gift for Robby
罗比的礼物

Little Robby,our neighbor's nephew,carefully spooned some of his water ration into a saucer and started for the door.How I hated this water rationing.We were forced to bathe without soap in the deep little pond we shared with Jessie,our cow.She was all we had now.Wells were dry,crops transformed to dust and blew away with our dreams,during the worst drought our small farming community had ever seen.

I held the screen open for Robby and watched,smiling,as he slowly sat on the steps.Dozens of bees circled his tousled brown curls in an angel's halo.He imitated their buzzing,which brought them to the saucer to sip the precious liquid.

His aunt's words echoed in my ears:

邻家侄子小罗比小心翼翼地用汤匙往碟子里舀了点定量配给他的水,然后动身朝大门走去。这样的定量配给供水,我真是厌恶透顶。连洗澡我们都只能和奶牛杰茜挤在一个小水塘里,肥皂当然没有,而这奶牛也只是我们仅有的了。水井干涸、庄稼绝收、地里尘土飞扬,收获的梦想也随之灰飞烟灭,我们农场区正经历前所未有的最严重的旱灾。

替罗比撩开了门帘,我笑着看他在台阶上慢慢坐下。一群蜜蜂绕着他的蓬头卷发,好像天使的光环。罗比也模仿它们嗡嗡作响,引得蜜蜂也飞到碟子里来享用这点宝贵的水。

此时,我耳边又回响起他大姨的一番话:

"I don't know what I was thinking when I took him in.Doctors say he wasn't hurt in the crash that killed my sister,but he can't talk.Oh,he makes noises all right,but they aren't human.He's in a world all his own, that boy,not like my children at all."

Why couldn't she see the wonderful gifts this four-year-old boy possessed?My heart ached for Robby.He had become the dearest part of our world,eagerly tending the garden with me and riding the tractor or pitching hay with my husband,Tom.He was blessed with a loving nature and a deep admiration for all living things,and I knew he could talk to animals.

We rejoiced in discoveries he joyfully shared with us.His inquisitive and often impish brown eyes mirrored an understanding of everything verbal.I longed to adopt him.His aunt had hinted often enough.We even called ourselves Mom and Dad to Robby,and before the drought had discussed adoption.But times were so bleak now that I couldn't approach the subject with Tom.The job he was forced to take in town to buy feed for Jessie and bare necessities for us had exacted its toll on his spirit.

Robby's aunt eagerly agreed to our request that he live with us for the summer.All his days were spent in our company anyway.I brushed away a tear,remembering how tiny and helpless he looked when she hastily put his hand in mine and gave me a rumpled brown paper bag.It contained two faded T-shirts we had bought him last year at the county fair and a hand-me-down pair of shorts.This and the clothes he wore were his only belongings,with the exception of one prized possession.

On a silken cord around his neck dangled a handcarved whistle. Tom had made it for him in case he was ever lost or in danger.After all, he could not call out for help.He knew perfectly well that the whistle was not a toy.It was for emergencies only,and to blow on it would bring us both running.I had told him the story of the boy who cried wolf,and I

"真不知当初收留他是怎么想的。我妹妹死于一场车祸,而医生说罗比没事,只是不会说话。哦,他要闹起来倒是挺好,不过,那可不是说话。和我的孩子们一点也不像,他是活在自己的世界里。"

为什么她看不出来这个4岁男孩拥有的天赋呢？我真为罗比心痛。后来他成了我们生活里最珍贵的一部分。有时他急着和我一起照料花园;有时和我丈夫汤姆一起开拖拉机;有时又一起堆干草。他天性仁慈,热爱自然万物,因此我觉得他肯定能通各种动物的语言。

他只要有了新发现,总是开心地和我们一起分享,我们也替他高兴。他那双褐色的眼睛,好奇而又顽皮,透出他对所有言语的理解。我曾盼着能收养罗比,他大姨也经常暗示此意。我们甚至称自己是他的爸妈,旱灾前也都谈过了收养的事情。然而现在日子如此凄凉,我也没法和汤姆再提此事。为了能给杰茜买些饲料,给我们买最低生活必需品,汤姆被迫在城里找了份工作,这已经让他精神不堪重负了。

当提出让罗比夏天和我们一起过,罗比大姨立即就同意了。毕竟,他在这里的所有日子都是和我们相伴度过的。我拭去眼泪,想起那天她匆忙把罗比交到我手上,他是那么的瘦小而无助。随同还递给我一个皱巴巴的棕色纸袋,里面装着两件褪色的T恤,那是去年我们在县里集市上给他挑的,还有一条半新的短裤,这些衣服和他身上穿的,是他的所有了。不过他还有一样宝贝。

他脖子上有一根丝绳,上面挂着一个手工雕刻的口哨。那是以前怕他走丢或有危险,汤姆做给他的,毕竟他没法开口说话求助别人。罗比很清楚这个口哨不是个玩具,只能紧急时才用,一旦吹响,我们都会跑去找他。我曾讲"狼来了"的故事给他听,看得出他明白

knew he understood me.

I sighed as I dried and put away the last supper dish.Tom came into the kitchen and picked up the dishpan.Every ounce of recycled water was saved for a tiny vegetable garden Robby had planted beside the porch.He was so proud of it,we tried desperately to save it.But without rain soon,it too would be lost.Tom put the pan on the counter and turned to me.

"You know,honey," he started,"I've been thinking a lot about Robby lately."

My heart began to pound in anticipation,but before he could continue,a shrill blast from the yard made us jump.My God! It's Robby's whistle! By the time we reached the door,the whistle was blowing at a feverish pace.Visions of a rattlesnake filled my head as we raced into the yard.When we reached him,Robby was pointing frantically skyward, and we couldn't pry the whistle from his grip.

Looking up,we saw the most magnificent sight.Rain clouds—gigantic rain clouds with black,ominous bottoms!

"Robby! Help me,quickly! We need all the pots and pans from the kitchen! "

The whistle dropped from his lips and he raced with me to the house.Tom ran for the barn to drag out an old washtub.When all the containers were placed in the yard,Robby ran back to the house.He emerged with three wooden spoons from my kitchen drawer and handed one to each of us.He picked up my big stock pot and sat down cross-legged.Turning it over,he began to beat a rhythm with his spoon.Tom and I each reached for a pot and joined in.

"Rain for Robby! Rain for Robby! " I chanted with each beat.

A drop of water splashed on my pot and then another.Soon the yard was enveloped in soaking,glorious rain.We all stood with faces held upward to feel the absolute luxury of it.Tom picked up Robby and

双语精华版·心灵鸡汤·

我的意思。

我边叹气，边擦干放好最后一个餐盘。这时，汤姆走进厨房，端起了洗碗盆。因为罗比在门廊边上弄了个小小的菜园，所以每一滴反复利用后的水都留下来浇灌。我们也竭尽全力要保住他那引以为荣的园子，可要再不下雨，这园子很快就会没了。汤姆把洗碗盆放在厨房餐台上，转向了我。

"亲爱的，"他说道，"我最近一直在考虑罗比的事情。"

我的心里不自觉地开始怦怦直跳，可汤姆还没来得及继续说下去，院子里传来了一声尖叫，我们都吃惊地跳了起来。天哪！罗比的哨子！我们跑到大门时，哨声已经非常急促。脑子想着罗比可能碰到响尾蛇了，我们急奔至院子里，来到罗比身边时，发现他发疯一样指向天空，嘴里牢牢含着口哨，而我们竟然无法撬开。

我们一抬头，看到了最为期待的一幕：乌云密布，大雨即将来临。

"罗比，快来帮我！我们把厨房所有的盆罐都拿出来！"

罗比终于松开了口哨，和我一起飞奔回屋。汤姆也赶紧跑到谷仓拖出了好久没用的洗衣盆。所有容器在院子里摆好后，罗比跑回房子。再回来时，手里多了3把厨房抽屉里的大木勺子，他递给我们一人一把。他拿起我的汤锅，翻转过来，盘腿坐下，开始用汤匙敲打节拍。见状我和汤姆也都各找一口汤锅加入进来。

"雨是为罗比下的！雨是为罗比下的！"我边敲边唱。

一滴雨水溅在我的锅上，接着，又一滴急速落下。很快院子就笼罩在瓢泼大雨中了。我们都抬头站着，尽情享受着久违而近乎奢侈的甘霖。汤姆抱起罗比绕着汤锅，纵情欢呼。开始还觉得声音比较温

danced about the pots,shouting and whooping.That's when I heard it—softly at first—then louder and louder:the most marvelous,boisterous,giggling laughter.Tom swung about to show me Robby's face.With head tilted back,he was laughing right out loud! I hugged them both,tears of joy mixing with the rain.Robby released his grip from Tom and clutched my neck.

Stretching out one tiny cupped hand to catch the downpour,he giggled again."Wain…Mom," he whispered.

Toni Fulco

和,随后越来越大,直至最后令人惊讶的哈哈大笑。汤姆旋转着,让我看罗比的脸蛋。他头朝后仰,纵情欢笑。我紧紧抱着他们俩,雨水夹着欢喜的泪水。罗比松开了汤姆,上来搂紧了我的脖子。

他伸出一只小手,窝着想要去接这倾盆大雨,又咯咯地笑起来。"雨……妈妈,"罗比轻声细语。

托尼·富尔科

"That's far enough for this year."

Reprinted by permission of Andrew Toos.

女性系列／挥洒四季的芬芳

The Best Badge of All

When I became a Girl Scout,my mother told me this story about her scout troop and what happened to them a long time ago,during World War Ⅱ:

On a chilly Saturday morning in December,the eleven-year-old girls in our troop gathered excitedly at the bus stop,where we met our leader, Mrs.Taylor.We carried large paper sacks filled with skillets,mixing bowls and assorted groceries.On this long-awaited day,the girls of Troop 11 were going to earn our cooking badges.

"Nothing tastes as good as the first meal you cook yourself,especially on an open fire," Mrs.Taylor smiled.

It would take three bus transfers to get us all the way out to the wilderness.As we boarded the first,we clutched our groceries as if they were bags of jewels.Several mothers had generously contributed precious ration stamps so we could buy the ingredients for a real breakfast:pancakes with actual butter,bacon,and even some brown sugar for homemade syrup! We scouts would earn our badges in spite of hardship,in spite of the war.In our minds,we were not only learning to cook in the wilderness;we were doing our parts to keep life going apace on the home front.

We finally arrived at Papango Park,a beautiful desert refuge filled with paloverde trees,smoky mesquite bushes and massive red rock formations.As we started hiking up the dirt road into the park,a U.S.Army truck filled with German prisoners of war passed us,heading into the park.

至高荣誉

在我加入女童子军时，母亲给我讲了下面的这个故事，那是关于她那时的童子军以及很久以前二战时的经历：

12月里的一个周六早上，天气很冷，不过我们这群才11岁大的童子军女孩子却来到公交车站，整队集合，心情激动，并见到了我们的头儿——泰勒夫人。我们都带来了大大的纸袋，装满了煎锅和面碗，还有各类烹饪原料。经过许久的期盼，今天我们第11小队的女孩们就要去赢取烹饪技能徽章了。

"什么美味都比不上你们自己煮的第一顿饭香，尤其是在野外煮出来的。"泰勒夫人笑道。

要换乘3次公交车才能最后到达野外。上第一辆时，我们牢牢抓着大纸袋，好像里面装有什么珠宝似的。有好几家孩子妈妈非常舍得，拿出了宝贵的定量配给券，我们这才得以购买一顿真正的早餐配料：涂着黄油的薄煎饼、熏肉，甚至还有一些用来自制糖水的红糖！不管日子多么艰辛，战争多么可怕，我们童子军一定要赢得我们的徽章。我们不但要学会在野外烧菜做饭，还要在后方尽自己的本分让生活继续下去，我们暗暗鼓劲。

终于来到了帕攀沟公园，这里是一处美丽的沙漠绿紫荆树、茂密的豆科灌木丛和大量的红色岩层。正当我泥路徒步进入公园时，一辆装满了德国战犯的美国陆′身边驶过，径直开进公园。

"There go those Germans!" one of the girls said,contemptuously."I hate them! "

"Why did they have to start the war?" another complained. "My dad's been gone for so long."

We all had fathers,brothers or uncles fighting in Europe.

Determinedly,we hiked to our campsite,and soon the bacon was sizzling in the skillets while the pancakes turned golden brown around the edges.

The meal was a success.Mrs.Taylor's prediction about our gastronomic delight was proved correct.

After the meal,one of the girls started a scouting song as we cleaned up our cooking site.One by one,we all joined in.Our leader started another song,and we continued wholeheartedly.

Then,unexpectedly,we heard male voices.A beautiful tune sung in deep,strong tones filled the December air and drifted down to us.

We looked up to see the cavernous natural shell in the red sediment boulders,called"Hole in the Rock", filled with the German prisoners and their guards.

As they finished their song,we began another.They reciprocated with another haunting melody.We couldn't understand a word they were singing,but to our delight,we continued exchanging songs throughout the clear desert morning.

Finally one of the girls began to sing *Silent Night*,and we all added our voices to the Christmas carol.A few moments of silence followed,and then…the familiar melody flowed back to us.

"How can they know our Christmas carols?" One of the girls asked our leader.They were our country's enemies!

We continued to listen in awe.For an odd,unforgettable moment,the men in the cave became somebody's fathers and brothers,just as they understood us to be beloved daughters and sisters.

"是德国佬！"一个女孩轻蔑地说道，"我恨死他们了！"

"为什么他们要挑起战争？"另一个女孩抱怨道，"我爸爸打仗已经去了很久了。"

的确，我们都有爸爸、哥哥或是叔叔们在欧洲打仗。

坚定步伐，我们来到了营地。不一会儿，煎锅里熏肉就开始嗞嗞作响，煎饼周边也慢慢烤得焦黄。

野炊非常成功。泰勒夫人先前提到的美食乐趣确实很有道理。

早餐过后，我们便开始清理野炊营地，这时有一个女孩开始唱起了童子军歌谣。一个接一个，不一会儿我们都跟着唱了起来。我们的头儿又起了另一首歌，大家也热情高涨地跟着唱起来。

突然，我们意外地听到了有男子的歌声。优美的旋律伴着浑厚、低沉的音调弥漫在这12月的天空，很快就飘向我们。

我们抬头望去，只见一个叫"岩洞"的红色沉积大石头，下面天然生成一个扇贝状空间，里面挤满了德国战犯和看守卫兵。

他们的歌声才落，我们又起了一首。他们接着又送上了一段难忘的旋律。尽管他们唱的我们一个字也听不懂，我们居然开心地和他们继续对唱，在这晴朗的沙漠绿洲上持续了一上午。

最后，一个女孩唱起了《平安夜》，大家紧跟着就都唱起了这首圣诞颂歌。这次唱完后却是一阵寂静，随后这熟悉的旋律又飘了回来。

"为什么他们也知道我们的圣诞颂歌？"一个小女孩问我们的头儿。他们可是我们国家的敌人啊！

我们怀着敬畏之情，继续在那静静地听着。那一刻，感觉如此奇怪，却又难以忘怀，洞里面的人仿佛成了我们某人的父亲或兄长，他们也把我们当成心爱的女儿或是小妹妹一样。

In the years that followed,others probably looked at our new badges as proof that we could cook over a fire.But to us,they were reminders of the need for peace,and a very strange transformation that happened one Christmastime.

Gerry Niskern

在后来的岁月里,别人都认为我们的新徽章是证明我们学会了在野外做饭,而对我们来说,那是提醒我们对和平的渴求,还有在那年圣诞我们心里奇怪的转变和升华。

格里·尼斯肯

"You are fat, jolly and love children."

Reprinted by permission of Randy Bisson.

My Dad, Charlie and Me

My father's long and successful career began in the days of vaudeville. The famous ventriloquist, Edgar Bergen and his equally famous wooden sidekick, Charlie McCarthy, delighted theater and later, radio and television audiences for decades. So when I was born, it was only natural that I was known in the press not as Candice Bergen, but as "Charlie's sister". As a little girl, I sometimes performed with Daddy and Charlie. I recited my well-learned lines with considerable poise and polish—a daughter determined to make good.

Many years later, in the summer of 1978, my father called a press conference at the Brown Derby in Beverly Hills to announce his retirement, half-wondering whether anyone would show up. He was surprised when the press conference, packed, was carried on the evening news.

His final appearance, he announced, would be a three-week engagement at Caesar's Palace in Las Vegas on a bill with Andy Williams. This was a serious risk for a man who, not six months before, had been hospitalized in coronary intensive care. But as soon as the offer had been made, he was hellbent on accepting it, determined, one last time, to "play the Palace on the top of the bill": Edgar Bergen and Charlie McCarthy just like way back when. Here was an opportunity to go out in style.

My mother went with him to Las Vegas, and on opening night my brother Kris and I were there to surprise him. We were sitting out front as the lights dimmed and the music started up, hoping he would make it smoothly through the routines, terrified that he might not.

The three of us barely breathed as the orchestra led into "Charlie My Boy", the familiar theme brought into America's living rooms by

父亲、查理和我

父亲漫长而成功的演艺生涯开始于杂耍盛行的年代。几十年来，著名的口技表演家埃德加·柏根和与他齐名的木偶搭档查理·麦卡锡深受剧院观众的喜爱，后来又为广播和电视观众带来愉悦。所以我一出生，很自然各大媒体就没当我是坎迪斯·柏根，而是"查理的妹妹"。很小的时候，我就时常随父亲和查理一起表演。我总是非常自信、优雅而出色地背诵那些熟记的诗句，所以我注定成为一个卓有成就的女儿。

多年以后，1978年夏天，父亲在好莱坞比佛利富人区著名的布朗·德比餐厅召开新闻发布会，宣布退休计划，同时也想看看哪些人会到场。结果新闻发布会现场人员爆满，当晚间新闻报道时，父亲都大吃一惊。

父亲宣布，他将在拉斯维加斯的恺撒皇宫大酒店与安迪·威廉姆斯，同期进行为期3周的告别演出。这对于一位老人，尤其是大约半年前还在医院接受心脏重症护理的父亲来说，有着很大的风险。然而一旦做出了决定，父亲就不顾一切地执行，坚定不移，最后一次一定要和搭档查理·麦卡锡，就像很久以前一样，"成为皇宫大酒店最出色的演员"。这也是成功退出演艺的一次好机会。

母亲陪他去了拉斯维加斯，在开幕之夜，我和哥哥克里斯也给了他一个惊喜。剧场灯光渐暗，音乐渐起，我们坐在最前排，希望他那些表演一切顺利，又害怕会有什么闪失。

当乐队奏起《查理，我的男孩》时，我们3人都屏住了呼吸。30年前，这首熟悉的旋律通过广播进入了美国的千家万户，直至那天晚

radio thirty years before.There were many there that night who remembered—people for whom Edgar and Charlie were old fireside friends—and as Bergen walked from the wings with McCarthy at his side,the applause was long and alive with memories.

My father stood straight and proud on the stage,his right hand on Charlie's back.For this occasion,his final farewell,he had insisted on playing again in white tie and tails.He was,after all,an elegant man,a poised and graceful presence commanding center stage.

"Well,Charlie—"

"Bergen,you old windbag,I'll kill ya,so help me,I'll mooowwww you down—"

And they slipped into the familiar patter of a partnership that had lasted sixty years.

The routine was flawless.Bergen reasoning,McCarthy saucy and razzing,the steady laughter of the audience,the frequent applause.Nothing could stop them,and the audience kept asking for more.

My mother sat still as a statue,her concentration locked on the man on the stage.Only her lips moved as she unconsciously mouthed the dialogue she had followed for thirty-five years,as if willing it to come out right.Each of us knew by heart the lines of the routines that had spanned our lives;but that night we heard them fresh,as if for the first time—perhaps because we sensed it would be the last.

The act ended with a sound track from their old radio shows,a montage of Bergen and McCarthy memories:John Barrymore jousting with Charlie;Marilyn Monroe and Charles McCarthy announcing their engagement;W.C.Fields threatening to split Charlie into Venetian blinds—flashbacks of famous voices from the past.Up on stage,Edgar and Charlie cocked their heads,swapped knowing glances and chuckled softly as they looked up,listening wistfully to their lives.

Then my father said simply,"In vaudeville,every act has to have a

双语精华版·心灵鸡汤·

上,许多观众都还记得,因为他们过去常常在家中炉火旁边收听这首曲子,埃德加和查理已经成为大家的炉边老友。而随着父亲和麦卡锡一起从幕后来到台前,掌声雷动,经久不息,激活了人们美好的回忆。

父亲右手搭在查理背上,英姿挺拔,在舞台上显得十分自豪。为了这次最后的告别,他坚持要穿上白西服,打上白领带,再演一次。事实上,他仍然是一个优雅绅士,自信优雅,傲立舞台。

"我说,查理——"

"柏根,你这个啰嗦的老家伙,我真想杀了你,快来帮我,我要毙了你——"

这样,他俩就渐渐进入60年来人们熟悉的搭档表演模式。

表演无懈可击,柏根据理力争,麦卡锡顽皮嘲弄,观众笑声不断,掌声此起彼伏。他们的表演轻松自如,观众却永不满足,要求更多加演。

母亲是纹丝不动,全心聚焦舞台上的父亲。只有她的嘴唇下意识在动,无声地说着她模仿了35年的对白,仿佛与台上的表演配合得恰到好处。这些伴随我们一生的表演台词,我们每个人都熟记于心,但那晚却好像是第一次听到,如此新颖,也许我们已经感觉到,这是最后一次了。

演出最后是以一段他们过去的广播表演录音来终场。这是一段对父亲和麦卡锡回忆的声音剪辑合成:约翰·巴里莫尔和查理的斗嘴;玛丽莲·梦露和查尔斯·麦卡锡宣布订婚;费尔兹威胁要把查理撕成百叶窗样的碎片,这些都是过去经典声音的回顾。此时舞台上,父亲和查理翘起头来,心照不宣地交换目光,仰望的时候轻声地笑,渴望聆听他们的生命之音。

随后父亲做了简洁的致辞:"在杂耍里,每一幕表演都有结束的

close,and I think,for me,the close has come and it's time to pack up my little friend and say good-bye.Good-night,God bless,and thank you all for listening." As the orchestra played his favorite,"*September Song*", he picked up Charlie and walked offstage.

The three of us smiled and cried,trying to compose ourselves before the house lights came up.The audience rose to its feet,applauding him with deep affection,grateful to share his farewell.

There were photographers in his dressing room backstage as we entered,and we had to press our way through the throng.He hugged Kris and my mother;then I came forward,wiping my eyes.We held each other tight.The love of a lifetime was squeezed into those moments.Once again I started sobbing,so proud of him,so happy for him,so sad.Knowing somehow that it was a last good-bye.His to an audience,ours to him.

The reviews of the show were unanimous,effusive in their praise. The next three days' performances went just as smoothly,with standing ovations at the end of each.

After the fourth night's performance,my father went to sleep in good spirits.My mother rose early,half opened the blinds and called to him.Several moments passed before she realized he was dead.He had gone peacefully while he slept.

For my father,there could have been no better ending;it was one he might have written himself. And who can say that he hadn't? There was the supreme sense of timing ingrained over sixty years of performing. Just as in vaudeville,he knew when to close.

Candice Bergen

时候,对我来说,我想这一时刻已经到来,该是收工说再见的时候了,晚安,上帝保佑,谢谢大家。"伴着乐队奏起父亲的最爱歌曲《九月之歌》,他和查理一起慢步走下舞台。

我们3个又哭又笑,并努力想使自己在场灯亮起之前恢复镇定。而全场观众早已起立,深情鼓掌,感谢父亲的告别演出。

来到父亲后台化妆间时,里面早已挤满了摄影记者,我们只好用力推挤进去。父亲激动地拥抱了克里斯和母亲。而我也擦了擦眼泪,向前一步,彼此紧紧地抱在了一起。一生的爱都凝聚在那一刻。我又一次不禁抽泣起来,太为父亲感到自豪、开心,却又太辛酸了。我已隐约知道,那是最后一次道别了,父亲与观众的,我们和父亲的。

对演出的评论全部都是热情洋溢的赞誉。接下来的3天表演也非常顺利,每次终场观众全体起立,报以热烈的掌声。

第4天晚上表演后,父亲欣然入睡。第2天母亲起得很早,半开了百叶窗,然后来喊父亲。过了好一会儿,母亲恍然,父亲已经辞世,在梦里安然离去。

对父亲来说,这可能是最好的结局了。这也许是他自己选择好的,谁又能说不是呢?父亲拥有60年演艺生涯烙下的超强时间感觉,就像在杂耍表演里,他总是知道适时谢幕。

坎迪斯·柏根

Veronica's Babies

When I was in third grade,Mrs.Margaret McNeil was my teacher. She was young,vibrant and very pretty.She taught me and all the other impressionable boys and girls in her class the basics.Even those kids who were perceptually impaired or had serious disabilities miraculously learned,too.Everyone mastered third-grade reading and writing thanks to Mrs. McNeil—and Veronica.

Veronica was a huge,variegated spider plant suspended in the window of our classroom in a large,glistening-white,hanging basket.Every year,it produced babies—little plantlets on slender stems that cascaded over the rim of the pot.When you learned to read and write to Mrs.McNeil's "satisfaction", you were awarded one of Veronica's babies.None of the students could wait to get one.

On the big day,first you watered Veronica,and then Mrs.McNeil handed you the special scissors.You got to snip off a baby and name it. With Mrs.McNeil guiding you,you next planted it in moist soil in a styrofoam cup and wrote its new name on the outside with a green marker.

I'll never forget that March day when I had learned to read and write well enough.I went through Mrs.McNeil's ritual and carried home a small plant.I named it Rose,after my mother.I was so proud because I was one of the first boys to get one.

By the time June rolled around,every boy and girl in the class had received one of Veronica's babies.Even Billy Acker,who was mildly retarded and struggled the hardest of all of us,did well enough to get one.

Over the summer,we all had to promise to write Mrs.McNeil a letter and let her know how Veronica's baby was doing.She advised us to

弗罗尼卡的宝贝

三年级时,玛格丽特·麦克尼尔夫人是我的老师。她年轻漂亮,充满活力。在课堂上,她教我和其他那些敏感的孩子们基础知识,甚至还有一些感觉受损或严重残疾的孩子,都在奇迹般地跟着学习。每一个掌握了三年级读写能力的学生都非常感谢麦克尼尔夫人,还有弗罗尼卡。

弗罗尼卡是一株巨大的杂色吊兰,悬挂在我们教室窗子上一个白闪闪的大吊篮里。它每年都要繁衍后代——细长茎干上的嫩枝垂挂在篮子边上。当你学习读写让麦克尼尔夫人"满意"时,她就奖励一根嫩芽——弗罗尼卡的宝贝。孩子们都急切地想得到一个小吊兰。

每逢节日时,你得首先替弗罗尼卡浇水,然后麦克尼尔夫人会递给你一把特殊的剪刀,用来剪下一根嫩芽,并且给它取个名字。在麦克尼尔夫人的指导下,接下来你就把它种在塑料杯子中潮湿的土壤里,再用绿色记号笔在杯子外面写上它的新名字。

我永远不会忘记,在3月的一天,我的读写学得非常好。终于如愿以偿,完成了麦克尼尔夫人奖赏的一系列活动,带了一株小吊兰回家。我给它取了我母亲的名字——罗斯。我非常自豪,因为我是最先获得小吊兰的男孩之一。

过了6月,班上每一个孩子都有了一株小吊兰。就连班上反应有点迟钝的比利·阿克,通过最辛苦的努力,也表现出色而获得了奖赏。

夏季里,我们都得答应给麦克尼尔夫人写信,告诉她小吊兰长

use a dictionary to help with difficult spellings.

I remember writing that my mom and dad helped me transplant the baby into a white hanging basket,and that its roots had grown really long.

During the summer,I kept my baby outside on our patio,and when fall arrived,I took it indoors to hang in front of my sliding glass door, where it got plenty of good light.

Years passed and Veronica's baby thrived.It produced babies,just as Veronica had done—many babies.I snipped them off and potted them up in hanging baskets,five to a basket.My dad would take them to work and sell them to his coworkers.With the extra money,I'd buy more hanging baskets and soil,and eventually I started a small business.

Thanks to Veronica's baby,I became interested in houseplants.Of course,my dad,who nurtured my interest in all kinds of plants,gets some of the credit,too.And while Mrs.McNeil first taught me to read and write well,it was Dad,again,who cultivated these skills in me.

When he called one weekend recently to tell me Mrs.McNeil had passed away,I knew I had to attend the wake.I journeyed home and sat with my wife,Carole,in a crowded funeral parlor.Mrs.McNeil lay there as if she were peacefully asleep.Her hair was silver,and there were many wrinkles on her powdered face,but other than that,she looked just as I remembered her.Hanging to her left by the window was Veronica,with many babies cascading over the rim of her basket.Veronica,unlike Mrs. McNeil,hadn't changed one bit.

Many people chatted about their remembrances of Mrs.McNeil,of third grade,of learning how to read and write better in order to get one of Veronica's babies,of her dedication.

When a vaguely familiar face rose to speak,the place grew suddenly silent.

"Hello,my name is Billy Acker," the man stammered. "Everyone

得怎么样了。她还建议我们使用词典来解决一些拼写难题。

我还记得在信里告诉麦克尼尔夫人,我的小吊兰的根实在长得太长了,我父母帮我把这个小宝贝移种到一个白色大吊篮里。

整个夏天,我把它都放在外面院子里,秋天来时,我就拿回屋内挂在玻璃拉门前面,这里光线照样充足。

很多年过去了,弗罗尼卡的宝贝小吊兰已经茁壮成长了,并且,就像弗罗尼卡一样,小吊兰也有了许多小嫩芽。我把它们小心剪下,栽在吊篮里,一个篮子5个。我父亲还把它们带到上班地方,卖给同事们。而挣得的钱,我又用来买更多的吊篮和泥土,最后我还开始做起了小买卖。

正是因为弗罗尼卡的宝贝小吊兰,我开始对室内植物产生了兴趣。当然,我父亲也应该表扬,正是他培养了我对各种植物的兴趣,同时,当麦克尼尔夫人先教会我读书写字时,也正是父亲又一次培养了我这些能力。

最近一个周末,父亲打电话告诉我说,麦克尼尔夫人已经去世了。我想我应该去悼念这位恩师。和妻子回到家乡,我们一起坐在殡仪馆里。麦克尼尔夫人安详地躺着,如静静地睡着了一样。除了满头银丝,面部多了皱纹之外,她和我的记忆里没什么两样。她左边窗上挂着的依旧是弗罗尼卡,许多嫩芽垂挂在篮子边上,和麦克尼尔夫人不同,它是一点也没变。

大家都开始谈起对麦克尼尔夫人的回忆,有三年级的事,有为了得到一株弗罗尼卡的宝贝小吊兰而更好地学习读写,有的还谈起了麦克尼尔夫人的奉献精神。

当一张模糊又有些熟悉的脸出现,并且开始讲话时,屋里突然都安静下来。

"你们好,我名叫比利·阿克,"这位男士结结巴巴地说道。"人人

told my mom and dad that I'd never be able to read and write because I was retarded.Ha!Mrs.McNeil taught me good how to read and write.She taught me real good."

He paused,and a large tear rolled down his cheek and stained the lapel of his gray suit."You know,I still have one of Veronica's babies."

He wiped his eyes with the back of his hand and continued."Every time I write or read an order in the shop,I can't help but think of Mrs. McNeil and how hard she worked with me after school.She taught me real good."

Many others spoke about Mrs.McNeil after Billy,but none matched him for his sincerity and simplicity.

Before we left,Carole and I talked to Mrs.McNeil's daughters and admired all the beautiful flower arrangements that lined the room.A good half of them were from Acker's Florist.A huge,heart-shaped spray of white carnations with a bold red banner caught our attention at the back of the room.Written in big black letters,it said:*If you can read this, thank a teacher.*Underneath it,in shaky,almost illegible penmanship,were the words:*Thank you Mrs. McNeil.Love,your student,Billy Acker.*

George M. Flynn

都对我父母说我绝对不会读书写字的,因为我反应迟钝。哈!是麦克尼尔夫人教会了我读书写字。她教得真好。"

顿了一下,一颗大滴泪珠从他脸上滑落,落在灰色西服的翻领上。"而且,我至今还有一株弗罗尼卡的宝贝小吊兰呢。"

他用手背擦了擦眼泪又继续说:"每次我在店里填写或查阅账单时,都不禁想起麦克尼尔夫人,是她在放学后还不辞辛苦地来教我。她教得真好。"

比利后面,其他许多人都怀念了麦克尼尔夫人,但都不如比利真诚和质朴。

离开之前,我和妻子同麦克尼尔夫人的几个女儿聊了一会,非常欣赏屋子里这些漂亮鲜花的布置。原来一大半都来自阿克花店。屋子后面,一大束带有大红色标语的心型白色康乃馨引起了我们的注意。上面用黑色大写字母写着:如果你能读懂这行字,感谢你的老师。这行字下面是用颤抖的、几乎认不出来的字体写的几个字:谢谢你,麦克尼尔夫人。爱你的学生,比利·阿克。

乔治·M.弗林

The Scar

His thumb softly rubbed the twisted flesh on my cheek.The plastic surgeon,a good fifteen years my senior,was a very attractive man.His masculinity and the intensity of his gaze seemed almost overpowering.

"Hmmm," he said quietly."Are you a model?"

*Is this a joke?Is he kidding?*I asked myself,and I searched his handsome face for signs of mockery.No way would anyone ever confuse me with a fashion model.I was ugly.My mother casually referred to my sister as her pretty child.Anyone could see I was homely.After all,I had the scar to prove it.

The accident happened in fourth grade,when a neighbor boy picked up a hunk of concrete and heaved the mass through the side of my face. An emergency room doctor stitched together the shreds of skin,pulling catgut through the tattered outside of my face and then suturing the shards of flesh inside my mouth.For the rest of the year,a huge bandage from cheekbone to jaw covered the raised angry welt.

A few weeks after the accident,an eye exam revealed I was nearsighted.Above the ungainly bandage sat a big,thick pair of glasses. Around my head,a short fuzzy glob of curls stood out like mold growing on old bread.To save money,Mom had taken me to a beauty school where a student cut my hair.The overzealous girl hacked away cheerfully.Globs of hair piled up on the floor.By the time her instructor wandered over,the damage was done.A quick conference followed,and we were given a coupon for a free styling on our next visit.

"Well," sighed my father that evening,"you'll always be pretty to me," and he hesitated,"even if you aren't to the rest of the world."

双语精华版·心灵鸡汤·

伤　痕

他用拇指轻轻地在我脸上，擦了擦有些扭曲变形的那块肉。这位整形医生，大我15岁，是个气度不凡的专家。凝望我时，有一股刚毅坚定的气势让我几乎透不过气来。

"嗯，"他轻声问道，"你是模特吗？"

是玩笑吗？他开玩笑吧？我不禁问自己，于是在他英俊的面容上找寻起嘲弄的痕迹。怎么也不会有人误认我是一个时装模特。因为我很丑。有时不经意间，我母亲也说我妹妹是个漂亮的孩子。谁都能看出来，我实在是不漂亮，因为我脸上的那道疤痕就是答案。

意外发生在我小学四年级那年。当时邻家的一个男孩捡起一大块混凝土，扔到我脸上。急诊医生把砸烂的皮肤缝合起来，缝线布满了我的烂脸，接着还要把嘴里的烂肉也缝起来。那年剩下的日子里，我一直缠着一个从颧骨直到下巴的大绷带，里面尽是发炎的肿包。

几周后视力检查，又发现我近视了，于是难看的绷带上又多了一副厚厚的大眼镜，头上还有一团短毛卷发，看起来就像变质的面包上长出了霉菌。那时，为了省点理发钱，母亲带我去美容学校，让里边的学生来剪。一位女生非常乐意，甚至有过分热情，在我头上一阵狂剪，不一会儿，地上就多了几堆头发。不过当美容老师过来看看时，这位学生还是紧张而弄伤了我的头。很快一番交涉后，美容学校给我们一张优惠券作为补偿，让我们下次免费来做头。

"唉，"那天晚上父亲一声叹息，"对我来说，你将永远是漂亮可爱的，"他又犹豫了一下，"即便其他人不这么认为。"

Right.Thanks.As if I couldn't hear the taunts of the other kids at school.As if I couldn't see how different I looked from the little girls whom the teachers fawned over.As if I didn't occasionally catch a glimpse of myself in the bathroom mirror.In a culture that values beauty, an ugly girl is an outcast.My looks caused me no end of pain.I sat in my room and sobbed every time my family watched a beauty pageant or a "talent" search show.

Eventually I decided that if I couldn't be pretty,I would at least be well-groomed.Over the course of years,I learned to style my hair,wear contact lenses and apply make-up.Watching what worked for other women,I learned to dress myself to best advantage.And now,I was engaged to be married.The scar,shrunken and faded with age,stood between me and a new life.

"Of course,I'm not a model," I replied with a small amount of in-dignation.

The plastic surgeon crossed his arms over his chest and looked at me appraisingly."Then why are you concerned about this scar?If there is no professional reason to have it removed,what brought you here today?"

Suddenly he represented all the men I'd ever known.The eight boys who turned me down when I invited them to the girls-ask-boys dance. The sporadic dates I'd had in college.The parade of men who had ig-nored me since then.The man whose ring I wore on my left hand.My hand rose to my face.The scar confirmed it;I was ugly.The room swam before me as my eyes filled with tears.

The doctor pulled a rolling stool up next to me and sat down.His knees almost touched mine.His voice was low and soft.

"Let me tell you what I see.I see a beautiful woman.Not a perfect woman,but a beautiful woman.Lauren Hutton has a gap between her front teeth.Elizabeth Taylor has a tiny,tiny scar on her forehead," he al-

好的。谢谢了。是让我装作听不见学校里其他孩子们的嘲弄,装成看不出来老师喜欢的那些小女孩和我有多么不一样,还是好像在浴室镜子里我从没偶尔瞥见过自己?在这个崇尚美貌的文化里,丑女孩终究会遭人冷落和遗弃。我的丑带给我无尽的痛苦。每次在家里收看选美或选秀节目时,我总是躲回自己的屋子,失声痛哭。

终于有一天,我决定,我不漂亮,但至少也要保持整洁体面。这些年来,我学会了给自己做发型,戴上隐形眼镜,抹上化妆品,看着别人如何打扮,我也学会了穿戴搭配得体。现在,我还订婚了。可是脸上的疤痕,虽然随着岁月逐渐缩小、变淡,但与我的新生活还是有些格格不入。

"我当然不是模特。"我有些愤愤不平地回了一句。

两臂交叉搭在胸前,整形医生开始审视我。"那你干嘛还在意这道疤痕呢?要是没什么特殊职业要求除疤,你今天来这儿是为什么呢?"

他的这番话,忽然间让我想起了我认识的那一个个臭男人。在玩女孩请男孩跳舞时,有8个男孩都拒绝了我;大学里那些时有时无的男友;后来对我始终视而不见的一大堆男人;还有那个给我左手戴上戒指的男人。想到这,我情不自禁用手捂住了脸。这脸上的疤痕清清楚楚地告诉他们:我真的很丑。此时,我眼里已经浸满泪水,眼前一片天旋地转。

医生赶忙拿了把旋转凳子在我身边坐下,靠得很近,膝盖都快碰到了。他说话的声音低沉而又柔和。

"让我来告诉你,我眼里的你是什么样的。我看到的是一位漂亮的女士,虽不是完美无缺,但真的挺漂亮。劳伦·赫顿的门牙中间有一道缝隙,伊丽莎白·泰勒额头也有一道小小的疤痕。"他的声音低

most whispered.Then he paused and handed me a mirror."I think to my-self how every remarkable woman has an imperfection,and I believe that imperfection makes her beauty more remarkable because it assures us she is human."

He pushed back the stool and stood up."I won't touch it.Don't let anyone fool with your face.You are delightful just the way you are. Beauty really does come from within a woman.Believe me.It is my busi-ness to know."

Then he left.

I turned to the face in the mirror.He was right.Somehow over the years,that ugly child had become a beautiful woman.Since that day in his office,as a woman who makes her living speaking before hundreds of people,I have been told many times by people of both sexes that I am beautiful.And,I know I am.

When I changed how I saw myself,others were forced to change how they saw me.The doctor didn't remove the scar on my face;he re-moved the scar on my heart.

Joanna Slan

柔到近乎耳语了。然后,他停了下来,递给我一面镜子。"我想对我来说,每一位女士再怎么美艳照人,都会有些瑕疵缺憾,而正是这凡人才有的瑕疵,却让她们的美丽更加动人。"

说完他朝后推开凳子,站了起来。"我不想碰你的疤痕。也别让任何人来嘲弄你的脸。现在的你就很讨人喜欢。女人的美丽其实是由内而外的。相信我,这可是我的专业知识。"

转身他就离开了。

我再一次仔细端详起镜子里这张脸,他说得很对。不知怎的,这些年来,原来那个难看的小女孩已经出落成了一个漂亮女人。自从那天离开那位整形医生的诊所后,我这个靠每天和成百人说话打交道来谋生的女人,也不知多少次被男男女女夸赞漂亮了。我想我的确是很漂亮。

当我改变看自己的方式时,其他人也都被迫改变了如何来看我。这位医生没有去除我脸上的疤痕;他却消除了我心头的伤痕。

乔安娜·斯兰

A First

I straightened my notebook and pen yet again,making sure the edge of the notebook lined up cleanly with my desk,the pen parallel to the notebook,uncapped and ready to write.But ready to write what?I glanced around in dismay at the bare conference room.My first day at my first job after graduate school and I was sitting in a conference room instead of an office.The walls were bare.No phone.No shelves.Just a round wooden table and four chairs.Oh,and me.

I glanced at my watch.Five minutes until I would walk down the hall and get my patient.My first real patient.After twelve years of regular school,four years of high school,four years of college and three years of graduate school,I was ready to begin my first day as a psychiatric physician's assistant.I slumped a little in my chair,gnawing on the end of a fingernail.

That morning,I had taken my thirteen-month-old to day care.While she was happy as a clam,racing into the room crowded with toys and games to sit down with "the gang"and eat breakfast,I was still wracked with doubt.Was putting her in day care so I could finish PA school a good decision?Was starting a new job,even though it was part time,the right thing to do?Even though I loved being a mom and while I had friends who were stay-at-home moms and I respected the incredible amount of work they did,there was a part of me that had always known I wanted to have a career.

But instead of appearing immediately after college,like a pot of gold at the end of the rainbow,my career had been elusive,involving jobs in sales,waitressing and reception before landing me in graduate school.

第一次

　　我把笔记本和钢笔又重新摆放了一下,确信笔记本的边儿正好与桌子笔直对齐,钢笔与笔记本平行,并揭开了笔帽做好书写的准备。但是准备写什么呢?我沮丧地扫了一眼空荡荡的会议室。这是我大学毕业后找的第一份工作,第一天上班就是坐在这间会议室而不是办公室里。墙壁光秃秃的。没有电话,没有隔板,只有一张木制的圆桌和4把椅子。哦,还有我。

　　我瞥了一眼手表。再过5分钟我就要走过大厅去给病人看病,我的第一个病人。在接受了12年常规基础教育,读了4年高中,4年大学和3年研究生之后,我为精神病临床医生助理的工作做好了第一天上班的准备。我在椅子里把身体朝后靠了靠,咬着手指尖。

　　那天早晨,我把13个月大的女儿送到了日间托儿所。当她像个涨潮时的蛤蜊一样开心地直奔那间堆满了玩具和游戏器材的房间,并和她的同伴坐下来吃早餐的时候,我却深受种种疑虑的折磨。为了能够完成医生助理学校的学业,我就把她送到日间托儿所是个明智的决定吗?开始一个新的工作,哪怕它并非全日制对吗?虽然我很喜欢做母亲,而且我有一些居家的母亲朋友,我尊重她们所做的难以计数的工作,但是我身体的某个部分总是提醒我——我其实还是挺想有自己的事业。

　　然而大学一毕业我没有直接找工作,就像那对想在彩虹的末端寻找一罐金子却最终没有结果的夫妇一样,我的经历曲折复杂,前途未卜。在读研究生之前,我做过销售和服务接待工作。作为一个年

女性系列／挥洒四季的芬芳

As a young girl who dreamed of great wealth and fame,had a strong desire to make a difference in people's lives,and had graduated from an Ivy League school,I hadn't expected to be beginning my career at this point—in my early thirties with a husband,a mortgage,a thirteen-month-old and thousands of dollars of debt.But here I was.A trickle of ice had been forming in my stomach over the years,growing with every moment of frustration.Now,it had hardened into a large mass of ice,establishing how important this would be.

Christina,my first real patient,was not what I expected.She was petite and dressed in pressed cotton pants and a light blue sweater.She smiled easily at me as I led her to the conference room.I couldn't imagine what she could possibly be here for—she seemed much less nervous than I.

I tried not to cringe as we settled into the conference room chairs. Surely the bare room and lack of a phone,books or diplomas belied my inexperience! If Christina noticed,she didn't let on,and as she began to talk,a story unfolded which belied her composed appearance.For her entire life,she had struggled with violent mood swings,at some moments feeling full of energy and passion,at other moments,depressed and suicidal.Tears poured down her face as she described her anger,which sometimes grew so severe she would scream at her family or even throw things.She couldn't handle stress and would retreat to her room and be unable to cope.Her marriage was rocky due to her volatile moods and her kids were starting to avoid her.She had been treated by other doctors for the depression,but that had only increased her anxiety and irritability. Christina was at the point where she had lost yet another job and was considering leaving her family so that at least their lives could return to normal.

As I questioned her further,it became apparent to me that the young woman in front of me likely had a bipolar disorder,or what is commonly

轻姑娘,我幻想成为有钱人和出名,我有强烈的欲望要生活得与常人不同,况且我还毕业于一所常春藤学校。我决不曾想到会在这个节骨眼上——在我30刚出头,有丈夫,有银行抵押贷款,有13个月大的女儿和好几千元债务的时刻开始自己的职业生涯。但是我已经置身其中不能自拔。多年以来,我的内心结出了一条冰河,并每每随着我的沮丧感在逐步扩大。现在它已经硬化成了一大块冰,而且日益显露出它的威力。

克里斯蒂娜,我的第一个病人,并不像我想象的那样。她身材娇小,穿着紧身的棉布裤子和一件淡蓝色的运动衫。当我把她带到会议室时,她轻松地朝我笑了笑。我想象不出她可能为了什么来到这里——她似乎要比我放松许多。

我们在会议室的椅子里坐定以后,我极力不让自己显出自卑的样子。空空的房间和缺少电话、图书或者奖状的确掩饰了我的经验不足。不过,即使克里斯蒂娜注意到这些的话,她也不会承认。随着开始谈论病情,掩盖在她平静外表下的故事就铺展开来。有生以来,她一直在跟一阵阵暴烈的情绪做斗争。有时她感到浑身充满力量和激情,有时则是情绪低落,想要结束自己的生命。说到她的气愤,如此剧烈的气愤,以至她向家人大喊大叫或者摔东西时,眼泪从她脸上喷涌而下。她无法驾驭自己的压抑感,每次只好退回自己的房间,对处理各种问题无能为力。她的婚姻由于她暴躁的情绪很不稳定,她的孩子们也开始逃避她。其他医生都对她的压抑感进行了治疗,但却都只是增添了她的焦虑不安和烦躁。克里斯蒂娜现在已经到了又丢掉一份工作,并正在考虑离开家庭,以便至少确保家人能够恢复正常生活的可悲地步。

我又向她提了些别的问题后发现,我面前的这个年轻女性明显可能患了躁狂与抑郁状态交替紊乱症,或者是人们平常说的躁狂抑

女性系列／挥洒四季的芬芳

known as manicdepressive illness.People with this illness have periods of depression,but they can also have periods of increased energy, talkativeness,anger or irritability and difficulty concentrating.Despite being treated by several doctors over the years,she had never been diagnosed with or treated for a bipolar illness.

At the conclusion of my questioning,I hesitated.How could I have noticed something that doctors had missed?First real patient,remember? Christina was looking at me expectantly. Waiting.I squelched the tight feeling in my chest and tried to smile reassuringly.Cautiously,I brought up the diagnosis of bipolar disorder and what it meant.We went over the treatments. With a slightly shaky hand,I wrote out a prescription for medication and gave her the name of a good therapist.

Two weeks later,Christina returned to my conference room.As before,she looked well put together in fashionable dark blue jeans and a button-down shirt.We sat down and I spent a moment writing the date in the chart and reviewing the medications I had prescribed.Then came the dreaded moment.It was time to ask the question.I tried to appear calm. "How are things going since your first visit?"I waited for the tears.

Christina looked down for a moment,then her eyes met mine,several tears already welling up at the corners."You've changed my life,"she said simply.She sniffed and pressed a knuckle to her left eye. "I don't know what you gave me,but it was magical.I have been less depressed. I'm not angry anymore.I'm not snapping at my kids.We actually went hiking this weekend and even when a snake almost bit my son on the ankle,I was able to remain calm and handle it.My thoughts aren't racing a mile a minute.I had the first good night's sleep I can ever remember."

I felt a grin forming and tried not to show my amazement. My treatment plan had actually worked! This was not the same woman who had come to me in tears just a few weeks earlier.

"I don't know how I can ever thank you,"she sniffed. "You've

双
语
精
华
版
·
心
灵
鸡
汤
·

郁症。得了这种病的人有一阵阵的郁闷期,但是他们仍然可以有浑身精力充沛,说话滔滔不绝,发怒或者烦躁,精力不能集中的时候。尽管几年来被好几个医生治疗过,但她从来没有被诊断出躁狂抑郁症并为此进行过治疗。

结束询问后,我犹豫不决。我怎么可能注意到别的医生忽略的东西呢?我还记得她是我的第一个病人吗?克里斯蒂娜期待地望着我。稍等一下。我抑制住内心的紧张感,极力给她一个让她宽心的微笑。我非常谨慎地思索躁狂抑郁症的诊断和它将带来的后果。我们一起重新回顾了以前的治疗。然后,我用略微有些颤抖的手写下了服用药物的处方,并把一个非常优秀的药剂师的名字告诉了她。

两周以后,克里斯蒂娜回到了我的会议室。她身穿时髦的暗蓝色牛仔裤和一件有纽扣领圈的衬衫,像上次一样看起来过得很好。我们坐下来,我花了点时间在表格上填写日期,接下来就询问我开过的处方服药的效果。然后那个可怕的时刻来到了。是问那个问题的时候了,我竭力保持镇静。"你第一次来过以后情况怎么样了?"我等着她的眼泪喷涌而出。

克里斯蒂娜的眼睛向下看了一会儿,后来她的目光触及到了我,有几滴眼泪已经涌出了眼角。"你改变了我的生活,"她简短地说。她吸着鼻子,用一个指关节按着左眼。"我不知道你给了我什么,但是它太神奇了。我的压抑感少了。我不再发火,不再对着孩子们粗声粗气地大声嚷嚷了。事实上,我们这个周末徒步旅行来着。当一条蛇差点咬到我儿子的脚踝时,我都能够保持镇静,从容不迫地处理这件事。我的思维不再每分钟狂奔一英里。晚上有了我记忆中的第一个好觉。"

我感到自己在咧着嘴笑,我可不想让我的吃惊表现出来。我的诊断计划真的奏效了!这已经不是几周前哭哭啼啼来到我这里的那个女人了。

"我真不知道该怎样感谢你,"她吸着鼻涕说。"你让我的家庭重

given me my family back.You've given me my hope back."

As I pressed a tissue into Christina's hands,I tried to hold back my own tears.There was an incredible shift in my stomach. The block of ice I had grown so accustomed to was starting to melt.I could feel the water trickling into my limbs,the cold in my gut replaced by warmth and comfort.Finally,it all clicked.All those years of struggling through jobs I hated,of wondering what my purpose was,of second-guessing my decisions,of dropping my daughter off at day care so I could finish school and start a job.They had led me here to this bare,ugly conference room. And I had changed a woman's life.A woman's entire future—and that of her family's.And she was only my first real patient!

Just think of how many more there were to come!

Rachel Byrne

新团聚。你让我重新有了自信。"

把一块纸巾塞到克里斯蒂娜手里的时候,我极力抑制住自己的泪水。我腹中有了一个让人不可思议的变化。我已经逐渐熟悉的那块冰开始融化。我能够感受到水慢慢地流淌进我的四肢,我内心深处的寒冷被温暖和宽慰取代。最终,冰块滴滴答答地全部融化。那么多年来为我痛恨的工作所做的奋斗,对我人生目标的犹豫不决,对所做决定的反复推测,对把女儿送到日间托儿所以便我完成学业开始工作的耿耿于怀都消释殆尽。正是它们引导我走进了这间空旷丑陋的会议室,于是我才能改变了一个女人的生活。一个女人的全部未来——还有她家庭的未来。而她只是我的第一个病人!

想想还有多少这样的事要接踵而来。

韦虹 译

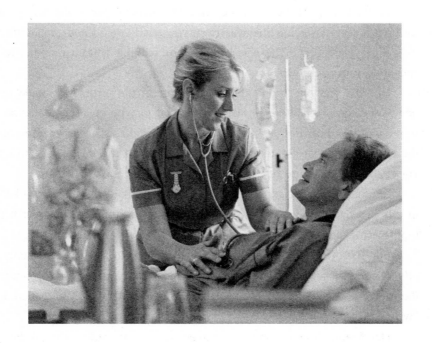

女性系列／挥洒四季的芬芳

· · · · · · · · · · · · · · · · ·

39

No Mistake

In 1951,Bette Nesmith worked in a Dallas bank,where she was glad to have a secretarial job.She was twenty-seven,divorced and the mother of a nine-year-old son.She was happy to be making $300 a month,a respectable sum back then.

But she had one problem—how to correct the errors she made on her new electric typewriter? She has learned to type on a manual typewriter,and was horrified at how many more mistakes she was making on the electric.It was a nightmare trying to correct all the mistakes with an eraser.she had to figure out another way.

She had some art experience,and she knew that artists who worked in oils just painted over errors,so she concocted a fluid to paint over her typing errors,and she put it in an empty bottle of fingernail polish.

For five years,Bette kept her new technique to herself.But finally, other secretaries began to notice her little bottle,and asked for some themselves.So she made up some bottle for her friends and called it "Mistake Out".

Her friends loved it and encouraged her to start selling the product. She approached various marketing agencies and companies,including IBM,but they turned her down.However,secretaries continued to like her product,so Bette Nesmith's kitchen became her first manufacturing facility,and she started selling it on her own.She didn't quit her day job,but worked long into the nights and early mornings mixing and packaging her product.

Orders began to trickle in,and she hired a college student to help the sales effort.It wasn't easy for these two inexperienced salespeople.

一劳永逸

1951年,贝特·内史密斯进入达拉斯一家银行做秘书工作。她已经27岁,离过婚,还带着9岁的儿子,能有这样一份工作,每月挣300美金,在当时已相当可观,所以她真的挺开心。

但是问题也随之而来,使用新电子打字机如果有错误该如何修改呢?过去学的是手动打字机,而现在的电子打字机上的错误率要高出许多,对此连她自己都觉得可怕。要是每处错误都用橡皮擦来改正,那简直令人恐怖。所以她必须得找出更好的方法。

好在她学过绘画,知道油画家总是在画错的地方再涂上一层,于是,她也试着调了一种液体来涂在打字错误处的上面,还把它装在一个空的指甲油瓶子里。

5年来,贝特都没跟别人透露这一新窍门。但是最后其他秘书们开始注意到她的空瓶子,于是都问她要点来用。所以她就做了一些送给她的朋友并取了名字叫"褪字灵"。

朋友们都很喜欢,并且鼓励她开始销售这一产品。她跑了多家市场机构和公司,包括大名鼎鼎的IBM公司,不过都遭到拒绝。但秘书们还是很喜欢她的产品,于是,她就开始在自家厨房生产并自己亲自去销售。由于白天还要上班,她只得下班后调制、包装她的产品,经常工作到深夜和凌晨。

订货单开始一个接一个地传来,她只好雇了一个大学生来帮她销售。因为两人都没多少推销经验,所以销售并不容易,经销商总是

Dealers kept telling them that people just wouldn't paint out their mistakes.Records show that from August 1959 to April 1960,the company's total income was $1,141,and its expenses were $1,217.

But Bette didn't give up.She went to a part-time secretarial job, managing to buy groceries and save $200 to pay a chemist to develop a faster-dying formula.

The new formula helped.Bette began traveling throughout the country,selling her little white bottles wherever she could.She'd arrive in a town,get the local phone book,and call every local office supply dealer. She visited individual stores and would leave a dozen bottles.Orders mushroomed,and what had become known as Liquid Paper began to take off.

When Bette Nesmith sold her enterprise,the Liquid Paper Corporation,in 1979,the tiny white bottles were earning $3.5 million annually on sales of $38 million.The buyer was the Gillette Company,and the sale price was $47.5 million.

Jennifer Read Hawthorne and Marci Shimoff
Adapted from a story in Bits & Pieces

说用户抱怨就是涂改不了错误。记录表明，从1959年8月到1960年4月，公司总收入为1141美元，而支出却是1217美元。

然而贝特并不放弃。她找了份兼职秘书工作，负责采购杂货，她还攒了200美元请一位化学专家来开发了快速上色的配方。

这一新配方的确奏效，贝特开始在全国各地推销她的小白瓶子。她每到一处就翻开电话簿，给每一位当地的供应商打电话联系。她还造访各个商店，赠送许多产品。这样一来，订货迅猛增长，另外新开发的液体纸也热销起来。

到1979年贝特出售她的液体纸公司时，那个小白瓶子已经有了3800万美元的销售额，每年给她带来了350万美元的利润。而最后的收购方是著名的吉列公司，收购价格竟高达4750万美元。

珍妮弗·里德·霍桑和玛茜·西莫夫
节选自《零碎故事集》

女性系列／挥洒四季的芬芳

Late for School

> *You are never too old to set another goal or to dream a new dream.*
>
> Les Brown

All my life,I've had this recurring dream that causes me to wake up feeling strange.In it,I am a little girl again,rushing about,trying to get ready for school.

"Hurry,Gin,you'll be late for school," my mother calls to me.

"I *am* hurrying,Mom! Where's my lunch?What did I do with my books?"

Deep inside I know where the dream comes from and what it means.It is God's way of reminding me of some unfinished business in my life.

I loved everything about school,even though the school I attended in Springfield,Ohio,in the 1920s was very strict.I loved books,teachers, even tests and homework.Most of all I longed to someday march down the aisle to the strains of*"Pomp and Circumstance"*. To me, that song was even more beautiful than*"Here Comes the Bride"*.

But there were problems.

The Great Depression hit the hardest at large,poor families like ours.With seven children,Mom and Dad had no money for things like fine school clothes.Every morning,I cut out strips of cardboard to stuff inside my shoes to cover the holes in the soles.There was no money for musical instruments or sports uniforms or after-school treats.We sang to

双语精华版·心灵鸡汤·

姗姗来迟

梦想不分老少，有志不在年高。

莱斯·布朗

在我这一生中，经常做同一个梦，惊醒后又觉得很奇怪。在梦里，我又变回了少女，为按时上学，忙得手忙脚乱。

"快点，金，你要迟到了！"妈妈在冲我大喊。

"我就好了，妈妈！午餐在哪？我的课本呢？"

我在内心深处很清楚这梦的由来和含义。这是上帝在告诫我：人生还有尚未完成的事业。

我喜欢学校里的一切，即使是20世纪20年代俄亥俄州斯普林菲尔德市我上的那所极为严格的学校也不例外。我喜欢课本，老师，甚至是各种考试和家庭作业。最想要做的还是有朝一日在学校毕业典礼上，和着《威风凛凛进行曲》，沿着礼堂中央过道，自豪地上台领取毕业证书。对我来说，听着那首毕业曲子比《婚礼进行曲》还要美妙幸福。

但是问题接踵而来。

大萧条时期的经济危机给了我们当头一棒，像我们这样的穷人家庭，谁都没能逃过一劫。家里有7个孩子，日子很拮据，我当然没法奢望父母能给我买件漂亮校服了。每天早上，我还要剪几条纸板塞进鞋子里，盖住鞋底的几个窟窿。没有钱置办乐器，买运动服，更没有放学后的活动器材。我们唱歌自娱自乐，玩抛石游戏、沙包游戏，

45

ourselves,played jacks or duck-on-the-rock,and munched on onions as we did homework.

These hardships I accepted.As long as I could go to school,I didn't mind too much how I looked or what I lacked.

What happened next was harder to accept.My brother Paul died of an infection after he accidentally stabbed himself in the eye with a fork. Then my father contracted tuberculosis and died.My sister,Margaret, caught the same disease,and soon she was gone,too.

The shock of these losses gave me an ulcer,and I fell behind in my schoolwork.Meanwhile,my widowed mother tried to keep going to the five dollars a week she made cleaning houses.Her face became a mask of despair.

One day I said to her,"Mom,I'm going to quit school and get a job to help out."

The look in her eyes was a mixture of grief and relief.

At fifteen,I dropped out of my beloved school and went to work in a bakery . My hope of walking down the aisle to "*Pomp and Circumstance*" was dead,or so I thought.

In 1940,I married Ed,a machinist,and we began our family.Then Ed decided to become a preacher,so we moved to Cincinnati,where he could attend the Cincinnati Bible Seminary.With the coming of children went the dream of schooling,forever.

Even so,I was determined that my children would have the education I had missed.I made sure the house was filled with books and magazines.I helped them with their homework and urged them to study hard.It paid off.All our six children eventually got some college training, and one of them is a college professor.

But Linda,our last child,had health problems.Juvenile arthritis in her hands and knees made it impossible for her to function in the typical classroom.Furthermore,the medications gave her cramps,

或者干脆边做家庭作业边大口啃洋葱。

吃这些苦我都没问题，只要还能上学，我不太在乎衣着难看还是家境贫寒。

不过接下来发生的更是难以接受。我的兄弟保罗不小心被叉子刺伤了眼睛，后来竟伤口感染而死。接着，我父亲患肺结核去世。我的姐姐，玛格丽特，随后得了同样的病，很快也离我而去。

我遭受了痛失亲人的沉重打击，从此一蹶不振，学校的学习也一落千丈。其间，我可怜的母亲只得忍着悲痛，帮人打扫屋子每周辛苦挣5美元来维持家用。她的脸上写满了绝望。

一天，我对她说："妈，我想退学，找份工作来帮家里渡过难关。"

母亲的眼神里充满了矛盾，既有些宽慰，又很痛心。

于是15岁那年，我辍学了。离开了我心爱的学校，进了一家面包店工作。我想这辈子，听着《威风凛凛进行曲》，参加学校毕业典礼的希望也随之成了泡影。

1940年，我嫁给了埃德，开始有了自己的家庭。埃德原本在厂里操控机器，后来决定成为一名传教士，所以我们搬到了辛辛那提，在那，我们可以进入辛辛那提圣经神学院学习。等到我生了几个孩子后，上学的梦想已是永远成空了。

即便这样，我还是坚持让我的孩子接受良好教育，弥补我失去的一切。我给家里买了很多书本杂志，帮助他们完成家庭作业，督促他们努力学习。辛苦终于有了回报，所有6个孩子最后都上了大学，其中一个还成了大学教授。

但是最后一个孩子琳达身体不好，孩提时落下的手脚关节炎，让她没法去一般学校上学。药物治疗后还带来一系列后遗症，如抽

stomach trouble and migraine headaches.

Teachers and principals were not always sympathetic.I lived in dread of the phone calls from school."Mom,I'm coming home."

Now Linda was nineteen,and still she did not have her high school diploma.She was repeating my own experience.

I prayed about this problem,and when we moved to Sturgis,Michigan,in 1979,I began to see an answer.I drove to the local high school to check it out.On the bulletin board,I spotted an announcement about evening courses.

*That's the answer,*I said to myself.*Linda always feels better in the evening,so I'll just sign her up for night school.*

Linda was busy filling out enrollment forms when the registrar looked at me with brown, persuasive eyes and said,"Mrs. Schantz, why don't *you* come back to school?"

I laughed in his face."Me?Ha! I'm an old woman.I'm fifty-five! "

But he persisted,and before I knew what I had done,I was enrolled for classes in English and crafts."This is only an experiment," I warned him,but he just smiled.

To my surprise,both Linda and I thrived in evening school.I went back again the next semester,and my grades steadily improved.

It was exciting,going to school again,but it was no game.Sitting in a class full of kids was awkward,but most of them were respectful and encouraging.During the day,I still had loads of housework to do and grandchildren to care for.Sometimes,I stayed up until two in the morning,adding columns of numbers for bookkeeping class.When the numbers didn't seem to work out,my eyes would cloud with tears and I would berate myself.*Why am I so dumb?*

But when I was down,Linda encouraged me. "Mom,you can't quit now! " And when she was down,I encouraged her.Together we would see this through.

搐、胃病和偏头痛。

校长和老师们并不总是那么关心和同情。我就怕琳达万一受不了，不知哪天会给我来电话："妈，我想回家。"

现在她也有19岁了，不过仍然没拿到高中毕业证书，正在重走我的老路。

我无数次祈祷能够解决这个问题，直到1979年我们搬到密歇根州的斯德基斯市后，我开始有了办法。一次我开车去当地一所高中咨询时，无意间在布告栏里看到了一则《夜校招生通告》。

就这么办了，我自言自语。琳达总是在晚上感觉要好些，所以我得赶快给她在夜校报名。

琳达正忙着填写招生表格，这时，学校的教导主任看着我，一双褐色的眼睛里面充满了期待，他劝说道："尚茨夫人，你为什么不也一起来上学？"

我冲他大笑起来。"我？哈哈！我这个老太太都55岁了！"

但最终在他的坚持下，我稀里糊涂就报了英语和工艺班。"这也就是试试啊。"我警告他，但他笑而不答。

让我惊讶的是，我和琳达在夜校表现都非常出色。于是，第二学期我又回来继续学习，各门成绩都有了稳步提高。

回到我心爱的学校，确实让人激动不已，不过学习也并不轻松。课堂上坐满了小孩，我在中间还是有些别扭，但多数孩子都很有礼貌，给我鼓劲加油。白天我有许多家庭作业要做，还要照看子女们的孩子。有时晚上熬到凌晨2点，我还在做会计课上的数字运算。当这些数字无法算出来时，我眼里充满泪水，十分自责。我怎么就这么笨呢？

还好，在我学习困难，心情郁闷时，琳达总是来鼓励我。"妈妈，你不能放弃！"而当她伤心时，我也同样激励她。我们俩在一起总能渡过难关。

At last, graduation was near, and the registrar called me into his office. I entered, trembling, afraid I had done something wrong.

He smiled and motioned for me to have a seat. "Mrs. Schantz," he began, "you have done very well in school."

I blushed with relief.

"As a matter of fact," he went on, "your classmates have voted unanimously for you to be class orator."

I was speechless.

He smiled again and handed me a piece of paper. "And here is a little reward for all your hard work."

I looked at the paper. It was a college scholarship for $3,000. "Thank you" was all I could think to say, and I said it over and over.

The night of graduation, I was terrified. Two hundred people were sitting out there, and public speaking was a brand-new experience for me. My mouth wrinkled as if I had been eating persimmons. My heart skipped beats, and I wanted to flee, but I couldn't! After all, my own children were sitting in that audience. I couldn't be a coward in front of them.

Then, when I heard the first strains of *"Pomp and Circumstance"*, my fears dissolved in a flood of delight. *I am graduating! And so is Linda!*

Somehow I got through the speech. I was startled by the applause, the first I ever remember receiving in my life.

Afterwards, roses arrived from my brothers and sisters throughout the Midwest. My husband gave me silk roses, "so they will not fade".

The local media showed up with cameras and recorders and lots of questions. There were tears and hugs and congratulations. I was proud of Linda, and a little afraid that I might have unintentionally stolen some of the attention that she deserved for her victory, but she seemed as proud as anyone of our dual success.

双
语
精
华
版
·
心
灵
鸡
汤
·

最后，毕业临近时，学校的教导主任让我去他的办公室。我进去时有些发抖，生怕自己做错了什么。

他笑着示意让我坐下。"尚茨夫人，"他开始说道，"你在这学习非常出色。"

听完这话，我终于放心了，但他的评价又让我惭愧，一下子脸都红了。

"事实上，"他继续说，"你的同学一致同意选你代表班级在毕业典礼上发言。"

我一时无语。

他又笑着递给我一张纸。"这是对你所有辛苦努力的一点奖励。"

我看了一眼，是一份大学奖学金，有3000美元。当时我所有能想到说的就是"谢谢"，我一遍又一遍地向他致谢。

毕业典礼当晚，我紧张极了。现场坐了有两百人，而公开演讲对我来说是一次全新的经历。我嘴皮发麻，就好像刚吃了许多青柿子，心里怦怦直跳，只想钻个洞逃走。但是我不能！我的子女们都在下面坐着，我不能在他们面前做个懦夫。

随后耳边第一次为我响起了《威风凛凛进行曲》，我开心的泪水翻涌而出。我毕业了！琳达也毕业了！

不知不觉，我就成功地结束了演讲。而后全场掌声雷动，让我大吃一惊，因为这是我这辈子第一次得到如此的荣耀。

后来，我那些在中西部的兄弟姐妹都寄来了玫瑰，向我表示祝贺。我丈夫也送了我一束丝绸玫瑰，说"这样就永不褪色，永不凋零"了。

当地媒体带着照相机、录音机也如约而至，对我进行了采访。泪水、拥抱和祝福接连不断，场面十分感人。我同样为女儿琳达感到骄傲，却又害怕我可能无意间影响了大家对她取得成功的关注，而她好像对我们俩的成功都感到无比自豪。

The class of '81 is history now,and I've gone on for some college education.

But sometimes,I sit down and put on the tape of my graduation speech.I hear myself say to the audience,"Don't ever underestimate your dreams in life.Anything can happen if you believe.Not a childish,magical belief.It means hard work,but never doubt that you can do it,with God's help."

And then,I remember the recurring dream—*Hurry,Gin,you'll be late for school*—and my eyes cloud over when I think of my mother.

Yes,Mom,I was late for school,but it was all the sweeter for waiting.I only wish you and Dad could have been there to see your daughter and granddaughter in all their *pomp and circumstance.*

Virginia Schantz
As told to Daniel Schantz

八一级高中已经成为过去,现在我又开始了大学学习。

有时我也静静地坐下来,听听我毕业演讲的磁带。我是这样说的,"绝不要低估你的人生梦想。只要你坚信梦想,一切皆有可能。这可不是幼稚或浪漫的想法,而是意味着艰辛努力。毋庸置疑,只要上帝与你同在,你就一定能够做到。"

然后我又一次记起了常做的那个梦——快点,金,你要迟到了——想起母亲,我不禁泪眼模糊。

是的,妈妈,我是上学迟到了,但经过这漫长的苦等,姗姗来迟的美好幸福就更加甜美了。我只希望你和爸爸在天堂里能看见你们的女儿和孙女都能够在盛大的庆典上,听着《威风凛凛进行曲》,迎接成功,实现梦想。

弗吉尼亚·尚茨
由丹尼尔·尚茨根据讲述整理

女性系列／挥洒四季的芬芳

He Taught Me to Fly

Everyone should carefully observe which way his heart draws him,and then choose that way with all his strength.

Hasidic Saying

My dad grew up not far from the Cabrini Green housing project in Chicago.The projects were built long after Dad moved out,but the tough, teeming neighborhood of his youth is not so very different from the neighborhood of today.It's still a place for people trying to find a way out of poverty and danger.To finally see that apartment house was to finally know the deepest part of my father.It was to finally understand why we spent so much time at odds.

Dad and I were always passionate about our feelings — we're Italian,after all — and when I reached my teen years,our arguments really heated up.I can't remember a meal from those years that we didn't argue through.Politics,feminism,the war in Vietnam.Our biggest fight, however,was an ongoing one.It was about my chosen profession.

"People like us aren't writers! " Dad would shout.

"Maybe people like *you* aren't writers," I would shoot back,"but people like *me* are! "

What I said was truer than I knew.

I grew up in a nice house with a lawn,a dog and lots of room to stretch out in.My only responsibilities were to get good grades and stay out of major trouble.Dad spent his youth squeezed into a tenement,taking care of a widowed mother who spoke no English,helping to parent

展翅高飞

每个人都要仔细观察自己的心灵轨迹，然后竭尽全力选择自己的人生道路。

　　　　　　　　　　海西狄克·塞茵

　　我父亲是在离芝加哥卡布里尼大型绿色公共住宅区不远的地方长大的。父亲从那个地区搬出来很长时间以后，大型住宅区才建造完成。那片地区在他年轻时就是拥挤不堪、暴力不断、犯罪频发，现在的情况也没什么大变样。这里的人们至今还在努力解决贫困、摆脱危险。只有看到那些公寓楼房，才能真正深入了解父亲的内心世界，也才能明白为什么我和父亲长期在不停地争吵。

　　父亲和我总是容易情绪激动，因为我们是意大利人。从我少年时期，我们的争论就已经白热化了。这些年来，我记得没有哪一餐不是在争吵中草草结束的。政治、女权、越战，都是我们争吵的对象，但是吵得最凶，也是不断升级的，还是关于我的择业问题。

　　"我们这样的人绝不可能当上作家。"父亲常这样咆哮。

　　"也许是你这样的人才当不了作家。"我奋力回击，"但是我这样的就行！"

　　实际上，我所说的比我知道的还要真实。

　　我成长的环境很好，漂亮的房子、草坪、小狗、宽敞的地方让我随处休息。我唯一的任务就是好好学习，取得好成绩，然后就无忧无虑了。可是父亲年轻时，一家人挤在一间狭小的出租屋里。他的母亲可怜守寡，又不会英语，自己下面还有两个弟妹，全靠他照顾。他还

55

two younger siblings—and earning enough money in whatever way he could to keep the family going.

Dad's dream was to move up and out of the old neighborhood,and after he married,he did.He drew a curtain over his past,never speaking of his growing-up days.Not to anyone.Ever.It was a point of pride with him that he allowed no one to know what he had suffered through.But by not knowing Dad's past,I could never really know him,or what drove him to want so much security for me.

As I persisted in my career,despite all the rejections,Mom told me Dad read and re-read everything I got published,although he never mentioned my work to me.Instead,he continually tried to steer me into a career he considered far safer—nursing or teaching or secretarial.

But in the last week of his life,as I sat by his bed,Dad opened up.It was as if he suddenly realized that soon it would be too late to let anyone know the truth.That's when he had me dig out a box of pictures he'd buried deep in the garage;that's when I finally saw what he and his brother and sister had looked like as children,and where they had lived.It was when I came face to face not only with Dad's old home,but with my father himself.

In those last days,Dad talked about everything.How it felt to carry buckets of coal up four flights of stairs and share one bathroom with five other families.he told me that he was always worried that his brother and sister wouldn't have enough to eat or that they wouldn't have enough warm clothes for winter,or that someone in the family would get sick and there wouldn't be enough money for medicine or doctors.He told me about the Saturdays he spent on a country club golf course,how wonderful the grass looked to him,and how he tried to get the men to use him as a caddie.After eighteen holes,if he was lucky, they'd toss him a quarter.

Dad told me how he'd wanted to protect me from poverty and

双语精华版·心灵鸡汤·

CHICKEN SOUP

要想尽一切办法挣够钱来维持家用。

当时父亲的梦想就是改善生活,搬出老城区,而这在他结婚后也实现了。不过他对年轻时的事情却讳莫如深,绝口不言。自己的痛苦从未对任何人提过,这正是父亲的自豪。然而,对父亲过去的一无所知,我就不能真正了解他,了解究竟是什么让他要对我如此保密。

就在我不顾大家反对,坚持自己的职业时,母亲悄悄告诉我,父亲虽然从不跟我提起写作,却把我发表的每一件作品都拿来一遍遍地仔细研读。而平时他还在继续努力劝导,想让我从事他认为更加安稳的职业,如护士、教师或秘书。

在他临终前一周里,我在他床边看护。他好像是突然意识到时日不多,向我敞开了心扉。他让我把深埋在车库地下的一箱子照片挖了出来,我终于看到了父亲和他的弟弟妹妹小时候的样子,还有他们当时生活的地方。此时,我不仅见到了父亲的老房子,而且真正开始了和父亲面对面地坦诚交流。

最后的几天,父亲几乎谈到了每件事情,有背着大量笨重的煤炭,上4层楼之后筋疲力尽,也有5家人合用一个厕所的尴尬处境。他总是担心弟弟妹妹平时吃不饱,冬天穿不暖,或是家人生病没钱买药请医生。每逢周六,他就去一个乡村俱乐部高尔夫球场。那儿青翠绿草,环境优美,而他就缠着在那打球的有钱人,当他们的球童。幸运的话,18个洞后,他们会丢给他一个25美分的硬币。

父亲告诉我他一直想让我衣食无忧,不用再去经历他的苦难岁

want,so I'd never have to go through what he had.He told me how important it was to him that I have something to fall back on.And I told Dad that what I'd fallen back on all these years was him.I told him my hopes and dreams had been built on his strong shoulders.I told him the roots he'd given me ran deep,and when he apologized for trying to clip my wings,I told him that he was the one who'd given me the chance to fly.Dad smiled at that and tried to nod,but I wasn't sure if he'd really understood what I'd meant.

But on the afternoon of the last day of his life,as Mom and I sat holding his hands,he beckoned the two hospice volunteers close. "You know my daughter," he whispered with great effort. "Well,I just want you to know—she's a writer."

It was the proudest moment of my life.

Cynthia Mercati

月,而且对他来说,让我有所依靠是多么重要。我也告诉父亲,是他坚强的肩膀撑起了我的希望和梦想,给我打下了坚实的基础。谈到当年想剪除我的翅羽,一切听他安排时,他向我道歉,我却说,正是他让我有了机会去飞翔。父亲听罢,微笑着想要点头,但我不确定他是否真的明白我的意思。

在他生命的最后一天中午,母亲和我坐在他身边,握住他的双手,但他却意外地招手让两位医院的临终护理义工靠近。"你们知道我女儿,"他费尽力气,也只是低声耳语,"哦,我是想让你们知道——她是个作家。"

这是我一生中最自豪的时刻。

辛西娅·莫卡提

The Real Thing

If I know what love is,it is because of you.

Herman Hesse

Cecile and I have been friends since college,for more than thirty years.Although we have never lived closer than 100 miles to each other, since we first met,our friendship has remained constant.We have seen each other through marriage,birth,divorce,the death of loved ones—all those times when you really need a friend.

In celebration of our friendship and our fiftieth birthday,Cecile and I took our first road trip together.We drove from my home in Texas to California and back.What a wonderful time we had!

The first day of our trip ended in Santa Fe,New Mexico.After the long drive,we were quite tired,so we decided to go to the restaurant near the hotel for dinner.We were seated in a rather quiet part of the dining room with only a few other patrons.We ordered our food and settled back to recount our day.As we talked,I glanced at the other people in the room.I noticed an attractive elderly couple sitting a short distance away from us.The gentleman was rather tall and athletic looking,with silver hair and a tanned complexion.The lady seated beside him was petite,well-dressed and lovely.What caught my immediate attention was the look of adoration on the woman's face.She sat,chin resting gently on her hands,and stared into the face of the man as he talked.She reminded me of a teenager in love!

I called Cecile's attention to the couple.As we watched,he reached

无尽的爱

如果我知道什么是爱，那是因为有你的存在。

赫尔曼·赫西

从大学算起，我和塞西尔的友谊已经有30多年了。虽然我们住在两地，之间距离也从没拉近到100英里以内，但从第一次认识开始，我们的友谊就一直深厚长久。在人生最需要友情的那些日子里，我们彼此见证对方从结婚到离婚，从子女出生到亲人离去。

为了庆祝友谊和我俩的50岁生日，塞西尔和我第一次结伴公路旅行。我们从我家乡得克萨斯州驱车往返于加利福尼亚州，美妙的行程真让人流连忘返！

在新墨西哥州首府圣达菲我们结束了第一天旅程。经过长途驱车，我们已是一身疲惫，所以决定就在旅馆附近找家餐厅。店里顾客不多，我们选了个安静的地方，免受打扰。点完饭菜，我们往后一靠，开始聊起这一天的见闻。一边聊天，我一边扫了一眼餐厅里的其他顾客。我注意到不远处有一对老夫妇，挺有意思。老头个子很高，体格健硕，古铜色的肌肤，一头银发。旁边的老太太身材娇小，穿着讲究，可爱动人。她脸上的爱慕之情立即引起我的注意，那位花白老头讲话时，她就双手微微托着下巴，两眼凝视，一片深情，让我联想起恋爱中少女的样子。

我不敢独享这温馨场面，于是让塞西尔也来关注这对老夫妇。继

over to place a gentle kiss on her cheek.She smiled.

"Now that's what I call real love! " I said with a sign."I imagine they've been married for a long time.They look so in love! "

"Or maybe,"remarked Cecile, "they haven't been together long.It could be they've just fallen in love."

"Well whatever the case,it's obvious they care a great deal for each other.They are in love."

Cecile and I watched surreptitiously and unashamedly eavesdropped on their conversation.He was explaining to her about a new business investment he was considering and asking her opinion.She smiled and agreed with whatever he said.When the waitress came to take their order,he ordered for her,reminding her that the veal was her favorite.He caressed her hand as he talked,and she listened raptly to his every word. We were enthralled by the poignant scene we were witnessing.

Then the scene changed.A perplexed look came over the finely wrinkled but beautiful face.She looked at the man and said in a sweet voice,"Do I know you?What it this place?Where are we?"

"Now,sweetheart,you know me.I'm Ralph,your husband.And we're in Santa Fe.We are going to see our son in Missouri tomorrow.Don't you remember?"

"Oh,I'm not sure.I seem to have forgotten," she said quietly.

"That's okay,sweetheart.You'll be all right.Just eat your dinner,and we'll go and get some rest." He reached over and caressed her cheek. "You sure do look pretty tonight."

Tears coursed down our cheeks as Cecile and I looked at each other. "We were right," she said quietly. "It is the real thing.That is love."

Frankie Germany

续看时,老头伸过头去,温柔地吻了老太太的面颊。她也幸福地笑了。

"那才是我所说的真爱!"我指着说道,"我想他们肯定是多年的夫妻了,看起来是多么恩爱。"

"或许,"塞西尔说,"他们在一起还没多久。可能刚刚坠入爱河。"

"不论哪种情形,很明显,他们相互关爱,心系对方,彼此深爱。"

我和塞西尔继续悄悄地偷听他们对话,丝毫没有觉得有什么不妥。老头向她解释他正考虑一项新的投资并且征求她的意见。无论他说什么,那位优雅的老太总是微笑着同意。当女招待过来点菜时,老头又为她点了些东西,并提醒她,小牛肉是她的最爱。他说话时还轻抚她的小手,她也十分默契地倾听他说的每一个字。这令人羡慕的一幕让我们看得是如痴如醉。

接下来场面发生了变化。她那皱纹细密但依旧漂亮的脸上掠过一丝困惑。她痴痴地望着对面的老头,甜甜地说道:"我认识你吗?这是什么地方?我们在哪?"

"我的甜心,你当然认识我。我是拉尔夫,你丈夫啊。我们在圣达菲。明天我们就要去密苏里看我们的儿子。你想不起来了吗?"

"哦,我弄不清楚。好像忘掉了。"她轻轻地念道。

"没事儿,亲爱的。你会好起来的。你吃饭吧,我们还要去好好睡一觉。"他伸过手来轻抚她的脸庞。"今晚,你看起来真漂亮。"

我和塞西尔相顾无言,唯有泪千行。她终于静静地说道:"我们是对的,那不是假的,是真爱。"

弗兰克·杰默尼

The Locket

As a seminar leader,I hear a lot of stories about people's lives and experiences.One day at the end of a seminar,a woman came up to me and told me about an event that changed her life—and in the telling, touched mine.

"I used to think I was just a nurse," she began,"until one day a couple of years ago.

"It was noontime and I was feeding 'the feeders',the elderly who cannot feed themselves.Messy work,keeping track of each one and making sure they keep the food in their mouths.I looked up as an elderly gentleman passed by the dining room doorway.He was on his way down the hall for a daily visit with his wife.

"Our eyes met over the distance,and I knew right then in my heart that I should be with them both that noon hour.My coworker covered for me,and I followed him down the corridor.

"When I entered the room,she was lying in bed,looking up at the ceiling with her arms across her chest.He was sitting in the chair at the end of the bed with his arms crossed,looking at the floor.

"I walked over to her and said,'Susan,is there anything you want to share today?If so,I came down to listen.'She tried to speak but her lips were dry and nothing came out.I bent over closer and asked again.

"'Susan,if you cannot say it with words,can you show me with your hands?'

"She carefully lifted her hands off her chest and held them up before her eyes.They were old hands,with leathery skin and swollen knuckles,worn from years of caring,working and living.She then grasped

心灵金盒

作为一名研讨会的培训主持人，我常常听到许多关于人生经历的感人故事。一天，研讨会结束后，一位女士前来找我，讲起了一次改变她人生的不寻常经历。她的讲述也同样深深地打动了我。

"我过去总认为我只不过是个护士而已，"她开始说道，"直到多年前的一天。"

"那是中午时候，我正在给那些无法自己进食的老年人喂饭。这是个苦差事，要仔细照看到每一位老人，还要确保食物入口，不能有一滴流出来。一位老先生经过餐厅入口处时，我抬头看了看，他正走过大厅，去探望他的妻子，每日如此。"

"和他目光接触时，我心里立刻明白，这个中午该去陪陪他们俩。于是我让同事替我一会儿，随后我也进了走廊。"

"当我走进房间时，老太太躺在床上，两臂交叉放在胸前，两眼向上望着天花板。而他在床尾坐在椅子上，两臂交叉，望着地上。"

"我走到她跟前，说道：'苏姗，今天有什么往事想要和我们分享的吗？如果有，我就来好好听听。'她努力想要说话，但嘴唇焦干，什么也没说出来。我弯腰凑近她，又问了一遍。"

"'苏姗，你要是说不出来，能用手示意一下吗？'"

"她小心把手从胸前拿开，撑着放在眼前。这一双手，经过多年家庭、工作和生活的艰辛磨难，已是皮肤粗糙，关节肿大。接着，她抓

the collar of her nightgown and began to pull.

"I unbuttoned the top buttons.She reached in and pulled out a long gold chain connected to a small gold locket.She held it up,and tears came to her eyes.

"Her husband got up from the end of the bed and came over.Sitting beside her,he took his hands and tenderly placed them around hers. 'There is a story about this locket,'he explained,and he began to tell it to me.

"'One day many months ago,we awoke early and I told Susan I could no longer care for her by myself.I could not carry her to the bathroom,keep the house clean,plus cook all the meals.My body could no longer do this.I,too,had aged.

"'We talked long and hard that morning.She told me to go to coffee club and ask where a good place might be.I didn't return until lunch time.We chose here from the advice of others.

"'On the first day,after all the forms,the weighing and the tests,the nurse told us that her fingers were so swollen that they would need to cut off her wedding rings.

"'After everyone left the room,we sat together and she asked me, "What do we do with a broken ring and a whole ring?" For I had chosen to take off my ring that day,too.

"'Both of these rings were old,more oval than round.Thin in some places and strong in other parts.We made a difficult decision.That was the hardest night in my entire life.It was the first time we had slept apart in forty-three years.

"'The next morning I took the two rings to the jewelers and had them melted.Half of that locket is my ring,and the other half is hers.The clasp is made from the engagement ring that I gave her when I proposed to her,down by the pond at the back of the farm on a warm summer's evening.She told me it was about time and answered yes.

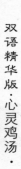

紧睡衣领子,开始用力拽扯。

"我帮她解开最上面的几个扣子。她伸手进去拽出一根长长的金项链,上面挂着一个小金盒子。她手拿着项链,眼里噙着泪水。"

"她丈夫立刻起身从床尾走过来,在她旁边坐下,轻柔地握住她的双手。'关于这个小金盒子还有一段故事。'他向我解释道,开始讲给我听。"

"'好几个月前的一天,我醒得很早,告诉她,我恐怕不能再亲自照看她了。像背她去卫生间,打扫房屋,还有一日三餐,这些我都做不了了。毕竟,我也上年纪了。'"

"'那天早上,我们好好地谈了很长时间,她让我去咖啡店问问有什么好地方可以安顿的。直到午饭时候我才回来。听了其他人的建议,我们最终选了你们这儿。'"

"'来这儿的头一天,填好表格,称完体重,做过体检,护士告诉我们,她的手指肿得厉害,必须剪开她的结婚戒指。'"

"'等大家都离开房间后,我们一起坐下来,她问我,"该怎么处理我这枚剪断了的戒指和你那枚完好的呢?"因为那天看她剪下了戒指,我也摘下了我的戒指。'"

"'这是两枚古朴的戒指,椭圆形状,有的部分纤细,有的厚实。我们做出了一个艰难的决定。那是我一辈子最煎熬的一个晚上,43年来,我们第一次分开睡了。'"

"'第2天一早,我带着两枚戒指去了珠宝店,把它们合二为一,熔炼在一起。小金盒一半是我的戒指,另一半是她的。钩扣是订婚戒指做成的。那是一个仲夏夜晚,在农场后面的池塘边上,我向她求婚时送给她的。她告诉我早就该来求婚了,接着就愉快地答应了。'"

"'On the inside it says *I love Susan* and on the other side it says *I love you Joseph*.We made this locket because we were afraid that one day we might not be able to say these words to each other.'

"He picked her up and held her gently in his arms.I knew that I was the channel,and they had the message.I slipped out the door and went back to feeding the feeders with more kindness in my heart.

"After lunch and the paperwork,I walked back down to their room. He was rocking her in his arms and singing the last verse of '*Amazing Grace*'.I waited while he laid her down,crossed her arms and closed her eyes.

"He turned to me at the door and said,'Thank you.She passed away just a little bit ago.Thank you very much.'

"I used to say I was 'just a nurse'or 'just a mom',but I don't anymore.No one is just an anything.Each of us has gifts and talents.We need not limit ourselves by such small definitions.I know what I can do when I listen to my heart and live from there."

As she finished her story,we hugged and she left.I stood in the doorway with thankfulness.

Geery Howe

"'金盒里面刻着:我爱苏珊,另一面刻着:我爱你,约瑟夫。我们做这个金盒就是害怕有一天我们都老得说不动这些话了。'"

"说到这里,他扶着她起来,轻轻地搂住她。我顿时明白,我当了一回心灵使者,让他们一起分享了美好的记忆。不忍心惊扰了此刻的温馨,我溜出了房门,回来继续我的工作,但心里面已是多了几分亲切。"

"吃过午饭,忙好文书事务,我又回到他们的房间,只见他抱着她,轻轻摇晃,嘴里唱着《奇异恩典》这首赞美诗的最后一句。接着,他把她轻轻放下,交叉双臂,帮她合上双眼。此时,我不敢打扰,只是在门边静静守候。"

"然后,他朝我走来,说道:'谢谢你。她就在刚才去世了。非常感谢你。'"

"以前我总是说'我不过就是个护士'或'就是孩子的妈妈',但自那以后我不再这样说了。一切都不是一成不变的,我们每个人都拥有天赋和才华,我们所要做的就是挣脱这些原先对我们定义的约束。当倾听我的心声,就能够感受到一股力量的支撑,我就能更加明白那些是我所能做的。"

听她讲完这个故事,我们相互拥抱。她走过以后,我还站在门口,心里充满了感激之情。

吉瑞·豪

The Dowry

In the faraway world of the South Pacific,there is an island named Nurabandi and,nearby,another one called Kiniwata.

The natives of these islands are all said to be very wonderful,to be fine and proud,but they still hold to the ageless custom of offering a dowry to a girl's family when a young man asks for her hand in marriage.

Johnny Lingo lived on the island of Nurabandi.He was handsome and rich and perhaps the smartest businessman on the entire island.Everyone knew that Johnny,a young bachelor,could have his pick of just about any of the single girls in the region.

But Johnny only had eyes for Sarita,who lived on Kiniwata,and some people had a hard time figuring that out.

Sarita,you see,was a rather plain,homely looking girl.When she walked,her shoulders slumped and her head ducked down just so.

Nonetheless,Johnny was deeply in love with Sarita and made arrangements to meet Sarita's father,a man named Sam Karoo,to ask for her hand in marriage and to discuss a proper dowry.

Now,the dowry was always paid in live cows because the animals were at such a premium on the small islands of the Pacific rim.History showed that some of the most beautiful South Pacific girls went for a dowry of four cows or,in a really rare instance,five.

Further,Johnny Lingo was the shrewdest trader on the island of Nurabandi and Sarita's daddy,bless his heart,was the worst of anyone on the island of Kiniwata.

Knowing this,a worried Sam Karoo sat down with his family the

结婚彩礼

在遥远的南太平洋地区,有一座岛屿,名叫努拉班迪岛,不远的地方还有一座,叫克尼瓦塔岛。

据说这些岛上的居民天性乐观、热情开朗,生活得自由自在,人人都感到幸福自豪,但他们却还保留这样的一个古老的风俗,当男子向女子求婚时,必须要向女方家人送上一份彩礼。

约翰尼·林戈就住在努拉班迪岛上。他英俊潇洒,十分有钱,极有可能是整个岛上最为精明能干的生意人。大家都认为,约翰尼这个钻石王老五,以他的条件可以自由挑选这里的任何一个单身女子作为他的妻子。

可是约翰尼偏偏只看中了住在克尼瓦塔岛上的女子莎丽塔,在别人看来这实在是不可思议。

因为莎丽塔相貌平平,极为普通,走路时还常常含胸低头,弓腰塌肩。

尽管这样,约翰尼仍然对莎丽塔一片痴情,并且安排好去拜见她的父亲,萨姆·卡鲁,郑重向莎丽塔求婚,同时商谈彩礼如何准备。

由于在太平洋地区的这些偏远小岛上,牲畜十分难得,所以现在彩礼就以奶牛来充当。过去南太平洋地区最漂亮的女孩子所要的彩礼一般为4头奶牛,最多也不过5头。

此外,约翰尼·林戈是努拉班迪岛上最精明的商人,而莎丽塔的父亲却是克尼瓦塔岛上生活最为贫困潦倒的。

萨姆·卡鲁知道两家的差距,在大家关注的会见前一天晚上,心

night before the, now-famous meeting and nervously plotted his strategy: He'd ask Johnny for three cows,but hold out for two until they were sure Johnny would give one.

The next day,at the very start of the meeting,Johnny Lingo looked Sam Karoo right in the eye and said evenly,"I would like to offer you eight cows as I ask your daughter,Sarita,to marry me."

Well,Sam stammered that would be just fine.Soon there was a dandy wedding,but nobody on any of the islands could figure out why on earth Johnny gave eight cows for Sarita.

Six months later,an American visitor,a gifted writer named Pat McGerr,met with Johnny Lingo at his beautiful home on Nurabandi and asked about the eight cows.

The writer had already been to the island of Kiniwata and had heard the villagers there still giggling over the fact that stupid ol' Sam had duped the wise Johnny out of eight cows for the homely and plain Sarita.

Yet in Nurabandi,no one dared laugh at Johnny Lingo because he was held in such high esteem.When the writer finally met Johnny,the new husband's eyes twinkled as he gently questioned the writer.

"I hear they speak of me on that island.My wife is from there."

"Yes,I know,"said the writer.

"So,tell me,what do they say?" asked Johnny.

The writer,struggling to be diplomatic,replied,"Well,that you were married to Sarita at festival time."

Johnny pressed on and on until the writer finally told him candidly, "They say you gave eight cows for your wife,and they wonder why you did that."

Right then,the most beautiful woman the writer had even seen came into the room to put flowers on the table.She was tall.And her shoulders were square.And her chin was straight.And,when her eyes caught Johnny's,there was an undeniable spark.

情变得沉重起来,紧张地开始和家人坐下来策划他的对策:他会首先要求约翰尼送上3头奶牛,否则,他就一定坚持要两头,一直到约翰尼明确表示只能给一头为止。

第2天,两人刚一会面,约翰尼就真诚地望着萨姆·卡鲁,平静地说道:"我想给你8头奶牛,请您把女儿莎丽塔许配给我。"

萨姆听完十分诧异,结结巴巴地就立刻说了句,那很好。很快,约翰尼和莎丽塔就举办了盛大的婚礼,但是岛上没人能想得出来,约翰尼·林戈究竟为什么要给莎丽塔8头奶牛作为彩礼。

6个月后,努拉班迪岛上来了位美国游客,名叫帕特·麦克格尔,是一位才华横溢的作家。她来到约翰尼漂亮的家里,见到了约翰尼,并问起了关于8头奶牛彩礼的事情。

这位作家先前已经去过了克尼瓦塔岛,听到当地村民至今还在笑谈,愚蠢的老萨姆用他其貌不扬的女儿从精明的约翰尼那里骗走了8头奶牛。

然而在努拉班迪岛上,没人敢嘲笑约翰尼·林戈,因为他在本地颇有威信,很受人们尊重。在帕特与约翰尼会面时,这一新婚丈夫,眼里难掩喜悦的神情,轻轻地问起这位作家。

"我听说那座岛上的人们在议论我。我妻子是那儿人。"

"是的,我知道。"作家答道。

"那就告诉我,他们都说了些什么?"约翰尼问道。

这位作家,竭力想说得圆滑些,不要太冒昧。她回答说:"哦,他们说你是在节日里娶了莎丽塔的。"

在约翰尼的一再追问下,这位作家才坦白地告诉他:"他们说你给你妻子8头牛作彩礼,他们想知道你为什么那么做。"

就在那时,一位女子走进屋来,把鲜花放在了桌子上。这位作家从没见过如此美貌的女子,个子高挑,肩膀宽平,下巴俏直。眼神与约翰尼交汇时,闪烁着迷人的火花。

"This is my wife,Sarita,"the now-amused Johnny said,and as Sarita excused herself,the writer was mystified.

And then Johnny began to explain.

"Do you ever think what it must mean to a woman to know her husband settled on the lowest price for which she could be bought?

"And then later,when the women talk among themselves,they boast what their husbands paid for them.One says four cows,another says three.But how does the woman feel who is bought for only one?" said Johnny.

"I wasn't going to let that happen to my Sarita.I wanted Sarita to be happy,yes,but it was more than that.You say she is different than you were told.That is true,but many things change a woman.

"Things happen inside and things happen outside,but what's most important is what she thinks about herself.In Kiniwata,Sarita believed she was worth nothing,but now she knows she is worth more than any woman on any of the islands."

Johnny Lingo paused just so and then added,"I wanted to marry Sarita from the beginning.I loved her and no other woman.But I also wanted to have an eight-cow wife,and,so you see,my dream came true."

Roy Exum

"这位就是我的妻子,莎丽塔。"约翰尼立刻开心地介绍。而当莎丽塔礼貌地离开时,这位作家深深地陷入了迷惑之中。

　　接下来,约翰尼开始了解释。

　　"你是否想过,如果一个女人知道她丈夫用很低的代价就把她娶来时,那对她是意味着什么?

　　"再往后,女人谈起她们自己时,就开始吹嘘起丈夫为她们付了多少彩礼。一个说4头奶牛,另一个说是3头,而只有一头奶牛就娶来的女子又会怎么想呢?"

　　"我不会让我的莎丽塔出现那样的事情。我只想莎丽塔开心快乐,是的,而且还不止这些。你说她跟你听到的完全不一样。是的,没错,但是很多事情都能改变一个女人。"

　　"有内在的变化,也有外在的,但最重要的是她是怎样看她自己的。在克尼瓦塔岛,莎丽塔认为她一无是处,但是现在她很清楚,她超过了任何一座岛上的任何一位女子。"

　　约翰尼·林戈顿了一下,又接着说:"从一开始我就想娶莎丽塔为妻,我爱她,对她忠贞不渝。但我也想有一位8头牛的妻子,所以你看,我现在梦想成真了。"

罗伊·埃克萨姆

I'll Never Understand My Wife

In every union there is a mystery.

Henri F.Amiel

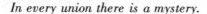

I'll never understand my wife.

The day she moved in with me,she started opening and closing my kitchen cabinets,gasping,"You don't have any shelf paper! We're going to have to get some shelf paper in here before I move my dishes in."

"But why?"I asked innocently.

"To keep the dishes clean,"she answered matter-of-factly.I didn't understand how the dust would magically migrate off the dishes if they had sticky blue paper under them,but I knew when to be quiet.

Then came the day when I left the toilet seat up.

"We never left the toilet seat up in my family," she scolded."It's impolite."

"It wasn't impolite in my family,"I said sheepishly.

"You're family didn't have cats."

In addition to these lessons,I also learned how I was supposed to squeeze the toothpaste tube,which towel to use after a shower and where the spoons are supposed to go when I set the table.I had no idea I was so uneducated.

Nope,I'll never understand my wife.

She alphabetizes her spices,washes dishes before sending them through the dishwasher,and sorts laundry into different piles before throwing it into the washing machine.Can you imagine?

双语精华版·心灵鸡汤·

琢磨不透的爱妻

在每个婚姻里，都有一些解不开的谜。

亨利·F·埃米尔

我永远也无法弄懂我的妻子。

搬来和我一起过的第一天，她就开始把我厨房的碗橱开了关，关了开，一阵乱翻，还惊叫起来："你橱架上面怎么一张垫纸都没有！放我的碗碟之前，我们一定得去买点放这儿。"

"为什么？"我傻乎乎地问。

"保持碗碟干净。"她一本正经地回答。我实在不明白，难道下面贴一张蓝色的垫纸，灰尘就会神秘地从碗碟上飘落下来吗？但我知道这个时候不该多嘴。

又有一天，我没把坐便器盖子放下来。

"在我家，我们绝不会忘了这事，"她严厉批评我。"这不礼貌。"

"而在我家，这没什么不礼貌的。"我难为情地回答。

"那是因为你们家没有养过猫。"

除了这些教训外，我还学会了该怎样挤牙膏，洗完澡该用哪条浴巾，还有摆饭桌时，各种汤匙该怎么放。真不知道我是这样的没教养。

不，我永远也无法琢磨透我的妻子。

她把调味品按字母顺序排列，自己把碗碟先洗一遍，再放进洗碗机，还有脏衣服分成几堆再扔进洗衣机。你能想象得到吗？

She wears pajamas to bed.I didn't think anyone in North America still wore pajamas to bed.She has a coat that makes her look like Sherlock Holmes."I could get you a new coat," I offered.

"No.This one was my grandmother's," she said,decisively ending the conversation.

Then,after we had kids,she acted even stranger.Wearing those pajamas all day long,eating breakfast at 1:00 P.M.,carrying around a diaper bag the size of a minivan,talking in one syllable paragraphs.

She carried our baby everywhere—on her back,on her front,in her arms,over her shoulder.She never set her down,even when other young mothers shook their heads as they set down the car seat with their baby in it,or peered down into their playpens.When an oddity she was,clutching that child.

My wife also chose to nurse her even when her friends told her not to bother.She picked up the baby whenever she cried,even though people told her it was healthy to let her wail.

"It's good for her lungs to cry," they would say.

"It's better for her heart to smile," she'd answer.

One day a friend of mine snickered at the bumper sticker my wife had put on the back of our car:"Being a Stay-at-Home Mom Is a Work of Heart."

"My wife must have put that on there," I said.

"My wife works," he boasted.

"So does mine," I said,smiling.

Once,I was filling out one of those warranty registration cards and I checked"homemaker" for my wife's occupation.Big mistake.She glanced over it and quickly corrected me. "I am not a homemaker.I am not a housewife.I am a mother."

"But there's no category for that," I stammered.

"Add one," she said.

她穿着睡衣睡裤上床睡觉，我觉得在北美谁都不会这样的了。她还有件外套穿起来就像大侦探福尔摩斯。"我给你买件新外套吧，"我建议她。

"不。这件可是我奶奶传给我的。"她说道，随即断然结束我们的谈话。

后来，我们有了孩子，她表现得就更像个陌生人了。整天穿着那几套睡衣，下午1点才吃早餐，随身带着巨大的尿布袋子，说话飞快，一口气讲完，都没停顿的。

她带孩子方式五花八门，后面背着，前面抱着，胳膊夹着，肩膀扛着。她从不把孩子放下来，这让其他年轻妈妈们极为不解。因为她们一般把汽车座椅放倒让孩子在里面玩，或者小心看着孩子在婴儿围栏里玩耍。而她总是奇怪地紧紧抓住孩子不放。

尽管有朋友建议她喂孩子别太麻烦了，她还是选择自己来母乳喂养。即使有人告诉她孩子啼哭有利身体健康，只要我们的孩子一哭，她总是抱她起来。

"啼哭有利于孩子的肺脏。"有人建议。

"微笑更有利于孩子的心脏。"她反驳道。

一天我的一个朋友对着我们车后她贴的保险杠贴纸一阵窃笑。上面写着："家庭主妇乃用心之作。"

"那肯定是我妻子贴上去的。"我说。

"我妻子在外面工作。"我朋友特别得意。

"我妻子在家里工作。"我笑着说道。

记得有一次，在填写一张产品保修单注册卡时，我在妻子的职业一项上面勾选了"全职主妇"。这下可犯大错了。她扫了一眼，迅速做了更正。"我不是全职主妇，我也不是家庭主妇，我是一位母亲。"

"但上面没这样的选项。"我有点结巴。

"那就添一个上去。"她说道。

I did.

And then one day,a few years later,she lay in bed smiling when I got up to go to work.

"What's wrong?" I asked.

"Nothing.Everything is wonderful.I didn't have to get up at all last night to calm the kids.And they didn't crawl in bed with us."

"Oh," I said,still not understanding.

"It was the first time I've slept through the night in four years." It was?Four years?That's a long time.I hadn't even noticed.Why hadn't she ever complained?I would have.

One day,in one thoughtless moment,I said something that sent her fleeing to the bedroom in tears.I went in to apologize.She knew I meant it because by then I was crying,too.

"I forgive you," she said.And you know what?She did.She never brought it up again.Not even when she got angry and could have hauled out the heavy artillery.She forgave,and she forgot.

Nope,I'll never understand my wife.And you know what?Our daughter is acting more and more like her mother every day.

If she turns out to be anything like her mom,someday there's going be one more lucky guy in this world,thankful for the shelf paper in his cupboard.

Steven James

于是我立刻照办。

几年后的一天清早，我起床准备去上班，她躺在床上冲我笑。

"有什么不对的吗？"我问道。

"没事。一切都挺好的。昨晚我用不着起来哄孩子，她们也没有在我们床上乱爬。"

"哦，"我说道，还没意识到什么。

"4年来，这是我第一次睡了个通宵安稳觉。"是吗？4年？真够长的。我根本都没注意到。为什么她从不抱怨呢？换了我肯定会。

有一天，我说了句没走脑子的胡话，把她气得跑回卧室，号啕大哭。我紧跟进去，向她赔礼道歉。她最后看出来我是真心悔过，因为那时，我也哭了起来。

"我原谅你。"她说。你知道接下来怎样？她真的做到了。即便是后来大发雷霆时，她再也没有翻起这件旧账。她原谅了，也忘记了。

不，我没法弄懂我的妻子。知道现在怎样了？我们女儿每天的表现，越来越像她妈妈了。

如果她变得跟她妈妈一模一样，那将来的某一天，这个世界上会有一个更加有福气的小伙子，来感谢她买的碗橱柜垫纸。

史蒂文·詹姆斯

Loving Donna

It has been said that love is not something you find;it's something you do.Loving Donna is the easiest thing I've ever done in my life.

We've been married to each other for twenty-one years,and we're still newlyweds,if you consider that marriage is supposed to be forever.

A year ago,when the phone rang and I answered it,the voice said, "This is Doctor Freeman.Your wife has breast cancer." He spoke matter-of-factly,not mincing any words,although I could tell from his tone that he was not in a matter-of-fact frame of mind.He is a warm,caring and kindly physician,and this was not an easy phone call to make.He talked to Donna for a few minutes,and when she hung up the phone,the color drained from her face,and we held each other and cried for about five minutes.

She sighed and said,"That's enough of that."

I looked at her."Okay," I said."We have cancer.We'll handle it."

In the twelve months since then,Donna has had chemotherapy,a mastectomy,a bone-marrow transplant and radiation.She lost her hair,she lost a breast,she lost her privacy,and she lost the comfort associated with the assumption that tomorrow always comes.Suddenly,all her tomorrows were put on hold,and doled out,piecemeal,until the supply could be reestablished.

But she never lost her dignity or her faith.She never gave up,and she never gave in.

We put a small sign on the wall beside her bed.It said:"Sometimes the Lord calms the storm.Sometimes he lets the storm rage and calms his child." The words of the small sign became our anthem.

深爱我的妻子唐娜

　　有人说,爱情不是你找到的某样东西,而是你去做的某件事情。而我这一生中做的最舒心的一件事情就是去深爱我的妻子唐娜。

　　虽然我们结婚已经21年,但如果你认为婚姻是永恒的话,那我们就还不过是新婚燕尔。

　　一年前的一天,电话突然响起,我拿起听筒,一个声音传来,"我是弗里曼医生,你妻子得了乳腺癌。"他在电话那头一本正经,逐字逐句地念出每一个字。其实从他异样的语调可以听出来,他早不再镇定自若。他是一位热情、亲切、有同情心的医生,对他来说,这可不是一个轻松的电话。接着,唐娜也听了一会儿,之后她挂上电话,脸色煞白,我们俩抱头痛哭足有5分钟。

　　她长叹了一声,看着我说道:"够了,就哭到这吧。"

　　我也望着她说:"好的,我们是有癌症,但我们一定能闯过去的。"

　　此后的12个月里,唐娜接受了各种治疗,包括化疗、乳房切除、骨髓移植和放射治疗,等等。结果是,她失去了头发、失去了一边乳房,失去了隐私,更失去了对未来的希望和信心而痛苦不安。顷刻间,她所有的明天都被推迟、肢解和粉碎了。唯有重建生命的源泉和生活的信心,明天才会再次出现。

　　但是,她从没有失去尊严和信念,她永不放弃,永不妥协。

　　我们在她的床边墙上贴了张纸条,上面写着:"有时上帝平息了风暴,有时上帝又让风暴咆哮而让他的孩子安静下来。"这两行字成了我们的战斗歌曲,时刻激励着我们。

The day she returned home after her mastectomy,she looked at herself in the mirror,carefully.Then she shrugged,said,"So that's what I look like," put on her pajamas and got into bed.She looked at herself and saw hope;I saw courage.

She was in the hospital for Easter,Mother's Day and a high school graduation.She missed a lot of other people's lives during an interminable list of medical procedures.

But she gained a lot,too.

She attended the wedding of one of our sons in a motorized wheelchair,wearing a wig and a padded bra,and,next to the bride,she was undoubtedly the most radiant woman there.

And she found out how much her extended family and her neighbors loved her,and how much she meant in the lives of all of us.We received notes and letters and phone calls and mysterious packages of homemade bread and cookies left on our doorstep.Donna said she didn't realize how many people cared about her.

One night,at the lowest point of her physical ordeal,I was in my usual chair in the quiet of her hospital room.She had finished four days of around-the-clock high-does chemotherapy.Her immune system had been destroyed.Her head was shiny-bald,her eyes glassy,her body thirty pounds lighter and wracked with waves of nausea.She woke up,and I reached over to touch her hand.I held it,gently,because her skin and veins and every part of her body were as fragile as the petals of a gardenia.If the bone marrow transplant didn't engraft,this was the beginning of the end.If the transplant worked,this was the bottom,and she could start climbing the steep road to recovery.

"Hi," I said."I love you."

She laughed."Yeah,sure you do.I'll bet you say that to all your girlfriends."

"Of course I do.Because you're all my girlfriends."

双语精华版·心灵鸡汤·

那天,她乳房切除愈后回到家里,仔细地端详起镜子里的自己。然后,她耸了耸肩,说了一句"这就是我的样子啦"就换上睡衣上床睡觉了。她在自己的身上看到了希望,而我却看到了她的勇气。

她住院期间,经历了没完没了的治疗过程,错过了外面的许多事情,没能分享许多其他人的精彩生活,从复活节到母亲节,还有一次高中毕业典礼遗憾地没能到场。

但是她也收获了许多。

她出席了我们一个儿子的婚礼,坐在机动轮椅上,戴着假发和加厚的胸罩,除了新娘之外,那天她无疑是最光彩照人的。

她还认识到,她的众多亲人和邻居们是多么爱她,她在我们所有人的生活中是多么重要。期间我们收到了大量的便条、信件和电话来问候,还有许多装着自制面包和糕点的神秘包裹放在我们家门口台阶上。唐娜说她从没意识到会有这么多人来关心她。

一天夜里,当我照常在她安静的病房里坐在椅子上时,她却在经历身体折磨最痛苦的时候。她刚刚结束了4天的全天不间断的大剂量的化疗。免疫系统遭到了破坏,头发完全脱落,目光呆滞,身体一下消瘦了30磅,还有一阵阵的恶心让她苦不堪言。她一醒过来,我就伸过去摸了摸她的手。我轻轻地握着,不敢多用劲,因为她的皮肤、血管以及身体的每一个部分,都像栀子花的花瓣那样脆弱。如果骨髓移植不能成功,那么这就是她的生命枯萎逝去的一个开始。如果骨髓移植手术成功,这就是她生命的一个新起点,她将开始在陡峭的崖壁上攀爬,努力到达巅峰,通向痊愈。

"嗨,"我说道,"我爱你。"

她笑着说:"是的,你当然爱我。我敢打赌,你对你所有的女朋友都这么说过。"

"我当然这么说。因为你就是我所有的女朋友。"

She smiled,the sedatives took over again,and she went back to sleep.Mercifully,she spent most of that week in a drug-induced mental twilight.

Ten days later,her bone marrow had engrafted,and her body was beginning to restore itself.A wonderful volunteer named Nancy came by Donna's room to teach her how to watercolor as part of her recovery therapy.I was in the room,and the lady handed me a brush and paper and paints with the simple command,"Paint something."

I have a great eye for beauty.I know it when I see it.But since elementary school,when I was young and innocent enough to believe that everything I painted was a work of art,I have learned that my hand-eye coordination is limited to the use of a computer keyboard and the TV remote control.I don't draw,and I don't paint.

So I dabbed some colors on the page,and I painted a bouquet of flowers that I pretended was something in the style that Picasso might have done and called"cubist" or Grandma Moses might have done and called"primitive".I was encouraged when Donna and Nancy both recognized them as daffodils,and that they could see seven of them,which is what I had intended.

I had remembered some lyrics from an old ballad that I'd heard more than forty years ago,so I wrote them on the bottom of the picture.I said:

> *I haven't any mansion;*
> *I haven't any land.*
> *Not one paper dollar to crinkle in my hand.*
> *But I can show you mornings on a thousand hills,*
> *And kiss you,and give you*
> *Seven daffodils.*

她笑了起来,不过此时镇静剂又起作用了,她于是慢慢睡去了。还算幸运,那一周,在药物的作用下,她一直都处于迷迷糊糊的状态,神智尚未完全清醒。

10天后,骨髓移植成功,她的身体开始慢慢地恢复。一名叫南希的出色的女义工来到唐娜的病房,教她水彩画,以辅助她的身体恢复。我也在病房里,南希就递给我画纸、画笔和颜料,然后简单地下了个命令:"画点什么。"

我有很高的审美眼光,只要一看就知道什么水平。小学时候,我太小、太天真,总是相信我画的每样东西都是艺术品,但即使从那时起,我就发现我的手眼协调能力其实不太好,也只限于操控电脑键盘和电视遥控器。于是我从不勾勒素描,也不涂彩上色。

所以我接过画笔只是在画纸上轻轻涂了点颜色,画出了一束鲜花,故意弄出点毕加索的立体派风格,或是摩西老太的乡村原始风格。当唐娜和南希都认出来画的是水仙花时,我深受鼓舞,特别是她们看出来我特意画了有7枝水仙花。

我还记得40多年前听的一首老歌的歌词,所以就在图画的下面把它写了下来。我说:

"我没有一座大房子;
我也没有一块土地。
手里没有一张钞票。
但是我能在千山万水间带你去看每一次朝阳,
我还要亲吻你,并给你带来
7枝水仙花。"

女性系列／挥洒四季的芬芳

She put my picture on the wall in her room,and it was like seeing my childhood dreams stuck to the refrigerator door once again.Only this time,it was about life and death and love and hope.

She's home now,and life goes on for us.Every day we laugh a little and sometimes we cry a little.And we love a lot.

I love her for all the best reasons that a man loves a woman.In the end,I love her because she makes more of my world and my life than I can make of them by myself.

She loves me for all the simple reasons that a woman loves a man. For quiet nights and sunny days.For shared laughter and common tears. For twenty-one years of dishes and diapers and going to work and coming home and seeing her own future when she looks into my eyes.

And for a picture of seven daffodils.

Ron G.Eggertsen

唐娜把我的画作挂在病房的墙上，我好像又一次看到小时候把许多的梦想写下来贴在冰箱门上一样。只是这一次，贴上去的是关于生与死、爱情和希望。

她现在终于回家了，我们的生活恢复了平常。每天我们都有哭有笑，彼此更加深爱着对方。

我爱她，有着所有男人爱上女人的最好理由。最终我爱上她，是因为她使我的生活更加丰富多彩。

她爱我，有着所有女人爱上男人的简单理由。为了静谧的星夜、灿烂的白天；为了共享欢笑和分担泪水；为了21年来她在家里的琐碎家务、我在外面的工作打拼，还有从我眼里能够看到她自己的未来。

当然最后还要有一张7枝水仙花的水彩画。

罗恩·C.埃格森

History and Chemistry

I heard some women talking in the beauty shop the other day,commiserating with one another because the romance,the spark,the zip had gone out of their marriages.There was no excitement anymore,they said, no spark.

"That's life," one said."It's inevitable.Time passes.Things change."

"I'd like to have that chemistry back," another said,sighing."I envy young lovers.Violins and fireworks."

I thought back to those early days of my own special romance, when I floated,rather than walked.I never got hungry and frequently forgot to eat.My hair was shiny,my skin was clear and I was considerate, warm-hearted and unfailingly good-humored.When my true love and I were apart,I spent every miserable moment thinking about him.I was wretched until we were together again,sometimes as long as two or three hours.Life was one glorious rush after another—when the phone would ring,or I'd hear him at the door,or when our hands would accidentally touch.

Now,this is the same man who today,remembers our wedding anniversary no more often than once every five years,who rarely closes a cupboard door or a drawer after he has opened one,and who resists replenishing his wardrobe until I have to secretly get rid of his more disreputable things to maintain family dignity.

I wouldn't say he's predictable,but he asks,"What did you make for lunch?" six days out of seven,after we agreed,upon his retirement,it was every person for himself at lunch time.Most recently he repeatedly asked,"What do you want for your birthday?" So often that finally,worn down,I named something.He gave me something else.

历久弥新的爱

几天前，我在美容院听到几位女士在聊天，谈到各自的婚姻危机，都不禁唏嘘不已，彼此安慰，因为浪漫、情调和活力都已渐渐淡出。她们表示，婚姻的激情已经消逝，爱情的火花早已熄灭。

"这就是人生，"一人说道，"你无法逃避。时光飞逝，今非昔比。"

"我想找回往日相恋的感觉，"另一人叹道，"我真羡慕现在的年轻恋人，激情似火。"

听完这番感慨，我不禁也回想起多年前我自己那段特别浪漫的热恋时光。那时我连走路都特别地轻盈，总是忘了吃饭时间，还没觉得过饿。我头发丝滑炫亮，皮肤也白皙嫩滑。我善解人意，为人热忱，心情永远轻松舒畅。而和我心爱的人分开时，我无时无刻不在痛苦地思念。哪怕有时分开只有两三个小时，我也心情郁闷，盼着我们早早相聚。那样的日子里，怦然心动的时刻一个接着一个，有电话响起时，还有听见他来到门口时，或是我们俩的手不经意碰到时。

虽然现在还是同样那个人，不过今天的他，四五年能记起一次结婚纪念日就不错了；在家里打开橱柜或抽屉后，几乎总是忘了关；他也从不愿给自己添几件像样衣服，弄得我只好背着他，扔掉那些难看的旧衣服，免得他在外面穿着丢人现眼。

我不敢说能够预知他接下来要说哪句话，但是他每周有6天都会来问我："你中午给我做了啥好吃的啊？"其实我们事先早就约定，退休以后午餐各自解决。最近他又再三问我："你想要什么生日礼物？"经过一再追问，我终于吃不消了，说了件我想要的。而他最后送给我的却是另外一件。

He enjoys TV or movies only if they have car chases,explosions or shootings every seven minutes,and then only at ear-shattering volume.He considers it his right,by virtue of being born male,to control the TV channel selector,and is hormonally incapable of speaking softly or closing the front door without causing the whole house to shudder.

However…this is also the man who,when I decide to go on a diet, says,"Why?You look good to me." Who gets out of bed on a chilly night to put an extra blanket on the bed because he knows I'm cold. Who gave me a stunning necklace for my above-mentioned birthday after I asked for foul-weather boating gear,telling me I should "just go ahead and get that other stuff" myself.

CHICKEN SOUP

He's a man with more integrity in his little finger than anyone I've ever known to have in their entire body,and who recently bragged to my in-laws that I supported him in the early,lean years of his career—thirty-four years after the fact.He's a man who,in spite of his own personal frugality left over from his poverty-stricken era,loans large sums of money to our adult children at the drop of a hat,with no time limits and no interest payments.He can always be counted on to be there in a crisis,to be calm,rational,strong,fair and loving.Over the years,he has held me in his arms when my mother died,has held my head when I threw up,my hand when I labored to give birth to our children,and my heart from the first time I saw him.

I remembered the women in the beauty shop the other day as I sat in the car waiting for him to return from an errand across the street.I caught a glimpse of a slender,good-looking,vigorous man on the side-walk.His head was lowered,hands in his pockets as he walked along, whistling.Very appealing.He raised his head and grinned.Zing!

The father of my children.The other name on my checking account. The man I fell in love with.

History and chemistry.It just doesn't get any better.

E.Lynne Wright

双语精华版·心灵鸡汤·

92

在家看电视、看电影时，只要是有精彩追车、每隔几分钟有爆炸枪击的画面，他就乐此不疲，还把音量开到震耳欲聋。仗着是家里的男子汉，他认为这当然是他的权利，霸住电视遥控器不放。说话时大叫大嚷，从不会压低嗓门，关大门时每次都大力使劲，震得房子直摇晃。

然而，也是这个男人，当我决定要节食瘦身，他却说："为什么？我看你挺好的。"寒夜里，只要觉得我有点冷，他就会立即起来给我再加床被子。在刚才讲我的生日时，我想要一件划船时穿的防雨外套，他却送了我一串项链，着实给了我一个惊喜，还说："其他什么的，还是你自己去买吧。"

他为人特别正直，在一些芝麻点大的事情上所表现出来的真诚，比起所有我认识的人一辈子的表现都要强。就在最近他还在我的公婆面前夸耀我，说起了34年前，在他早期生意惨淡时我给他的莫大支持。他还是一个既节俭而又慷慨的人，受过去穷日子的影响，他自己非常节约，可是当我们的孩子长大过后，日子拮据时，他总是大笔地借钱给他们，不假思索，而且没有时限、没有利息。每逢有危机麻烦时，他总能让我们信赖、依靠，因为他镇定、理性、坚强、公正，而且深爱着我们。这些年来，当我母亲去世时，他把我抱在怀里；当我恶心呕吐时，他把我的头轻轻地捧起；当我每次辛苦分娩时，他都紧张地抓住我的手；而当我第一次见到他时，他就永远地偷走了我的心。

一天，他过街为我买东西，而我坐在车里等他回来时，我不由得想起了那天在美容院的几位女士。突然，我瞥见人行道上有一位身材瘦长、相貌英俊、充满活力的男士。他低着头，手插在口袋里，边走还边吹着口哨，非常吸引人。这时，他一抬头，飞快地冲我咧嘴一笑，吓得我尖叫一声。

居然是他！我孩子的父亲，我存折上的另一个名字，我深爱的男人。

虽然时过境迁，爱情却历久弥新。没有什么比这更加美妙了。

E·林恩.赖特

True Intimacy

Love cures people—both the ones who give it and the ones who receive it.

Karl Menninger

After two twelve-hour surgeries in seven days to rebuild my degenerating spine,all I remember is pain.The maximum pain medications barely dented my agony and,in my daze,I thought surely the entire ordeal would kill me.

The day came when I had no words,no identity,no reason left,so I screamed.I remember none of it,but I am sure it was one of those times when I fought everything I could fight,and screaming rolled out like a war cry.And I thrashed,threatening to pull tubes and needles out of arms, neck and legs.

My husband,because he loved me and suffered with me,held my hand,paced,felt powerless and pled with God to remove my agony and give it to him.The nurse,starched and efficient,bent over me and said to take some deep breaths and stop fighting.As she explained crisply,"You will hurt yourself and undo the surgery done to help you.So stop,or we'll have to stop you."

It was like speaking to me in another language that I neither understood nor cared to learn.Somewhere inside the fire raging in my body, her words only made me fight harder.

Finally,to my husband,she said, "Listen,I know this must be very hard on you.Why don't you run on back to the hotel and rest a bit? We'll take care of your wife.Don't you worry."

体贴入微

爱是一剂良药,奉献者和接受者皆然。

卡尔·门宁格

　　一周以来,为了挽救正在恶化的脊椎骨,我经历了两次各12小时的大手术,随后的记忆就只有疼痛了。大剂量的止疼用药,也不能减轻我的痛苦。在恍惚中,我感到我快要被折磨致死了。

　　那天我没法说出话来,想不起来自己是谁,早已失去了理智,所以我就大声尖叫起来。现在我是什么都不记得了,不过我很清楚,我很多次都是竭尽全力去抗争一切,而这一次的尖叫出来就如同战斗打响时士兵的呐喊声。同时,我还翻来覆去,威胁要把手臂、脖子和腿上所有的插管和针头都拔掉。

　　此时,疼爱我的丈夫正和我一起分担痛苦煎熬,一会儿拽住我的手,一会儿又来回踱步,感到无能为力,只好恳求上帝把我的痛苦转给他。护士见状立刻做出了职业反应,弯腰凑近我,让我深呼吸,不要挣扎。她很干脆地解释说:"你这样会弄伤自己,破坏手术效果,影响你的恢复。所以,要么自己安静,要么我们让你安静。"

　　这番话就好像是用其他某种语言跟我说的,我既听不懂,也不想搞懂。不过我内心却更加来火,她的话让我挣扎得更加厉害。

　　最后,她对我丈夫说:"听着,我知道这对你来说太残酷了。你为什么不回旅馆休息一会?别担心,我们会照看好你妻子的。"

"But what will you do?Surely no more drugs," he said wearily.

"You just run along.We'll tie her to the bed,and when she finds she can't move,she'll stop all this."

He stood by my bedside listening to these words.He looked at me—his wife,his friend,his lover—and with tears streaming,he said to the nurse,"Oh,no,you will never tie down my Jean.I will lay my body on top of hers and she will recognize me and she will rest."

The nurse,her mouth agape and her eyes wide,was horrified.When she found her voice,she stammered,"What are you saying?You absolutely *cannot* even lie in her bed,much less lie on top of her! Why,you'll pull the rest of the tubes out,and besides,the whole thing is against hospital rules." She shook,she was so shocked,as she added,"You cannot do any such thing! "

My husband,this man who understood intimacy and love,stood,all six feet,three inches of him,looked that nurse straight in the eye and said,almost in a whisper,"Oh,no,not to my Jean.I *can* do this and I *will* do this." And he *did* do this and I,recognizing him,found peace in the recognition.I let go.I slept.Such power there is in love.

Jean Brody

"但是,你们打算怎么办呢?坚决不能再用镇静药物了。"他无力地说。

　　"你只管走吧。我们会把她绑在床上,她发现自己不能动了,自然就会停下来。"

　　站在床边听完这些话,他深情地望着我——他的妻子、朋友、爱人,终于忍不住泪如泉涌。他转向护士,"哦,不,你别想把我的琼绑起来。我来躺在她的身上,她知道是我就会停下来的。"

　　护士听完后,目瞪口呆,大吃一惊。好容易恍过神来,她结巴地说:"你说什么?你绝对不能躺在她床上,更别说在她身上了。为什么,这样你会碰掉她的剩下的插管,而且这些都不符合医院规定。"她身体微颤了一下,实在是太震惊了,于是又添了一句,"绝不许你这样做!"

　　我丈夫对我体贴入微,疼爱有加,1米9的大高个,此时却无奈地盯着护士,几乎是在低声哀求:"哦,不,不要那样对我的琼。我能这么做的,我也要这样做。"然后,他就真的上了病床。当我感觉到是他在我身上时,顿时安静下来,不再挣扎。爱的魔力让我渐渐地安然入睡。

　　　　　　　　　　　　　　　　　　琼·布罗迪

女性系列／挥洒四季的芬芳

Second Skin

I looked on child rearing not only as a work of love and duty but as a profession that was fully as interesting and challenging as any honorable profession in the world, and one that demanded the best I could bring to it.

Rose Kennedy

My favorite pair of old jeans will never fit me again. I have finally accepted this immutable truth. After nurturing and giving birth to two babies, my body has undergone a metamorphosis. I may have returned to my pre-baby weight, but subtle shifts and expansions have taken place—my own version of continental drift. As a teenager, I never understood the difference between junior and misses sizing; misses clothing just looked old. Now it is all too clear that wasp waists and micro-fannies are but the fleeting trappings of youth. But that's okay, because while the jeans no longer button, the life I exchanged for them fits better than they ever did.

For me, this is a barefoot, shorts and T-shirt time of life. I have slipped so easily into young motherhood; it is the most comfortable role I have ever worn. No tough seams, no snagging zippers. Just a feeling that I have stepped out of the dressing room in something that finally feels right.

I love the feel of this baby on my hip, his soft head a perfect fit under my chin, his tiny hands splayed out like small pink starfish against my arms. I love the way my eight-year-old daughter walks alongside us as we cross the grocery store's sunny parking lot. On gorgeous spring

第二个春天

> 我从不把抚养孩子看做是爱的工作和义务，我把这当成世界上崇高的事业，一种充满乐趣和挑战，需要我全身心投入的事业。
>
> 罗斯·肯尼迪

我最喜欢的一条旧牛仔裤再也穿不上了。我终于接受了这个无法改变的事实。生完两个孩子，接着又辛勤地哺育，我的身体已经变形，不成样子了。我本可以恢复到生育之前的体重的，但身体细微的变化和发胖已经开始，这也许是我身上的板块漂移吧。在少女时代，我一直都没弄懂，女装的小码和均码有什么区别。现在总算明白了，瘦臀蜂腰对姑娘来说不过是昙花一现。但是没关系，因为当牛仔裤不合身而扣不上时，我以此为代价换来了更适合我的新生活。

对我来说，这是成天在家光脚，穿着短裤和T恤的日子。不经意间，我已经成为年轻的妈妈了。这是一个让我听着最舒服的人生角色。再不用穿那些缝得紧紧的衣服，也不用为拉链常坏而郁闷了。只有一种感觉，我走出了更衣室，终于换上了合适的衣服了。

我喜欢这种感觉。孩子贴着我的髋部，柔软的小脑袋搭在我下巴下面尤其合适，他张开嫩嫩的小手，扒在我胳膊上，活像粉红色的小海星。我也喜欢8岁的女儿走在我们身边的样子，我们全家一起穿过杂货店外洒满阳光的停车场。在春暖花开、阳光灿烂的日子里，微

99

days,the breeze lifts her wispy ponytail,and we laugh at how the sunshine makes the baby sniff and squint.I am constantly reaching out to touch them,the way a seamstress would two lengths of perfect silk,envisioning what might be made from them,yet hesitant to alter them,to lose the weight of their wholeness in my hands.

On those rare mornings when I wake up before they do,I go into their rooms and watch them sleeping,their faces creased and rosy.Finally,they squirm and stretch themselves awake,reaching out for a hug.I gather them up,bury my face in them and breathe deeply.They are like towels just pulled from the dryer,tumbled warm and cottony.

Sometimes,I follow the sound of girlish voices to my daughter's room,where she and her friends play dressup,knee-deep in garage-sale chiffon,trying life on for size.Fussing and preening in front of the mirror,they drape themselves in cheap beads and adjust tiaras made of sequins and cardboard.I watch these little girls with their lank,shiny hair that no rubber bands or barrettes seem able to tame.They are constantly pushing errant strands behind their ears,and in that grown-up gesture,I see glimpses of the women they will become.I know that too soon these clouds of organdy and lace will settle permanently into their battered boxes,the ones that have served as treasure chests and princess thrones. They will become the hand-me-downs of my daughter's girlhood,handed back to me.

For now,though,my children curl around me on the sofa in the evening,often falling asleep,limbs limp and soft against me like the folds of a well-worn nightgown.For now,we still adorn each other,and they are content to be clothed in my embrace.I know there will be times that will wear like scratchy wool sweaters and four-inch heels.We will have to try on new looks together,tugging and scrunching,trying to keep the basic fabric intact.By then,we will have woven a complicated tapestry with its own peculiar pattern,its snags and pulls and tears.

风轻轻掠起她的小马尾辫子,我们在一旁看着阳光下的她,眯起了小眼,嗅着阳光的味道。我常常伸手去轻抚他们,就像女裁缝手摸着两段上等丝绸,遐想用它做出华美服饰,却又犹豫不决,舍不得动它们一下,同样,我也怕孩子在我手里失去天真无邪的完美。

有几个难得的早上,他们醒来之前,我起床去到他们屋里,望着他们酣睡的样子,浑然不知红扑扑的小脸蛋都压出一道道线条。终于,他们迷迷糊糊地开始蠕动,伸着懒腰醒了过来,伸手就要我抱。我把他们放在一起,脸紧紧地贴着他们,用力嗅闻他们身上的味道。他们就像刚从干衣机里拿出来的毛巾,乱乱的、暖暖的、软软的。

有时候,我跟着女孩子大叫的声音来到女儿的房间,看她和朋友们正在玩穿衣扮相游戏,屋子乱得像修理厂,薄绸衣裳在地上堆得已没过了膝盖,她们还在不停地试着各种衣服。站在镜子前她们精心地装扮自己,身上挂满了便宜的珠子,头上戴着纸板和各种亮片做成的头饰。看着这些女孩子,头发细直闪亮,好像没什么橡皮筋或发卡能把它们打理好。于是她们常常把几缕凌乱的头发捋到耳后,看到这个像大人般的手势,我眼前不禁闪过了她们将来长成成熟女人的样子。我知道,很快,这些蝉翼薄纱衣裳和便宜链子,就会永远地放入她们自己的旧箱子,而这箱子也曾经是她们游戏时的珠宝箱和公主的宝座。慢慢地它们将成为我女儿少女时代的旧衣裳,最后又交还给我。

虽然眼下我的孩子喜欢在晚上,坐在沙发上,依偎在我旁边。她们常常就这样睡着了,手脚松弛无力,就像穿得很旧的睡衣一样,外面软绵绵的。现在,我们还常常相互打扮,她们也总是要钻到我的怀里来。不过我知道某一天,她们也会开始穿上毛糙的羊毛衫和4英寸高的高跟鞋,这些时刻慢慢都会到来的。所以我们必须一起来尝试新的样式,揉搓拽拉,努力保持布料完好无缺。到那时,我们将编出一幅复杂的挂毯,上面是我们自己的独特样式,当然也有抽丝和钩破的地方。

But I will not forget *this* time,of drowsy heads against my shoulder, of footy pajamas and mother-daughter dresses,of small hands clasped in mine.*This* time fits me.I plan to wear it well.

Caroline Castle Hicks

但我不会忘记她熟睡时，一次次用头磨蹭我的肩膀；不会忘记那连体小睡衣和母女亲子连衣裙；不会忘记她那小手在我手里紧紧抓着。这一切我已经习惯了，并将珍藏在记忆里。

卡罗琳·卡斯尔·希克斯

THE FAMILY CIRCUS

"Was there an older generation when you were little, Mommy?"

女性系列／挥洒四季的芬芳

Parental Justice

Many people know me as Whoopi Goldberg,the comedienne,but few know my work—what I've gone through—as Whoopi Goldberg,the mother.

One night when my daughter was maybe thirteen or fourteen,she came downstairs and told me she was going out,and it was none of my business where.I looked this child over,this little version of me.She was wearing three pieces of cloth.The cloth itself was all shiny and nice and fine,but it wasn't covering enough to suit a mother.It wasn't even close. Okay,in my time I wore a mini so small that all I needed to do was sneeze and you would have known exactly what color my panties were, but here was my barely teenage daughter,looking like a grown woman, dressed like Madonna used to dress.I completely flipped.

Before my mother could come out of my mouth,she was in my ear. I heard her chuckling in the corner,laughing at me over the way our situation had turned.This was parental justice.Her laugh took me back, and I got angry."Why are you laughing?" I shot back.

"Because it's funny," she said."Because it's funny to see you like this now."

Funny?I'm trying to explain to this child that she can't go out look- ing like this.She can't go out looking like this because you don't know what invitation someone is going to pick up from this.

That line—*you don't know what invitation someone is going to pick up from this*—was one of my mother's,and I wanted to take it right back as soon as I'd said it.My mother looked over at me and smiled,

父母的眼光

　　许多人都知道我是喜剧女演员,伍比·戈德堡,但是很少有人知道作为一个母亲,伍比·戈德堡所经历过的工作。

　　我女儿大概只有十三四岁时,一天夜里,她下楼来告诉我,马上要出门,她去哪儿却叫我别管。我把这孩子上下打量一番,仿佛看到了我自己小时候的一些影子。她穿的衣服只由3块布片拼成。布料本身很闪亮,质地也不错,只是以一个母亲的眼光来看,这实在太暴露了,而且衣服也不够紧了。当然在我那个时代,要是穿这么暴露的迷你裙,我肯定会感冒打喷嚏,而你甚至可以清楚地看见我内裤的颜色。但是现在却是我的女儿,她只是个少女,看上去像个大姑娘,穿得像麦当娜过去的打扮。我听完顿时七窍生烟。

　　正准备去跟她说当年我母亲是怎么教育我的,她倒先出声了。我听见她在角落里咯咯地笑,仿佛是在嘲笑我还没注意到母女对峙局面突然发生了变化。这可是父母的眼光。她的笑声把我从过去拉回现实,让我感到非常恼火。"你为什么要笑?"我开始反击。

　　"因为这很好笑,"她说,"因为看你现在这样很好笑。"

　　好笑?我正准备跟这孩子解释,她不能穿成这样就出门。因为你不知道别人看到你的穿着会怎么想,这很容易让人误解,给你带来麻烦。

　　"因为你不知道别人看到你的穿着会怎么想,这很容易让人误解,给你带来麻烦。"这句话曾是我母亲说给我听的,而我现在就想讲给我女儿听。当年,我母亲上下打量了我,然后笑了起来。刚开

and at first I tried not to smile back,but it was too late.I had to smile too.It wasn't one of those let-me-laugh-along-with-you kind of smiles,or one of those gee-ain't-we-funny kind of smiles,but the kind of smile that comes from knowing.

I got it.Finally.I understood.It was a smile of recognition,and maybe a little surrender.I reconnected to everything that passed between us,and I could see what was coming.I wanted to tell my mother how sorry I was for putting her through all of those motions,for not recognizing that she had something to offer beyond what I could see.But she knew.She smiled back and she knew.

I turned to my kid and said,"You know what?Go out.Just go."

And she did.She looked at me funny—suspicious—but she went out like she has planned.And then she came back,about twenty minutes later. "You know what?"　she said. "It's cold out there.I think I'm going to change,put a little more on."

It happens,but it takes time.I watch now as my daughter goes through it for herself,with her own kids,and I try not to chuckle.I know someday she'll hear me coming out of her mouth and she'll look over with one of those knowing smiles and start to laugh,because we all get it,eventually.

Whoopi Goldberg

始我憋住不想对我母亲笑,但已经太晚了。我禁不住地也笑了出来。这不是那种"让我和你一起笑"的随便笑笑,也不是那种"闹着玩"的开玩笑,而是彼此太了解了才有的会心一笑。

我明白了,终于弄懂了,母亲的笑包含了一种认可,也许还有点对我屈服的意味。我再结合过去和我母亲相处的所有事情,我知道下一步我该做什么了。我想告诉母亲,我真的很对不起,因为我让她心里难过半天,因为我没看出来,她要告诉我许多我不知道的东西。但她明白我的心思。她又对我笑了,她是真的明白。

我回过神来,对我的孩子说:"你知道什么?出去。赶紧走吧。"

然后她真照着做了。她看了看我,有点好笑,心里又有点将信将疑,但她还是出去了,就像她原计划那样。大约20分钟后,她又回来了。"你知道什么?"她说,"外面挺冷。我想我打算换件衣裳,该多穿点了。"

这样的事情总是发生,不过要隔很长时间才有。当我女儿在她的孩子身上,自己也来经历一遍此类事情时,我会在旁边看着,而且努力憋住不要笑。我知道将来某一天,她会把我的例子说出来,带着这样的会心一笑,也上下打量孩子,然后开始大笑,最终我们都大笑了起来。

伍比·戈德堡

Snowballs and Lilacs

What would I want engraved on my gravestone for posterity?"Mother."

Jessica Lange

I set the big,manila envelope on my mother's table,continuing our ordinary conversation,trying to draw away from the importance of this package and its contents.Through sentences of chit-chat,I worked up the courage from within,until I finally asked her to open it.She did,with a Norwegian sparkle in her blue eyes,expecting a surprise.She grew quiet as she pulled out the picture inside,and saw my own dark brown eyes staring back at her in the face of another woman.The resemblance was startling,and realization swept across her face as she turned to me with joy and wonder and whispered,"Is this your *real* mother?"

Biting my lip,a trick I had learned from her to hold back the tears,I realized this wonderful woman of substance in front of me had never seemed more precious than at this moment.A flash of all the years she had spent caring for my brothers and me flickered through my mind,as well as the life she led—a life that knew no other way than to put her children and others first on a daily basis.With the knowledge of what was truly"real", I answered her with borrowed wisdom and responded, "Yes,it's a picture of my birth mother."

My search for her had been a need for self-fulfillment,to answer all those nagging questions once wondered.My inquiry had brought feelings of guilt as well.Although my parents had always encouraged me to look,

石莲与丁香

我要在自己的墓碑上刻着"母亲"两字以鉴后人。

杰西卡·兰格

我把一个黄色的大信封放在母亲的桌上，继续我们的日常谈话，尽量避免提起这个包裹和里面内容的重要性。几句闲聊过后，我终于忍不住鼓起勇气，让她打开看看。她照我的话做了，挪威人蓝色的眼睛里闪烁着火花，期待有意外的内容出现。当她从里面抽出相片时，渐渐没了言语，怔怔地看着我那双深褐色的眼睛，在相片上另一个女人的脸上正凝视着她。两人相貌如此相似，令人难以置信。不过很快她脸上掠过了理解的神情，高兴而又好奇地向我轻声问道："是你的真正的母亲吗？"

要不是从她那学会一招，咬住嘴唇来止住泪水，我早就泪如泉涌了。我已经意识到，眼前这位极好的有钱妇人，此刻显得格外高尚。这些年来她一直照顾我们姐弟俩的情景顿时又浮现在我眼前，我也想起了她为了养育儿女所过的那种辛苦生活。明白了她说的"真正"是什么意思，我借用了别人的妙语回答："是的，这是我亲生母亲的相片。"

寻找我的生母也是为了让自己的想法兑现，解决萦绕在心头的许多疑问。不过寻访的过程还是让我平添了不少内疚感。虽然父母一直都支持我去找找看，说他们也很好奇，但我还是不愿他们俩在

saying that they were just as curious,I didn't want either one of them to be hurt in the process,or to think that I loved them any less.I secretly marveled at their encouragement,and the confidence that it represented in my steadfast love for them.But after a lifetime of unconditional love and bonding,they had well earned that security.

My mother's eyes saddened as I told her that my birth mother had died;both my mother and I had often hoped for the day when we would be able to thank her personally.Now that connection would never come.

On Memorial Day,I took my two young sons to the cemetery to place flowers on my birth mother's grave.We first stopped at the gravesides of my grandparents.My mother had obviously been there,having left her homemade bouquet of snowballs and lilacs—an annual tradition of hers.Year after year,I had found comfort in those flowers,always there,loved ones always remembered.They reminded me of my mother in their simple but Godgiven beauty.I smiled as I thought of the daffodils she gave me each birthday—one for each year of my life.When I was younger,Mom's time-honored yellow tradition had been taken for granted.Now at the age of thirty-five,I counted each one,each flower so significant.Nothing would make me happier than to adopt a little girl and continue that tradition with her.

But now was not the time to be a daughter dabbling in daydreams, but to be a mother myself.My sons tugged on my hands,playing tug-of-war with my thoughts.We hurried off to our last stop,my birth mother's grave.Our pace slowed as we neared the general location,and we solemnly walked through row after row of beautifully decorated tombstones.I knew we were looking for a plain simple stone,without flowers.

I had formed friendships in the last several months with my birth sisters and brother.Although they deeply loved my birth mother,I knew they were not ones to visit cemeteries.Somehow that made it even more important that I come.She definitely deserved flowers,to be remembered, and so very much more.But after half an hour of searching unsuccess-

此期间有谁受到伤害,或是认为我对他们的爱有任何减少。我暗暗敬佩他们对我的鼓励和自信,相信我对他们坚贞不移的感情。他们也有理由对我放心,因为这一辈子他们给予我无私的爱,和我建立了浓郁的亲情。

我接着告诉母亲,我生母已经去世了,她听完两眼顿时忧郁起来,有些难过;母亲和我都经常期盼有这么一天,我们能够亲自去谢谢她。现在看来,一同前往是再也不可能了。

阵亡将士纪念日那天,我带着两个儿子到墓地,想在我生母的坟前献上一些鲜花。我们首先来到我祖父母的坟墓边上。显然我母亲刚才来过,献上了一个自制的花束,包着她每年的传统——石莲与丁香花。年复一年,那里总是有这两种鲜花,带给我慰藉,让我想起心爱的人。它们都很普通,却有着天赐的纯美。我笑着想起了每次生日她送的水仙花,一枝代表一年。我还年轻的时候,从没把母亲送生日黄水仙的传统当回事。现在我已经有35岁了,我数着每一枝水仙,都觉得那么意味深长。没有什么比收养一个小女孩,并继续我母亲的传统还能让我更加幸福了。

但是现在自己都做了母亲,早已不是当年的女儿,成天做着白日梦,什么都想试。我的两个儿子拖着我的手,把我从胡思乱想中拽了回来。我们加快步伐,前往最后一站——我亲生母亲的坟墓。快要接近时,我们放慢了脚步,庄重地走过一排排装饰漂亮的墓碑。我知道,我们在找一块朴素、简单的墓碑,应该没有鲜花。

在刚刚过去的几个月里,我和几个亲兄妹关系处得挺好。虽然他们深爱我的生母,但我知道,他们是不会来墓地祭拜她的。这样我的到来就更显得重要了。她的确值得我献上鲜花,值得我永远记住,而且更加值得我为她这么做。可是找了半个小时候,还是没有结果,

fully,my sons were growing impatient,so I decided I would have to come back by myself.We were just about to leave when I spotted it.

Not her name.Not an empty stone.But the same simple bouquet of snowballs and lilacs that I had seen earlier,the ones most assuredly that had been placed there by my mother.Mom had already been there,in the morning's early hours,to show her gratitude and the respect she felt for the importance of this woman's life,and the great gift she had given.

As I knelt and closely looked at the dates,I noticed the epitaph, which so appropriately read, "Beloved Mother".Biting my lip,I couldn't hold back the tears as I honored this remarkable woman who had given me life,and my own beloved mother,who had given that life such meaning.

Lisa Marie Finley

我的两个儿子也已经渐渐失去了耐心,所以决定下次我自己再来一趟。正打算离开时,我突然把它找出来了。

上面没有她的名字,也不是一块无字碑。只有一束石莲和丁香花,和我先前看到的一样简单,毫无疑问,这是我母亲刚才放上去的。原来母亲今天早上已经提前来过这里了,向我生母表达了她的感激之情,她对我生母光辉一生的尊敬,更感谢我生母送给她的一份厚礼,那就是我。

当我跪下仔细查看立碑日期时,我注意到了墓志铭,上面非常合适地写着:"亲爱的母亲"。当我向这位给了我生命的、杰出的女性,还有一位赋予我生命精彩意义的我亲爱的母亲同时表达我的敬意时,咬住嘴唇来止住眼泪的办法已经不再奏效,我已然是泪流满面。

莉萨·玛丽·芬利

双语精华版·心灵鸡汤·

"This is the perfect watch for mothers.
Every day is thirty-six hours."

Reprinted by permission of Randy Glasbergen.

When Did She Really Grow Up?

Every night after I tucked her into bed,I sang to her,a silly song,a made-up song,our song."Stay little,stay little,little little stay;little stay little stay little."

She would giggle and I would smile.The next morning I would say: "Look at you.You grew.The song didn't work."

I sang that song for years,and every time I finished,she crossed her heart and promised she wouldn't grow any more.

Then one night,I stopped singing it.Who knows why.Maybe her door was closed.Maybe she was studying.Maybe she was on the phone talking to someone.Or maybe I realized it was time to give her permission to grow.

It seems to me now that our song must have had some magic because all the nights I sang it,she remained a baby...four,five,six,seven, eight,nine,ten.They felt the same.They even looked the same.She got taller and her feet got bigger and some teeth fell out and new ones grew in,but she still had to be reminded to brush them and her hair and to take a shower every now and then.

She played with dolls and Play-Doh.Though Candy Land was abandoned for Monopoly and Clue,across a table,there she still was.For years,she was like those wooden dolls that nest one inside the other, identical in everything but size.

Or at least that's how I saw her.She roller-skated and ice-skated and did cartwheels in shopping malls and blew bubbles and drew pictures,which we hung on the refrigerator.She devoured Yodels and

她何时长大

每天夜里,把她放进被窝后,我就开始唱歌哄她睡觉,这是一首有点无聊的、自己瞎编的,一首我们俩的歌曲。"不要长大,不要长大,不要,不要长大,不要长大。"

唱得她咯咯直笑,我也笑了。第2天早上我总对她说:"看看你,你又长了一点。我唱的歌没起作用。"

多年以来,我一直唱着这首歌谣,每次唱完,她就开始画十字,发誓不再长大。

后来,不知从哪天夜里起,我就没再唱起过了。谁知道为什么。可能是她的房门关了,或许是她正在做功课,也许是正在和别人通电话,还有可能是我认为该是时候,允许她长大了。

现在我看来,好像当时那首歌谣应该是有些魔力的,我夜夜唱起时,她就没变过,4岁、5岁、6岁、7岁、8岁、9岁,一直到10岁,都还是我的小宝贝。夜夜感觉不变,夜夜甚至看起来都一样。她个子渐渐长高,鞋子越穿越大,也开始换牙了,但有时还是要我提醒她刷牙、梳头,或是该冲澡了。

她以前喜欢洋娃娃和橡皮泥。桌子上的棋盘游戏也从糖果乐园换成了垄断大亨和谜案线索,她还是没变。这些年来,她就像俄罗斯木头娃娃,一个套着一个,样子完全一样,只是尺寸有大有小。

至少,我是这样看她的。她渐渐学会了溜旱冰、真冰滑冰,骑在大卖场的购物车上滑行,吹泡泡和画画,画完后我们就贴在冰箱上。她吃起刨冰来狼吞虎咽,周日上午总是早早起来看电视连续剧《大

女性系列／挥洒四季的芬芳

slushes and woke early on Sunday mornings to watch *Davey and Go-liath.*

She never slept through the night,not at ten months,not at ten years. When she was small,she'd wake and cry and I'd take her into bed with me.When she got bigger,she'd wake and make her way down the hall, and in the morning,I would find her lying beside me.

She used to put notes under my pillow before she went to bed.I used to put notes in her bologna sandwiches before she went to school. She used to wait by the phone when I was away.I used to wait at the bus stop for her to come home.

The song,the notes,the waking up to find her next to me,the waiting at the bus stop—all these things ended a long time ago.Upstairs now is a young woman,a grown-up.She has been grown up for a while.Everyone else has seen this—everyone but me.

I look at her today,one week before she graduates from high school,and I am proud of her,proud of the person she has become.But I'm sad,too—not for her,but for me.There has been a child in this house for twenty-five years.First one grew up,then the other,but there was always this one…the baby.

Now the baby is grown.And despite what people tell me—*you don't lose them,they go away but they come home again,you'll like the quiet when she's gone,the next part of life is the best*—I know that what lies ahead won't be like what was.

I loved what was.I loved it when she toddled into my office and set up her toy typewriter next to mine.I loved watching her run down the hall at nursery school straight into my arms,after a separation of just two-and-a-half hours.I loved taking her to buy stickers and for walks and to movies.I loved driving her to gymnastics and listening to her friends.I loved being the one she raced to when she was happy or frightened or sad.I loved being the center of her world.

卫和戈里亚》。

　　从小她夜里睡觉就是断断续续的,无论是才10个月,还是10岁时都一样。一点大的时候,她一醒过来就又哭又闹,我只好把她抱到我床上带她睡。大一点后,她夜里醒来,自己跑过门厅,第二天早上,我会发现她就又躺在我的身旁。

　　过去她常常睡前在我枕头底下留一张便条。我也常在她上学前,丢一张纸条在她的博洛尼亚红肠三明治里。我出门时,她总是守在电话旁边。她要是出去,我也常在公交车站等她回家。

　　那首歌谣,那些便条,早上醒来发现她躺在我身边,还有在公交车站的等候,许久以前,这些经历就已经结束了。现在楼上的已是一位年轻姑娘,一个大人了。她长大成人也不是刚刚的事了,其他人都看见了,唯独我没有。

　　一周以后,她就要高中毕业了,望着今天的她,我为她感到自豪,为她长大而骄傲。但是我也感到有些难过,不是为了她,而是为我的。25年来,这屋子里一直住着一个小女孩。一次次地不断成长,但永远都是我的宝贝。

　　现在这个小宝贝已经长大了。尽管别人都这么对我说,你不会失去他们的,他们暂时离开,但将来会回来的,你也会习惯下半生最美好的一面——宁静。

　　我喜欢过去的这一切。我喜欢她摇摇晃晃地来到我的书房,在我旁边摆弄她的玩具打字机。我喜欢看着她在托儿所里,跑出大厅,直扑到我怀里,虽然分开只有两个半小时,已是很想妈妈了。我喜欢带她出去买贴画、散步和看电影。我喜欢开车送她去练健身操,听她的朋友聊天。我喜欢在她开心、害怕或难过时,都等着她向我飞跑过来。我喜欢成为她世界的中心。

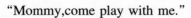

"Mommy,come play with me."

"Mommy,I'm home."

"Mommy,I love you the best and the widest."

What replaces these things?

"What to see my cap and gown?" she says now,peeking into my office.She holds it up.She smiles.She's happy.I'm happy for her.She kisses me on the cheek and says,"I love you,Mom." And then she walks upstairs.

I sit at my desk and though my heart hurts,I smile.I think what a privilege motherhood is,and how very lucky I am.

Beverly Beckham

"妈咪,来和我玩。"

"妈咪,我回家了。"

"妈咪,我最最爱你了。"

这些又有什么能够替代呢?

"看看我的毕业礼服和礼帽。"她正说着,朝我的书房里面瞥了一眼。她举了起来,开心地笑了。我也为她感到高兴。她过来在我脸颊上亲了一下,说了一句,"我爱你,妈咪。"然后上楼去了。

我坐在书桌前,虽然有些伤感,但我还是笑了起来。我觉得做母亲是无上光荣的,而我又是如此的幸运。

贝弗利·贝克汉姆

THE FAMILY CIRCUS　　　　By Bil Keane

女性系列／挥洒四季的芬芳

"Their mommies write their names on their
shirts so they won't lose them."

Reprinted by permission of Bil Keane.

Children on Loan

I am not good at returning things.Take library books.I have no intention of keeping them,but it takes a jolt to separate us—like a call from the librarian.Today,they sit awaiting return three days early. Because today,I'm painfully aware of the passage of time.In thirty minutes,assuming my son is packed—and he will be—Christopher Paul("the best boy of all," he'd tease his sisters)leaves for his last year of college. He's our youngest,the last to leave home.By now,I tell myself,I am used to these departures.*I am used to these departures.I am used to these departures...*

Only this one is for keeps.Next May,there will be no bags of soiled laundry coming home.Chris won't be coming home at all.After graduation,it's marriage to Pam—the sunny Californian,adorable and already beloved by us all—and on to start their life together a thousand miles away.Every tick of our copper kitchen clock says,*This—is—it.Empty—nest.*

My sister,the research chemist,calls. "For Pete's sake,you knew it was coming."

"So is the end of the world,but who's ready for it?"

"You really are in a mood."

My silence speaks for itself.Who knows us as well as our sisters?

"After all," she adds,"he'll be home for the holidays.Anyway,you wouldn't want to keep him forever."

My sister does not read me well at all.I find myself caressing my chunky Timex as tenderly as I would a newborn's head.We've ticked away a lot of time together—waiting outside schools,athletic fields,piano lessons,rehearsals,practices.Later,awake in bed,listening for his first car

双语精华版·心灵鸡汤·

恩赐的孩子

　　还给别人东西的时候我总觉得有些割舍不下。就拿从图书馆借来的书说吧，我也没想留住不还，但真要还时，我还是心头一颤，就像听到图书管理员大喝一声一样。今天就有人坐在那等着要我归还东西了。因为感到了时间的匆匆流逝，我今天心里特别难过。再过30分钟，假如儿子整理好行李——他应该要准备好了——克里斯托弗·保罗（他常嘲弄几个姐姐，并自诩是"最好的男孩"。）就要离开家，去完成大学最后一年学业了。他是我们家的老幺，也是最后一个离开家的。到如今，我只好一遍遍地念叨："我早已习惯了这样的离别，我早已习惯了这样的离别，我早已习惯了这样的离别……"

　　只是这一次是永远的离别了。明年5月将不会再有他的一包包脏衣服送回家来洗了。克里斯不会再回这个家了。大学毕业后，他要和帕姆结婚。她来自加利福尼亚，性情开朗，可爱迷人，我们都很喜欢她。从此，克里斯要在1000英里以外的地方开始他们的新生活了。我们厨房那面铜制挂钟的每一次滴答声，都在告诉我，这一刻终于要来到了。只留下一间空空的房子。

　　我妹妹是个负责研发的化学家，她给我打了电话，说："看在彼得的分上，你知道这一刻即将到来。"

　　"世界末日要是来临的话，谁会有准备呢？"

　　"你真是有点不对劲了。"

　　我的沉默表明了这一点。除了姐妹还有谁知我的心？

　　"毕竟，"她补了一句，"节假日他会回家来的，再说了，你也不想一辈子把他留在身边吧。"

　　我妹妹还是不懂我的心情。我只好轻轻地抚摸手上那块结实的天美时表，像是抚摸新生儿的头。这表伴我一起度过了许多时间，如为了儿子等候在学校外面、运动场外、钢琴课时、彩排时和练习时。后来，我醒着躺在床上，听儿子把他第一辆车开进院子里的行车道。

to pull into the drive.Waiting as time dragged by.Now,in take-off time, seconds spring ahead.

The doorbell summons me to a girl selling candy for her school band.The six chocolate bars are my excuse to visit Chris's room with him still in it.Boxes block the doorway.A barricade?Walls easily erect themselves at times like these.At his "Hi,Mom," I try to read his voice. Glad I'm here?Resentful of intrusion?

He's tossing items into a carton labeled MED.CAB.SUPPLIES. Glancing down on stomach soothers,skin scrubbers,lens solution,musky colognes,I'm reminded of the bottle of cheap aftershave he was so thrilled to find in his stocking one long-ago Christmas.He used it up in a week,but his room reeked all winter."Ever try this?" he asks now,hold- ing up a new brand of tooth gel.I smile brightly as I shake my head,but I have the ugly urge to snatch his alien brand and write TRAITOR on his suitcase.We all use Crest.We've always used Crest!

I realize my hand still clutches a damp tissue when I find myself using it to wipe his battered alarm clock.A wasted effort.Not only is it no longer smeared with peanut butter or sticky with Coke,I notice it is among the abandoned.

"This still dependable?"

"Never failed me yet."

Which means just fifteen minutes to go. "Time for a quick cup of coffee?" I would climb a Brazilian mountain and hand-pick beans to buy more time.

"Sure." He smiles in the lopsided way I love.He'll make a hand- some bridegroom,but I really didn't have that in mind when I nagged him into slimming down in eighth grade.

It's been a long time since I stood watching coffee perk.I remember putting his early bottle on to warm,then starting the coffee.We snuggled cheek to cheek,waiting for our morning brews.He was warm with baby- sleep,I with mother-love.Neither of us minded the wait.

Now,sitting across from Chris as I gulp from my hot mug,I have to

以前等候他的时候,时间一点一滴慢慢地熬过,如今儿子要出发了,时间却一眨眼便已溜走。

突然,门铃想起来,我过去开门一看,原来是一个小女孩在推销糖果来为学校的乐队筹钱。我买了6块巧克力并以此为借口,打算到克里斯房间去看看。不巧几个箱子挡在了门口。给我设置一个路障?这四面墙壁有时也像路障一样隔在我们之间。只听他问了声好,"嗨,妈妈。"于是我又开始努力解读他的声音。是很高兴我来呢?还是对我突然闯进来很不高兴呢?

他正在往一只纸板箱里扔东西,箱子外面标着"药柜必备品"的字样。我往下扫了一眼,有胃痛药、皮肤护理器,隐形眼镜护理液,还有麝香味的古龙香水。这让我想起好多年前的一次圣诞节,他在长袜里面找到这瓶便宜的,剃须后使用的香水礼物,于是便欣喜若狂。他一周就用完了,结果使他的房间整个冬天臭气熏天。"试过这个吗?"他在问我,手上拿着一支新牌子的牙膏。我边摇头边爽朗地笑了。但是我脑子里突然冒出一个邪恶的念头,想冲上去,夺下那支古怪的牙膏,在他的手提箱上用牙膏写上"叛徒"两个大字。因为我们都用佳洁士,我们一直都用佳洁士!

看到他的老闹钟,我不禁上去帮他擦了擦,这时我才意识到手里一直抓着一块湿纸巾。真是浪费体力。不仅闹钟上没了以前常抹上的花生油或粘粘的可乐,我还注意到它已经放在不要的一堆东西里面了。

"这钟走得还准吗?"

"还从没误过事呢。"

那不就只有15分钟就要走了吗?我着急地问:"有时间赶紧来杯咖啡吗?"天哪,我真想登上巴西的高山,亲手采摘咖啡豆,这一切只为换来更多的时间。

"没问题。"他撇着嘴在笑,我很喜欢他这样。他会成为一个英俊的新郎,但他上8年级时,我可没这样想过,那时,他被我责骂之后,日渐消瘦,不太好看。

有很长一段时间,我都是站在那儿看着煮咖啡。我记得以前总是把他的瓶子先热一热,然后开始煮咖啡。接下来,我就把他抱在我怀里,脸贴着脸相互依偎在一起,等待我们早上的咖啡煮好。在我怀里,他很暖和,睡得也香。而因为这浓浓的母爱,我心里很温暖。我们谁都不介意等待的时间。

现在,我坐在克里斯对面,拿起热杯子,猛喝了一大口。既有咖

content myself with coffee and conversation.As appreciative as I am for our small talk,I'm aware of resenting it.More meaningful words could be said.I see by his watch that it's time for him to go.His hands are exactly like my father's.Odd I never noticed before.What else have I missed?

His eyes grow sober as he begins to speak of yesterday and seeing Pam off to her college,how they worked at keeping it light.I detect a message here for me,too.God knows I'm trying.And I wouldn't mind a little help from the Man Upstairs right now.*You got me into this,*I tell him.*You let me share in your birthing business,but you messed up on the motherhood bit—or else I didn't read the fine print at the end.*

"Well…"Chris stands and shoves in his chair.Never once has he shoved in his chair."Now it's *This is it,old chair.So long,old kitchen,old mother…*"

I stand,too,but let my chair be.He bends over and gives me a kiss. It's always a sweet surprise,the firm kiss that shows he's not afraid of affection between us.Does he know how much it means?

"Hey…I'll call once I'm settled," he says,and his sensitivity triggers my tears.

"I really am trying to keep it light," I choke out with a tight laugh.

"Mom,it isn't as though…"

"I know.I know."

Three minutes A.D.—After Departure—I've blown my nose,repaired my make-up and am armed with my books.As I head for the door,my eyes happen to light on the plaque above it.It's hung there for years,overlooked as we hastily,purposefully,moved through our lives as a family.The line from Tennyson must have been waiting for just this moment.

God gives us love.Something to love,he lends us.

Children on loan.And I've never been good at returning things.

Norma R.Larson

啡喝着,又与儿子聊着,我应该知足了。然而,就像对刚才我们的闲聊心存感激一样,我觉得自己开始有些恼火了。我们应该多说一些有意义的话才对。看他的手表,我知道时间到了,他该走了。他那双手,和我父亲的简直一模一样。奇怪的是我以前从来没注意到。还有什么东西我错过了?

提到昨天送帕姆返校时,他变得严肃而冷静,说他俩当时都努力地表现出轻松的样子。我觉察出来,这话是讲给我听的。上帝证明,我已经很努力了。现在楼上面前的这个人,你就是稍微帮我一下,我也不会介意的。我真想告诉他,是你把我弄成这样的。我当初为你怀胎分娩,吃尽了苦头,你不能这样粗暴对待母亲对你应有的眷恋之情,否则我就后悔为你做出如此牺牲,就像签协议时最后忘了审读细则条款那样,后悔莫及。

"好吧……"克里斯站起来,用力把椅子推进去。他从来没有一次这样推过椅子。他接着说:"现在,我该……就放这儿吧,我的旧椅子。再见了,我曾经的厨房,还有我的老妈妈……"

我也立即起身,但没动椅子。他突然俯身亲吻我。他每次吻我都是一次甜蜜的惊喜。这深深的一吻,袒露了他的心声,他并不回避我们之间的亲密感情。但他知道这感情对我有多重要吗?

"嗨……我一安顿下来就打电话。"他说道。此时我已经无法自控,眼泪被他的敏感打开了闸门,奔流而下。

"我是真的想尽量放松些。"我哽咽了一下,挤出一点笑声。

"妈,这不是像你想的……"

"我知道,我知道。"

离别后3分钟——他才走了3分钟,我就已经清好了鼻子,补好了妆,拿起了我的书。朝门边走去的时候,我一抬头正好看到门上的匾。在上面挂了这么多年,这匾见证了我们一家人忙碌而坚定地走过我们的人生。匾上丁尼生的诗句静候了多年,用在此时正是恰到好处。

"爱是上帝赐给我们的,所爱的是上帝借给我们的。"

我的孩子也是租来的。归还的时候,我总是难以割舍。

诺尔马·R.拉森

It's Really Christmas Now

The Sunday before Christmas last year,my husband,a police officer in Arlington,Texas,and I were just leaving for church when the phone rang.*Probably someone wanting Lee,who has already worked a lot of extra hours,to put in some more,*I thought.I looked at him and commanded,"We're going to church! "

"I'll leave in five minutes and be there in about twenty," I heard him tell the caller.I seethed,but his next words stopped me short.

"A Wish with Wings was broken into last night,and the presents are gone," he told me."I have to go.I'll call you later." I was dumbfounded.

A Wish with Wings—Lee serves on the administrative board—is an organization in our area that grants wishes for children with devastating illnesses.Each year Wish also gives a Christmas party,where gifts are distributed.Some 170 donated gifts had been wrapped and were ready for the party,which was to be held that evening,less than nine hours away.

In a daze,I dressed our two children—Ben,just seventeen months, and five-year-old Kate—and we went to church.In between services,I told friends and the pastors about what had happened.The president of our Sunday school gave me forty dollars to buy more presents.One teacher said her class was bringing gifts to donate to another charitable organization and they would be happy to give some of them to Wish.

At 10:30 A.M.,I phoned Lee at the Wish office.He was busy making other calls,so I packed up the kids and headed in his direction.I arrived at a barren scene.Shattered glass covered the front office where the thief had broken the door.The chill that pervaded the room was caused not only by the cold wind coming through the broken door but also by the dashed

难忘的圣诞节

去年圣诞节前的最后一个星期天,我和丈夫李,正要出门上教堂去,电话突然响起来。丈夫是得克萨斯州阿灵顿市的一名警员,也许电话是找他的,都已经加班很长时间了,难道是又要他去忙了,我心里嘀咕。于是我盯着他,给他下了命令,"我们去教堂!"

"我5分钟后出门,约20分钟后到。"我听见他对电话那头说。这让我气得直发抖,不过他接下来的一番解释,顿时让我怒气全无。

"放飞希望"机构的办公室昨晚被盗,圣诞礼物不翼而飞。"他告诉我。"我得走了。待会儿给你电话。"我听得目瞪口呆。

"放飞希望"是我们地区的一个慈善机构,专门帮助那些身患重病的儿童实现他们的愿望,李是该机构行政处的成员之一。每年他们都要举办一个圣诞晚会,同时分发许多礼物。还有不到9个小时的时间,这一次的晚会就要在当晚举行,大家捐赠的170份礼物原来已是包装精美,等候分发了。

此时,我心神恍惚,慌忙帮两个孩子穿好衣服,他们一个名叫本,才17个月大,另一个是5岁的凯特,然后我们就赶快去了教堂。在教堂仪式中间休息时,我同教友和牧师们说起了昨晚发生的窃案。周日学校的校长知道后立刻给了我40美元,让我再去买些礼物。一位教师说她班上的学生正准备给另外一个慈善机构捐赠礼物,他们愿意把其中一部分捐给"放飞希望"。

上午10点半,我给李在"放飞希望"的办公室打电话。他正在忙着处理许多其他的电话,所以我就带上孩子,直奔他办公室去了。到了那儿时,只见现场一片狼藉。窃贼从对外事务的办公室破门而入,地上到处都是碎玻璃。冷风穿过破门吹得屋内阵阵寒意,而屋里

hopes of the several people who stood inside—including Pat Skaggs, the founder of Wish, and Adrena Martinez, the administrative assistant.

Looking out at the parking lot, I was startled to see a news crew from a local television station unloading a camera. Then I learned that Lee's first phone calls had been to the local radio and TV stations.

A few minutes later, a family who had heard a radio report arrived with gifts, already wrapped. Other people soon followed. One was a little boy who had brought things from his own room.

CHICKEN SOUP

I left to get lunch for my kids and some drinks for the workers. When I got back, I found the volunteers eating pizzas that had been donated by a local pizza place. More strangers had arrived, offering gifts and labor. A glass-repair company had fixed the door and refused payment. We began to feel hope: Maybe we could still have the party!

Lee was fielding phone calls, sometimes with a receiver in each ear. Ben was fussing, so I headed home with him, hoping he could take a nap and I could find a baby-sitter.

Meanwhile, the city came alive. Two other police officers were going from church to church to spread the news. Lee told me later of a man who came directly from church, complete with coat and tie, and went to work on the floor, wrapping presents. A third officer, whose wife is deejay for a local radio station, put on his uniform and stood outside the station collecting gifts while his wife made a plea on the air. The fire department agreed to be a drop-off point for gifts. Lee called and asked me to bring our van so it could be used to pick them up.

The clock was ticking. It was mid-afternoon, and 6:00 P.M.—the scheduled time of the party—was not far away. I couldn't find a sitter, and my son started running a fever of 103 °F, so I took him with me to the Wish building just long enough to trade cars with Lee.

Nothing I had ever witnessed could have prepared me for what I saw there—people lined up at the door, arms laden with gifts. One family in which the father had been laid off brought the presents from under

站着的几个人脸上的失望神情,更是让我感到寒心。他们包括,机构的创始人帕特·斯卡格斯和行政助理阿德伦娜·马丁内斯。

再往外看停车场时,我大吃一惊,居然看见当地电视台的一个新闻报道组,正从车上拿出照相机,准备采访。我这才明白,李最初几个电话是打给当地电台和电视台的。

几分钟过后,有一户人家才听完广播,就包好礼物送了过来。很快,其他人也陆续赶来。其中还有一个小男孩,从自己家里带来了礼物。

我离开了一会,给我的孩子弄了点午餐,也给现场的工作人员买了些饮料。等我再回来时,我发现当地一家比萨店送来了比萨饼,在场的义工们已经吃上了。越来越多不相识的人纷纷赶来,送上礼物,提供帮助。一家玻璃维修公司也来免费把门修好了。我们开始觉得大有希望:也许我们还能如期举办圣诞晚会呢!

打来的咨询电话接连不断,李一刻不停地接听,有时两边耳朵上都放着听筒。本在一边不停地吵闹,我只好送他回家,希望他睡一会儿,好让我能找个保姆来带他。

在此期间,整个城市都动员起来了。另外两个警员正挨个向各个教堂通报此事。李后来告诉我,一位先生获悉此事后,从教堂直接赶来,西服领带,穿得整整齐齐,二话没说就在地上开始帮忙包装礼物。第三位警员的妻子是当地电台的音乐主持人,当妻子在节目中向听众呼吁捐赠时,他就穿好制服站在电台外面收集捐来的礼物。消防局也同意临时作为礼物收集站。李打电话让我把我们的小货车开去,用来接运礼物。

时间一分一秒地过去了,从下午3点到下午6点,距离晚会开幕的预定时间越来越近。我找不到保姆,儿子却开始高热到华氏103度,所以我只好又带着他回到"希望"机构办公楼,正好能把小货车交给李,拿回我的轿车。

对当时的场景我毫无心理准备,只见人们怀抱着许多礼物,在门口排队等候捐赠。有一户家庭,尽管父亲已经下岗,他们还是自己

their own tree.It was like a scene from *It's a Wonderful Life.*

Inside,Lee was still on the phone.Outside,volunteers were loading vans with wrapped gifts to be taken to the party site,an Elks lodge six miles away.By 5:50 P.M.—just before the first of the more than 100 children arrived—enough presents had been delivered to the lodge. Somehow,workers had matched up the donated items with the young-sters' wishes,so many received just what they wanted.Their faces shone with delight as they opened the packages.For some,it would be their last Christmas.

Those presents,however,were only a small portion of what came in during the day.Wish had lost 170 gifts in the robbery,but more than 1,500 had been donated! Lee decided to spend the night at the office to guard the surplus,so I packed some food and a sleeping bag and drove them down to the office.There,gifts were stacked to the ceiling,filling every available inch of space except for a small pathway that had been cleared to the back office.

Lee spent a quiet night,but the phone started ringing again at 6:30 A.M..The first caller wanted to make a donation,so Lee started to give him directions. "You'd better give me the mailing address,"the caller said. "I'm in Philadelphia."The story had been picked up by the national news.Soon calls were coming from all over the country.

By midday,the Wish office was again filled with workers,this time picking up the extra gifts to take to other charitable organizations so they could distribute them before Christmas,just two days away.Pat and Adrena,whose faces had been tear-stained twenty-four hours earlier,were now filled with joy.

When Lee was interviewed for the local news,he summed up every-one's feeling:"It's really Christmas now." We had all caught the spirit—and the meaning—of the season.

Kitsy Jones

准备了礼物送来。此情此景，就像老电影《风云人物》里的一幕。

大楼里面，李还在忙着接听电话，大楼外面，义工们正在把包好了的礼物装上小货车，准备送往6英里外的晚会现场——"糜鹿会场"。下午5点50分，恰好在100多个儿童到达之前，足够的礼物已经送抵会场。不一会儿，工作人员就把捐赠的礼物和这些儿童的愿望一一搭配好，大多数小孩都收到了他们希望等到的礼物。当他们拆开包装时，孩子们的脸上洋溢着喜悦的神情。对有些孩子来说，这也许是他们最后一个圣诞节了。

而这些礼物只不过是那天大家捐赠的其中一小部分而已。"希望"机构在窃案中被盗走了170份礼物，却收到了超过1500份礼物。李决定晚上留在办公室看守多余的礼物，所以我给他带了些吃的，拿了一个睡袋就驱车前往他的办公室。在那，我看见礼物堆到了屋顶，除了留下一条通往后厅的狭小过道外，房间的每个角落都挤满了礼物。

那天晚上办公室里非常安静，不过，第二天早上6点30分，电话再次响起。第一个打进电话的就想要捐赠，于是李开始告诉他前往路线。"你最好还是给我邮寄地址吧，"打电话的人说。"我在费城。"原来全国新闻里面报道了这个故事。很快，许多电话从全国各地打来。

到了中午，"希望"机构办公室又挤满了工作人员，这一次，他们正在挑选多余的礼物送给其他慈善机构，以便能在两天后的圣诞节前派发出去。24小时之前，帕特和阿德伦娜还是泪流满面，现在他们已经是满脸欢笑了。

当李接受当地新闻采访时，他概括了大家的感受："现在才是真正的圣诞节。"我们大家也都感受到了这浓浓的节日气氛，还有，这节日的深远意义。

基特西·琼斯

One Life at a Time

As our car slowly made its way through the crowded streets of Dhaka,Bangladesh's capital of 2 million people,I thought I knew what to expect.As leader of the American Voluntary Medical Team (AVMT),I had seen great suffering and devastation in Iraq,Nicaragua and Calcutta. But I wasn't prepared for what I saw in Bangladesh.

I traveled there with a group of AVMT doctors,nurses and other volunteers after a series of devastating cyclones hit the tiny country in 1991.More than 100,000 people had been killed,and now,because flood-ing had wiped out clean water and sanitation systems,thousands more were dying from diarrhea and dehydration.Children were dying from polio and tetanus,diseases nearly forgotten in the United States.

As we drove to the hospital where we were to set up a clinic,I thought I knew what we were up against:humid,scorching days,heavy rains and crowded conditions.After all,since Bangladesh became inde-pendent from Pakistan more than twenty years earlier,some 125 million people live in an area slightly smaller than the state of Wisconsin.

I glanced out the window at the street teeming with people:men talking in groups,women dressed in bright red and yellow saris,and chil-dren chasing each other,darting in between the many carts and rick-shaws.

Then I looked more closely.The people were walking through raw sewage.A man stepped over a body in a doorway,just as one of the many body carts pulled up to haul it away.At a busy corner,I saw a woman standing very still,holding a small bundle,a baby.As I watched her face,she pulled her shawl back slightly,and I clearly saw her baby

施善一生

当我们来到有200万人口的孟加拉首都达卡，汽车在拥挤的街道上缓慢穿行时，我想我知道该有何期待。作为美国医疗志愿小组的领导，我在伊拉克、尼加拉瓜和加尔各答等地，已经见过了大量的苦难和荒废的场景。但是我在孟加拉的所见所闻还是让我措手不及。

我当时率领一批美国医疗志愿小组的医生、护士以及其他志愿者前往孟加拉，在此之前，1991年一系列毁灭性的龙卷风刚刚袭击了这个弹丸之地。灾害夺走了超过10万人的生命，现在，因为洪水冲毁了卫生和供水系统，成千上万的人又将死于痢疾和缺水。大批儿童还将死于小儿麻痹症和破伤风，而这些疾病在美国早已绝迹了。

我们打算在当地一家医院里设立诊所，就在我们驱车前往时，我想到了我们面临的各种困难：潮湿、炎热、大雨和拥挤不堪的条件。毕竟，从20多年前孟加拉脱离巴基斯坦获得独立时起，就有大约125 000 000人，挤在这个比威斯康星州还略小一点的地区。

我透过窗户朝外略微看了看，只见街上密密麻麻，人头攒动：男人们三五成群，聊天说话，妇女穿着鲜红色或黄色的莎丽服饰，儿童则相互追逐嬉戏，急速穿梭在成堆的马车和人力三轮车之间。

接着我又更仔细地观察起来。街上污水横流，人们也就在上面走过。当一辆运尸推车在门口正要把地上一具尸体拖走时，一个男的就从尸体上一跃而过。在一个热闹的角落，我看见一位妇人伫足在那里，怀里抱着个小包袱，是一个婴儿。这时，她轻轻地把披肩往

was dead.I suddenly thought of my own healthy children at home,and tears stung my eyes.I'd never seen anything so horrible.

The following day,I decided to ride out to Mother Teresa's orphanage in old Dhaka.A friend had asked me before I left home to visit and see what medical help they needed.Two of the Little Sisters of the Poor greeted me at the gate and immediately led me to the infant floor.I was astonished to find 160 babies,mostly girls,squalling for attention from the few hardworking sisters.

"There are so many," I said,amazed.

"Some were given up because their parents couldn't feed them," one sister said.

"And others were abandoned because they are girls," said another. She explained that often females are aborted or killed at birth because they are considered inferior in the male-dominated culture.What little food there is must go to males.

The irony struck me hard.These baby girls were society's throwaways,yet what had I seen today?Women everywhere:working in the rice fields outside the city,herding children through crowded Dhaka,trying to earn a living by selling trinkets on the street,and here,at the orphanage, caring for the forgotten.

"A couple of the babies have serious medical problems," the sister said."Would you like to see them?"

I followed her down a row of basket-style cribs to the tiny,sick little girls,both about two months old.One had a heart condition,the other,a severe cleft lip and palate.

"We can't do much more for them," the sister said."Please help them.Whatever you can do will be a blessing."

I held each baby,stroking each girl's soft,dark hair and gazing into their small faces.How my heart ached for these innocent angels.What kind of a future did they face,if they had a future at all?

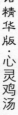
双语精华版·心灵鸡汤·

后拉,我这才看清她抱的是个死婴。见状,我突然想起我家里健康可爱的孩子们,不禁淌下泪水,刺痛了双眼。这是我见过的最恐怖的一幕。

第二天,我决定驱车前往老达卡城区穷人圣母特里萨修女的孤儿院。我离家之前有一位朋友托我来这里拜访,并看看他们需要些什么医疗帮助。安贫小姊妹会的两位修女来到大门口迎接我,并立刻带我去婴儿区。我惊讶地发现,里面竟然有160个婴儿,而且大多数都是女孩,孩子们正在哇哇地大声啼哭,渴望得到几个不辞辛劳的修女的关照。

"这太多了。"我惊叹道。

"有些是因为父母没法养活而被抛弃的。"一个修女说。

"其他的就因为是女孩而被丢弃了。"另一个补充说。她接着解释道,女孩经常被堕胎打掉,或生下来就被弄死,因为在男人主宰的世界里,她们被看做是低人一等。仅有的少量食物都必须留给男性。

如此可笑的说法强烈地刺激了我。这些女婴都是社会的弃儿,那我今天看到的都是什么?妇女随处可见:城外稻田里劳作的,拥挤的达卡城里带着成群孩子的,街上靠卖小饰物来谋生的,还有这,在孤儿院里照看弃婴的修女们。

"许多婴儿都重病在身,"这位修女说,"你能看看吗?"

我随她沿着一排篮子样式的婴儿床,走到两个才两个月大的患病女婴跟前,她们瘦弱不堪。一个有心脏病,另一个患有严重的唇裂。

"除了照看他们,其他的我们就无能为力了。"修女说道。"请帮帮她们吧。不论做点什么都将是她们的福音。"

两个女婴我各抱了一会,抚摸着她们黑色柔软的头发,凝视着她们的小脸蛋。我内心在为这些纯真的天使感到颤痛。如果她们还有未来,那将是什么样的未来呢?

"I'll see what we can do," I said.

When I returned to the clinic,hundreds were waiting for treatment and much work needed to be done.I'm not a medical person,so my job is varied:I run the pharmacy,track down medicine when we run out,negotiate with local officials for equipment or transportation,and scout the patient line for critical cases.

By day's end,my head was swimming.The helpless babies' cries and the hundreds of faces on the streets and in our clinic all seemed to express the same thing—hopelessness.The thought startled me.*These people are without hope.*Even Calcutta had not seemed so bleak.*Without hope.*I repeated the words in my mind,and my heart sank.So much of what AVMT tries to do is give hope.

My inspiration was a woman who had dedicated her life to giving hope to others—my grandmother.We called her Lulu Belle,and she practically ran the Mississippi River town of Cairo,Illinois.She wasn't the mayor or a town official,but if a jobless man came to her back door, she'd call everyone she knew until she found the man work.Once,I came through her kitchen door and was startled to find a table full of strangers eating supper.

"A new family in town,Cindy,"she said,as she set the mashed potatoes on the table and headed to the stove for the gravy. "Just tryin'to give 'em a good start." I later learned the man hadn't yet found work, and Lulu Belle was making sure his family had at least one hot meal every day.

Lulu Belle had great faith,and it made her stronger than any woman I knew.Her favorite *Bible* verse was a simple one："Do unto others as you would have them do unto you." She believed that if you treated people right,the way you would want to be treated,God would do the rest.So she never worried about where the job or the food would come from—she knew God would provide it.

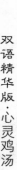

"我会考虑我们能做点什么。"我说。

回到诊所,成百的病人在等待治疗,有大量的工作需要完成。我不是医疗人员,因此我的工作很不固定:有时在药房里忙,有时药售完了又要四处求购,有时还要和当地官员商谈设备和交通问题,有时又在病人排得长长的队伍里找出高危病人,提前救治。

这样一天下来,我头昏眼花,天旋地转。婴儿无助的啼哭声,诊所里和大街上那无数张迷茫的脸都好像在跟我诉说着同一件事——绝望。这个想法让我大吃一惊,这些人都是没有希望的。即便是在加尔各答,也好像没有如此惨淡无望。"没有希望。"我脑子里不停地重复,心情也很低落。这样看来,我们美国医疗志愿小组要努力去做的应该是把希望带给他们。

我的灵感来自我祖母,她一辈子都致力于为别人播撒希望。我们都叫她露露·贝尔,她住在伊利诺伊州的密西西比河边一个名叫开罗的小镇,她不是镇长,也不是什么官员,但她实际上却对当地事务热心负责。如果有失业的人悄悄来到她家后门求助,她会找所有认识的人来帮忙,直到别人找到了工作。有一次,我经过她的厨房,吃惊地发现一桌陌生人在吃晚饭。

"他们家刚搬来镇上,辛迪。"她边说边把土豆泥放在桌上,到炉灶上去取肉汁。"我只是想让他们有一个好的开始。"后来我得知,那家男主人还没找着工作,我祖母就保证他家每天至少能吃上一顿热饭。

祖母有着很坚定不移的信念,这也让她比我所认识的任何女子都坚强。她最喜欢《圣经》里面很简单的一句话:"对待别人要像你想别人对待你那样。"她坚信,如果你对别人很好,就像你想别人怎么对你一样,剩下的就交给上帝来成全我们了。因此,她从不担心工作和食物,她知道上帝会恩赐给她的。

But God seemed so far away in Bangladesh.I struggled with that thought at our morning meeting.We were set up in a clinic near Rangpur,in the northern part of the country,and our team had gathered to go over the day's schedule.At the meeting's end I told them what I tell every team:"Remember,we're here to give hope." But the words caught a little in my throat as I wondered how we would do it.Where would hope come from for these people,especially the women,so overwhelmed by disease,poverty and circumstance?

Already, 8,000 people were lined up for treatment.Scouting the line, I noticed something peculiar.All of them were men,many quite healthy. Not until I reached the end of the line did I see any women and children,and most of them looked very sick,some near death.My heart pounded as I realized what was happening.The men expected to be seen first,even if they were perfectly healthy.The women could wait.

I wondered what I should do.I remembered the woman I'd seen on the street,holding her dead baby,perhaps because she couldn't get care quickly enough.I thought of the abandoned babies in the orphanage,and anger and frustration welled up inside me.

Maybe a bit of Lulu Belle was with me as I rushed past the line and back inside the clinic to tell the doctor in charge what was going on.He was as upset as I was.

"Well,what do you think?" he asked."We can either see all these well men,or we can get the sick women and children up front."

"Let's do it," I said."Let's do what we came here for."

I ran back outside and asked the interpreter to tell the men at the front to step aside.He did,and immediately I heard a disgruntled murmuring rumble through the crowd.The men were angry and the women were afraid to come forward.The interpreter repeated the announcement, and as we tried to get the crowd to move,a scuffle broke out and soon soldiers appeared,their guns strapped across their chests.They tried to restore order,but several men still pushed to the front of the line.

但是在孟加拉，上帝似乎离我们很远。在我们早上会议时，我一直在跟这播撒希望的想法作斗争。这一次我们被派往孟加拉北部的兰普尔市的一个诊所，我们小组提前集合起来研究一天的工作计划。会议结束时，我重复了一遍对每个小组我都要提醒的话："记住，我们来这是带给他们希望的。"但是，在考虑如何具体实施时，我欲言又止。对当地这些人来说，希望从何而来？尤其是妇女们，她们还长期遭受疾病、贫穷和悲惨命运的压迫。

已经有8 000人在排队等候治疗。在检查候诊队伍时，我注意到有些古怪的事情，排队的都是男人，其中许多还很健康。直到队伍的最后，我才看见有妇女和儿童，而且多数患病，有些甚至生命垂危。当我意识到这是怎么回事时，我气得心里怦怦直跳。这些男人即使身体完全健康，也希望最先接受诊断，而妇女则只能等。

我考虑这该怎么办。我想起在街上看到的那个母亲，也许就是因为没有及时救治，最后只能两手捧着她死去的孩子，我还想到孤儿院里的那些弃婴。顿时，我怒火中烧，忍无可忍。

也许是受坚强的祖母的影响，我飞速跑回诊所，告诉主治医生怎么回事。他听完后和我一样恼火。

"那你看怎么办？"他问道，"我们要么诊治这些身体棒棒的男人，要么把患病的妇女儿童放到前面来。"

"就这么办，"我说。"让我们开始做来这儿真正该做的吧。"

我立刻跑了出去，要求翻译告诉前面的男人们，让他们靠边站。他照着做了，立刻人群中传来闹哄哄的、不满的吵嚷声。男人们非常愤怒，妇女们也不敢向前。翻译重复了一遍决定。就在我们上前尽力想让他们挪动时，人群当中爆发了冲突，荷枪实弹的士兵很快赶到。他们努力恢复秩序，但还是有几名男子仍然在往前挤。

"Tell them no," I said to the interpreter,gathering all the courage I had."Tell them we treat the sick women and children first or we fold up the clinic."

The men looked at me for a moment,then backed down and began letting the women forward.The fear and sadness I'd seen on the women's faces gave way to joy as they rushed to enter the clinic first. They smiled at me,grasping my hands and arms in thanks.

As one woman stretched out her hand to give me a flower,our eyes met,and I saw something incredible:hope.Now I understood.We didn't have to pull off a miracle.It was what my grandmother believed about doing unto others what was right.And out of that simple act,God had brought life-affirming hope.

Our doctors and nurses saved lives that day,and treated thousands during our two weeks in Bangladesh.When it was time to come home,I returned by way of the orphanage,to bring the two sick babies I'd seen back to the United States for treatment.On the plane home,I knew I'd have a surprise for my husband—that we would be adopting one of them,now our beautiful Bridget.

Several months later,I had the privilege of meeting with Mother Teresa about Calcutta's medical needs.In her beautifully simple way,she crystallized what I had felt in Bangladesh.

"How do you deal with the overwhelming needs,the disease,the death?" I asked.

"You look into one face," she said,her voice filled with peace,"and you continue the work." And know that God will do the rest.

Cindy Hensley McCain

As told to Gina Bridgeman

"告诉他们绝对不行。"我鼓起所有勇气,态度坚决地对翻译说,"跟他们说,我们先看患病的妇女儿童,否则我们就关闭诊所。"

这几名男子看了我一会儿,然后朝后走开,让妇女们上前。她们迅速跑过来进了诊所,脸上已不再是我先前见到的恐惧和悲伤,而是满心欢喜了。她们冲我微笑,心存感激地抓住我的胳膊和手。

一位女子伸出手来,递给我一朵鲜花,然后,我们目光交汇时,在她眼里我看到了某种神奇的东西:希望。现在我明白了,我们没必要去创造一个奇迹,只要像我祖母信奉的那样对别人好。就做这么简单的一次善事之后,上帝就已经带来了希望,让人们对人生充满了信心。

当天,我们的医生和护士挽救了许多生命,而在孟加拉的两周时间里,我们救治了成百上千的当地人。快结束回国时,我又去了孤儿院,把我先前见到的两个患病女婴带回美国救治。在回国的飞机上,我在想我给丈夫带来了一个惊喜,因为我们将收养其中一个女孩,也就是我们家现在漂亮的布里奇特。

几个月后,我很荣幸地与圣母特里萨修女会见,商谈加尔各答的医疗需求。其间,她以简单而精彩的方法,概括了我在孟加拉的感受,让我更加清楚明白。

"你如何能解决这无数的贫困、疾病和死亡问题?"我问道。

"你先分析身边某一个人的困难,"她心平气和地说道,"然后你接着做下去。"我知道接下来上帝就会帮助成就其余的事了。

辛迪·汉斯莱·麦凯恩
由吉纳·布里奇曼根据讲述整理

I Did My Best

To live in the hearts of those we leave behind is not to die.

Thomas Campbell

[EDITORS' NOTE:*Princess Diana was loved around the world for her humanitarian and compassionate work.Her easy rapport with people in need and her warm,understanding heart touched millions of lives. Here she describes the incident that turned the attention of the world to the cause of AIDS.*]

I had always wanted to hug people in hospital beds.A visit to an AIDS hospice in 1991,with Mrs.Bush,was a stepping stone for me.This particular man,who was so ill,started crying when I sat on his bed,and he held my hand,and I thought *Diana,do it,just do it,*and I gave him an enormous hug.It was just so touching because he clung to me and he cried.I thought,*Wonderful!*

On the other side of the room,a very young man,who I can only describe as beautiful,lying in his bed,told me he was going to die about Christmas.His friend,a man sitting in a chair by his bed,was crying his eyes out."Why not me?" he said.I put my hand out to him and said:"It's not supposed to be easy,all this.Isn't it extraordinary,wherever I go,it's always those like you,sitting in a chair,who have to go through such hell,whereas those who accept they are going to die are calm?"

He said:"I didn't know that happened."

And I said:"Well,it does;you're not the only one.It's wonderful that

献上所有爱心

活在后人心中，我们终获永生。

托马斯·坎贝尔

编者按：黛安娜王妃积极从事人道主义和慈善事业，从而赢得全世界人民的爱戴。她同情、关心、理解危难中的人们，这深深地感动了亿万人民。她在本文描述了一次偶然机会让全世界都来关注艾滋病事业。

我有个夙愿，一直想要去拥抱医院病床上的病人。1991年，我和布什夫人去艾滋病安养院探望病人，这成了我实现夙愿的一块垫脚石。我见到的这名男子病得很重，当我坐到他病床边上时，他开始哭了起来，紧紧地拽住我的手。我当时在想，赶快，赶快行动吧，于是我终于给了他一个真诚而有力的拥抱。他紧紧地抱着我，眼泪止不住地往下淌，场面实在是太感人了。我想，这真是太激动了。

病房另一边住的男子非常年轻，我只能用俊美来描述他。躺在病床上，他告诉我，圣诞节前后他将离开人世。旁边的一位男士是他朋友，坐在床边的椅子上，眼睛都哭肿了。"为什么不是我呢？"他说。我把手伸过去给他，对他说："这些都不容易。这难道还不够令人惊叹吗？不论我到哪，都能见到像你这样的，坐在椅子上，不得不经历地狱似的苦难，而那些病人们还能平静地接受他们即将离开人世的现实。"

他接着说道："我不知道真会发生这样的事。"

我又说道："是的，是这样的；你也不是唯一的经历者。你现在陪

you're actually by his bed.You'll learn so much from watching your friend."

He was crying and clung on to my hand,and I felt so comfortable in there.I just hated being taken away.

When I go into the Palace for a garden party or summit meeting dinner,I am a very different person.I conform to what's expected of me; but when I come to the hospice,I know when I turn my light off at night,I did my best.

Diana,Princess of Wales

伴在他床边,这就很让人欣慰了。在看护你的朋友这一过程中,你能领悟到许多东西。"

他抓住我的手不放,眼泪还在翻涌而出。在那里,我心情也感到了无比的放松,丝毫不想离开。

当我进入王宫,参加花园聚会或高层会面后的宴会,我就成了另外一个人,我遵从大家对我的期望。当我来到医院探望病人时,我知道,当我生命之灯熄灭时,我已经献上了所有的爱心。

威尔士王妃 黛安娜

A Reason to Live

In October 1986,farmer Darrell Adams needed help with the corn harvest.He asked his wife,Marilyn,if eleven-year-old Keith,Marilyn's son and Darrell's stepson,could stay home from school to help.Darrell's request wasn't an unusual one in farm country,where children are often needed to help bring in the crops.

Marilyn stifled a sense of foreboding and gave her permission.*Staying home from school to help with the harvest is a rite of passage for a farm kid,*she told herself.Keith had shown his mother he knew the rules of working safely around farm machinery,and the boy was proud that Darrell had asked for his help.

Before she left for a computer class in Des Moines the next morning,Marilyn fixed a big farm breakfast for Keith and Darrell.As she walked out the door she told them,"You guys be careful today.I don't know what I'd do without either one of you."

Later that afternoon,when Darrell rolled his combine into the farmyard to unload more corn,he found Keith curled in the fetal position at the bottom of the grain wagon,14,000 pounds of corn on top of him and kernels clogging his throat.In a panic,Darrell rushed Keith to the nearby medical clinic,where medics did what they could for the boy while a hospital helicopter flew to the rescue.

Marilyn had been rousted from her computer class to take the telephone call all parents fear.She was driven to the hospital,dread cloaking her like a shroud.Darrell,who had been driven to the hospital by clinic personnel,met her there.

"I killed him!I killed him!"He cried,as he buried his face in his big,

重生的理由

　　1986年10月,农场主达雷尔·亚当斯急需人手来帮他收割玉米。他问妻子,玛里琳,能否让她的儿子,11岁的基思,也就是他的继子,别上学在家帮他干几天农活。在乡下农场里,经常会要求孩子们来帮忙收获庄稼,所以,达雷尔的要求也不过分。

　　玛里琳打消了心头闪过的不详预感,同意了他的要求。收获季节停学在家帮忙,这是农家子弟必经之事,她这样说服自己。基思以前也在他妈妈面前表现过,他对农场机械的安全操作规则比较了解,当达雷尔请他帮忙时,这小男孩还显得很自豪。

　　第2天早上去得梅因上电脑课之前,玛里琳为基思和达雷尔准备了一份丰盛的农场早餐。就在走出大门时,她还不忘叮嘱他们,"你们俩今天要小心点。你们俩没了谁我都没法活了。"

　　那天下午,当达雷尔把联合收割机开进农场院子里来卸下玉米时,他突然发现基思被卷进玉米脱粒机底部的漏斗口处,14 000磅重的玉米压在他上面,喉咙里面还卡住了许多玉米粒。达雷尔惊恐万分,抱起基思就往附近的诊所跑,诊所的医生立即竭力抢救,医院的直升机也飞来援救。

　　玛里琳从电脑课上被喊出来,接到了一个所有父母都害怕听到的电话。随后,玛里琳被送往医院,惊恐失色,脸色煞白,像盖了块裹尸布。达雷尔已经由门诊医护人员送到医院,现在见到了玛里琳。

　　"是我害了他!是我害了他!"达雷尔号啕大哭,把脸深深地埋

rough farmers' hands.

At Keith's bedside,Marilyn anxiously examined her son,his eighty-pound body shaking from shock,his face almost covered by the oxygen mask.Keith was hooked up to every medical device imaginable and an intravenous bag hung from a metal stand over his head.As Marilyn brushed her son's hair from his forehead,she noticed that his face felt cold and clammy.She felt his arms,legs and feet—they were like ice.

Stricken and helpless,Marilyn sat and prayed for Keith,who had read the Bible cover to cover and wanted to be a minister.Several hours into her vigil,she leaned over and spoke to her son.

"Keith,"she said."We have to talk to Jesus now."

A single tear fell from the corner of the boy's left eye and ran down his cheek.

At 2:30 A.M.,with Marilyn on one side of his bed and his grandmother on the other,Keith stopped trembling.Marilyn felt her precious boy slip away to a place beyond pain and suffering.Her only son was gone.

Marilyn sank into sorrow so deep that even her family's love and concern could not reach her.She stopped going to church because all she did was cry.She couldn't drag herself to school programs or go to parent-teacher conferences.Her remaining daughters had to parent her. She watched,numb with grief,as she and Darrell grew apart.

It was a request for help from her daughter,Kelly,that started Marilyn on her road to recovery.Kelly had joined FFA,Future Farmers of America,which teaches young people about agriculture and related occupations.Her younger brother's death had spurred Kelly to do a presentation on the dangers of grain wagons.

Together,mother and daughter researched the subject and found a recommendation that warning decals should be placed on the side of grain wagons.No one,they found to their surprise and consternation,had

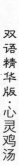

进了他那双农民的粗糙大手里。

在基思的床边，玛里琳焦急地观察他的儿子，他80磅的身体因为休克而颤抖，面部几乎被氧气面罩完全遮住。他身上接上了各种可能的医疗设备，头上方的金属支架上还挂着一个静脉输液袋。玛里琳用手把儿子的头发从额头往后梳时，感觉到潮湿冰冷。她又摸了他的胳膊、大腿和脚，它们都已经像冰一样了。

悲伤无助的玛里琳只好坐下来为基思祈祷。基思曾经一页一页地仔细读过《圣经》，还想长大了当一名牧师。几个小时的祈祷后，玛里琳靠近儿子，开始对儿子说话。

"基思，"她说，"我们现在必须和耶稣谈谈。"

一滴眼泪从孩子的左眼角流出，顺着脸颊滑落下来。

凌晨2:30分，玛里琳和孩子的祖母分别站在病床的两边，看着基思停止了颤抖。玛里琳觉得她的爱子已经悄悄地离开她们，去了一个没有痛苦不用受难的地方。她唯一的儿子没了。

此后，玛里琳深深地陷入丧子之痛，对家人的关爱也不再理睬。她也不再去教堂了，因为她所能做的就只是独自哭泣。她再也没去过学校或参加教师家长会了。剩下的几个女儿不得不反过来照顾她。她成天发呆，哑然发愣，与达雷尔也渐渐疏远了。

直到后来，是女儿凯利要求帮助的一个请求，开始了玛里琳慢慢的恢复过程。凯利加入了美国未来农场主组织，这个组织专门教授年轻人农业知识和相关的职业。弟弟的意外死亡促进了凯利举办了一个关于脱粒机的危险的讲座。

就此主题，母女一起做调查研究，发现了一条重要的指导建议，即脱粒机边上应该贴上警示标记。令他们感到更加意外和可怕的

followed up on the recommendation.No one,that is,until Marilyn Adams decided that she and her family would do it.

Marilyn realized she could resurrect her son's memory,if not his life,by spreading the word about the dangers of farming for children.A woman with a mission,Marilyn channeled her profound sense of loss into starting an organization called Farm Safety For Just Kids.

Her employer donated enough money to print the warning decals Marilyn and her family had designed,sitting around their kitchen table. Iowa FFA chapters distributed thousands of these decals,sticking them on grain wagons while farmers waited in line to unload at grain eleva- tors across Iowa.Marilyn felt reborn.She had found a reason to live and a way to keep Keith's memory alive.

Marilyn knew that there was still a lot of hard work ahead.Garner- ing the support of the Iowa Farm Safety Council,she did a radio inter- view,and then a couple of articles appeared in farm magazines on Mari- lyn and her fledgling organization.The publicity prompted a flood of phone calls from the public and the media.

"The phone just rang and rang and rang.We couldn't even eat din- ner.A lot of people called who'd lost a child in a farming accident.They wanted to talk to me and reach out.Many of the people who get in- volved in Farm Safety For Just Kids have also lost children in farm ac- cidents—it helps them in their grief.Any time a grieving parent calls me, I put them to work.It gives us something positive to do in our lives.That was when I began to feel I had a purpose in life,like I could begin to nurture again," Marilyn recalls.

Marilyn tirelessly traveled the country,talking to businesses.She eventually lined up enough financial support so she could quit her job and work on farm safety issues full-time.She convinced then-First Lady Barbara Bush to be honorary chairwoman of Farm Safety For Just Kids.

"Nobody says'no'to Marilyn Adams," Mrs.Bush said.

双语精华版·心灵鸡汤·

是,在玛里琳·亚当斯决定她和家人开始这么做之前,居然没有任何人采用过这条指导建议。

玛里琳意识到,即使她不能挽回儿子的生命,她也要通过宣传儿童农耕的危险,来唤起她对儿子的美好回忆。带着强烈的使命感,她化悲痛为力量,开始创办了一个组织,取名为"儿童农场安全"。

玛里琳和家人围坐在厨房餐桌上设计出警示标记贴纸,随后,她的老板捐了大笔的钱使之得以印制出来。美国未来农场主组织在艾奥瓦州的分部发放了几千张这样的贴纸,并且在整个州当农民在谷物吊车旁排队卸下玉米时,把警示标记贴在他们的脱粒机上面。这样一来,玛里琳找到了重生的感觉,同时也找到一个活下来的理由和永远保留对基思回忆的方法。

玛里琳很清楚前面仍然还有大量的艰苦工作。在艾奥瓦州农场安全委员会的支持下,她参加了一个电台专访,接着,一些农业杂志对玛里琳和她新创办的组织进行了几次文章报道。知名度有了很大提高,随之而来的就是来自公众和媒体的大量电话。

"电话响个没完没了,我们都没办法吃饭。很多在农耕事故中失去孩子的家长打来电话。他们想和我交流,并提供帮助。许多加入'儿童农场安全'的人都曾在农耕事故中失去过孩子。这样的活动有利于他们从痛苦中解脱出来。任何时候如果有伤心的父母打来电话,我都让他们去参加这项活动。这给我们的生活增添了积极力量。从那时起,我开始感觉到生活有了目标,如同重新开始哺育一个孩子那样。"玛里琳回忆起当时的情况。

玛里琳不知疲倦地穿梭在全国各地,同不计其数的公司企业商谈赞助事宜。最后她筹集到足够的资金,于是她辞去了工作,专门关注解决农场安全问题。她还说服了当时的第一夫人——芭芭拉·布什出任该组织的荣誉主席。

"没人能对玛里琳·亚当斯说'不'。"布什夫人这样评价。

Over the last ten years,the organization has grown enormously. Today Farm Safety For Just Kids has a staff of nine,an annual budget of $750,000 and seventy-seven chapters in the United States and Canada.

And recently,a study found that farm accidents claimed the lives of 39 percent fewer children since the founding of Farm Safety For Just Kids.There are many reasons for the decline,but most of the experts a-gree that Farm Safety For Just Kids is one of them.

Fulfilled with her success,her family whole and happy once more—Marilyn and Darrell even had another baby—Mayilyn seems at peace. When asked how she envisioned Keith in heaven,Marilyn laughed and said,"I believe he's very busy pointing his mother in the right direction."

Jerry Perkins

在过去的10年时间里,该组织发展十分迅猛。今天,它已扩大为有9个工作人员,年预算达到75万美元,在全美和加拿大有77个分部的组织。

最近,一项研究表明自从建立"儿童农场安全"组织起,儿童在农场的意外死亡率已经下降了39%。这里面有多方面的因素,但大多数专家都认为"儿童农场安全"组织的努力是其中之一。

事业上的成功,让玛里琳一家人又团聚在了一起,生活也再现幸福和美满,玛里琳和达雷尔甚至又添了一个孩子,玛里琳自己也渐渐恢复了平和。当被问起怎样怀念天堂里的基思时,玛里琳笑着说道:"相信他现在正忙着给他妈妈指引正确的方向。"

杰里·珀金斯

女性系列／挥洒四季的芬芳

The Night I Wrote My Pulitzer Prize Winner

> *I long to accomplish a great and noble task,but it is my chief duty to accomplish small tasks as if they were great and noble.*
>
> Helen Keller

As a writer,I've felt that someday,somewhere my work would touch human hearts,bridge continents,unite generations.One night,it did.

I'm at McKelvey's Tavern,sipping Amber Bock.The Blues Band is on a break.A small,white-haired man sits two barstools away.

"I've got ten kids," he boasts."And two grandbabies on the way. My youngest daughter is in the Army.I think the world of that girl.Last five years,she's been in Germany."

"Does she call you?"

"Sometimes.But with her schedule and the time difference,we don't talk much anymore." His lips tighten as he looks into his beer."It costs a bundle to phone over there.She tells me,'Call collect,Dad.'Nah,I can't put that expense on her."

"Write a letter," I suggest.

"Can't hold a pen," he says."I've had four strokes.My arm is paralyzed." To show me,he lifts the lifeless limb with his good hand.

I grab my journal,open to a clean page,and lean forward,pen in hand."What's her name?"

"Suzie."

双
语
精
华
版
·
心
灵
鸡
汤
·

我的普利策①之夜

> 我渴望成就大事业，但我主要还是把小事情当做大事
> 业来完成。
>
> 海伦·凯勒

作为作家，我感到总有一天，在某个地方，我的作品能够动人心弦，飞越大洲，世代相传。终于有一天夜里，我真的做到了。

当时，我在一家名叫麦凯尔维的酒馆里，小口品着琥珀黑啤。蓝调乐队的表演已经结束。在我附近隔着两个高脚凳的地方，有一个白发苍苍的小老头在那坐着。

"我有10个子女，"他得意地说，"还有两个他们的孩子就要出世了。我最小的女儿正在陆军服役。我对她是疼爱有加。过去5年，她都在德国。"

"她给你来过电话吗？"

"有时吧。但她的安排很紧，又有时差影响，我们谈的也不多。"说罢他便嘴唇紧闭，眼睛望着啤酒。过了一会，他接着说："打越洋电话要花不少钱。她劝我，'打对方付费电话吧，爸爸。'不，我不能让她来承担这笔开销。"

"那就写信。"我建议他。

"我拿不动笔了，"他说道，"经过4次中风，我一只胳膊都麻痹了。"说着就用他那只好手拎起一只废胳膊来给我看。

我抓起我的日记本，翻到空白页，朝前微倾，手握着笔，问："她叫什么名字？"

"苏茜。"

I look into his bloodshot eyes and ask, "Shall I start with 'Dear Suzie,' 'Hi Suzie,' or 'Suzie,how the heck are ya?'?"

"All of that." He grins,exhales smoke.

"Dear Suzie," I slowly repeat,then pen the words. "You talk,I'll write."

He presses the bit stub of his cigarette into the small tin ashtray, reaches for another Camel,lights up and inhales. "Tell her I'm down to one pack a day...and...I eat every day...at the Senior Center.The food is wonderful.Spaghetti,cake,ice cream.All you can eat." He adds with a chuckle,"Just no beer."

I listen and write nonstop.

"Tell her I think the world of her.Tell her Jen and Dave are getting married and Pat and Tim are getting divorced.Tell her Uncle Wilbur is still up on Doe Island,workin' the pumpkin patch.That's where all my kids grew up."

As I listen,a kind of intimacy opens between the wizened-faced man and me.

"Tell her not to worry.I've got no complaints.I dance every night I can." His eyes sparkle. "Tell her to remember Grandpa Jones.He died jogging—at 104.That gives me more than twenty years.Tell her...I think the world of her." His voice quivers.He gulps his beer,wipes his mouth.

Two blank lines remain on the second side of the paper.I pick up his limp arm,place my pen in his rigid hand,and squeeze his fingers. "You sign it," I urge.

To add leverage,he couches his left hand around his writing hand.I watch him etch each stroke.The scribble reads "Jove Da".I knew he means "Love,Dad". The pen rolls out of his hand.His right arm flops to his side.With his left arm,he reaches a finger beneath his glasses,wipes a tear.

"Thanks," he says in a half-whisper,than clears his throat.

望着他那双布满血丝的眼睛，我继续问："开头我是写'亲爱的苏茜'，'嗨，苏茜'还是'苏茜，你还好吗？'"

"都行。"他咧嘴一笑，烟雾随之吐出。

"亲爱的苏茜，"我慢慢地重复一遍，然后提笔写下来。我又提醒他："你说我写。"

他把抽完的烟蒂放在锡制烟灰缸里按灭，又伸手拿了一支"骆驼"牌香烟，点燃吸了起来，继续说："告诉她，我现在抽烟已经降到一天一包了……还有……我每天吃饭……在老年中心。吃得挺好。有意大利面条、蛋糕，还有冰淇淋，随便你吃。"然后他咯咯地笑起来，补充了一句，"就是没有啤酒。"

我认真听着，不停在写。

"跟她说，我非常爱她。告诉她，简和戴夫快结婚了，帕特和蒂姆要离婚了。威尔伯叔叔还住在鹿岛，忙他那块小南瓜地。我所有孩子都在那儿长大的。"

听着听着，眼前这位面容消瘦，皱纹密布的老人和我已渐渐亲近起来。

"叫她别担心，我身体很好，每天晚上我还坚持跳舞呢。"他眼里闪着激动神情。"告诉她，别忘了怀念琼斯爷爷。他在一次慢跑过程中与世长辞了，享年104岁。比我要大20岁。跟她说……我真的爱她。"说到这，他声音有些颤抖，紧接着他把啤酒一饮而尽，擦了擦嘴。

第二页纸还剩两行空着，于是我拿起他那无力的手臂，把钢笔塞进僵硬的手里，轻轻地捏起他的手指。"你来签名吧。"我劝他。

为了更好地支撑住，他把左手垫在握笔的右手下面。我看他一笔一画地艰难写下，潦草的字迹显示好像是"爱你的爷爷"。我知道他的意思是"爱你的爸爸"。写完后，钢笔就从手里滚了下来，右手臂也砰地一声落下。他用左手伸出一根手指到眼镜底下，擦拭了一滴泪珠。

"谢谢你。"他边清嗓子，边轻声说道。

"No big deal.I write in this journal every day." I pat his shoulder and leave,saying, "When the Blues Band plays next Saturday,you bring Suzie's address.I'll bring a stamped envelope."

On the way home,I wept.I knew I had just written my Pulitzer Prize winner.

Shinan Barclay

　　"这不算什么。我每天都在这本日记本上写东西。"我说着就拍拍他肩膀，准备离开，"下周六蓝调乐队再来表演时，你把苏茜的地址带来给我，我给你准备信封，贴好邮票。"

　　回家的路上，我不禁落泪。因为我知道，我已经写出了能获普利策大奖的作品。

茜南·巴克利

注释：
　　① 由美国历史上著名的新闻工作者约瑟夫·普利策设立的每年颁给在新闻、文学及音乐等领域取得成就的美国人的若干奖金。

CHICKEN SOUP

Low-Fat and Happy

They can conquer who believe they can.

Virgil

When you're a kid,it's tough being different.By the time I was ten,I was taller than most kids and overweight.It was then that I began to hide my eating.I felt bad enough about my size,but when the others laughed at me,it only made me feel worse,and I turned to food for comfort.

For a time I tried slumping,so that I'd be closer to my friends' sizes,but my mother wouldn't allow it.Mom always said to me, "Be proud of your height.You've never seen a short model,have you?" *That* got my attention.To me,the word "model" stood for beauty,which certainly wasn't included in the vocabulary I would have used to describe myself.

One day,I was crying about how some of my friends got attention from boys that I didn't.Mom sat me down again.I remember the soft, comforting look in her beautiful baby-blue eyes as she told me the story of *The Ugly Duckling*—how the little bird's beauty was revealed when its time arrived.Mom told me that we all have our time on earth to shine. "This is their time," she said. "Your time will come when you become a woman." I listened to Mama's story over and over throughout my growing-up years,but my time never really seemed to come.

Grown and married,I started to have my babies.After the birth of each of my three sons,I always hung on to twenty pounds.When I got pregnant with my last son,I went into the pregnancy weighing 209.After

双语精华版·心灵鸡汤·

减肥与快乐

相信自己，你就能战胜一切。

维吉尔

在孩提时代，如果你与众不同，那将会麻烦不断。10岁时，我就比大多数同龄人个子高，比他们重。从那时起，我就开始把我的那份食物藏起来。我对自己的体形很不满意，可是当其他人嘲笑我时，我感觉更加糟糕，只好又吃起来，以求安慰。

有一阵子，我试着弯腰弓背，希望能更接近我朋友们的体形，但遭到母亲的严厉禁止。她总是对我说："个子高，你应该感到自豪才对。你从没见过矮个的模特，不是吗？"这话很是吸引我。对我来说，模特一词代表着美丽，当然，我并不用美丽来形容我自己。

后来有一天，因为我几个朋友都得到了男孩子的关注，而我没有，所以我伤心地哭了起来。母亲又让我好好坐下来。我至今还记得，她当时说话时，那双浅蓝色漂亮的眼睛里充满了温柔和抚慰。她给我讲了《丑小鸭》的故事，描述了在时机成熟后，丑小鸭的美丽终于被发现，变成了美丽天鹅。母亲告诉我，我们每个人在世上都有自己光耀的时刻。"这是她们的时刻，"她说，"当你长大变成女人，你的时刻将会来临。"在我成长的岁月里，我一遍又一遍地听着母亲的故事，只是我的时刻好像从没真正来临。

长大后就结婚了，接着我有了自己的孩子。我有3个儿子，每次生育过后，我总要多出20磅来。到了怀小儿子时，我已重达209磅。之

that,for a period of eight years,I gave up on ever being a normal weight again.I was the first to crack jokes about my size,laughing with the others on the outside but crying intensely on the inside.I hid my eating binges from my family,hating myself for what I was doing,but unable to control myself.

At the age of thirty-four,I weighed 300 pounds.I was in pain twenty-four hours a day,with degenerative disc problems.My body felt stretched and crushed all at the same time.Stepping on the scales at 300 pounds was a turning point in my life.The scale registered that enormous number,but I felt like a zero.And I realized with startling clarity that if I didn't gain control of my life,I wouldn't be around much longer.I thought of my precious sons—I wouldn't be there to watch them grow up.I'd miss their first crushes,first headaches,proms,driver's licenses, graduations,weddings—I'd never hold my grandbabies.At that moment,I knew I had two choices:live or die.Something inside me broke free and I heard myself screaming,"I'm going to live! I deserve to live,live,*live!*"

I screamed loud enough to awaken a new me.How I wanted to live that day! I had a drive inside I'd never felt before.I knew then that I was going to do everything in my power to win this battle.I wasn't going to give up on me ever again.

This powerful force inside me for life was a force of love as well.I felt a spark of love for myself—as I was—that had been gone for a long time.I decided,for the first time ever,that I was going to lose weight the healthy way.In the past,I had abused diets as much as I'd abused food.I had starved the weight off to the point of losing my hair and developing blurred vision.

This time,I would set small goals,so that when I reached them it would give me the confidence to continue.I learned to prepare and enjoy low-fat,healthy foods.I also developed a new way to talk to myself about food.When food"called out to me", instead of saying,*Go ahead,girl,eat.*

后的8年里，我打消了再恢复到正常体重的念头。我自己首先拿我的体形跟别人开玩笑，表面上我和别人一起纵声大笑，内心里我却在放声痛哭。我有时又背着家人狼吞虎咽，我恨自己这样，却又不能自拔。

34岁那年，我体重300磅。椎间盘问题逐渐严重，一天24小时，我都在痛苦之中。由于肥胖，我就感觉到身体同时在被拽扯和挤压。拖着300磅踏上磅秤的那一刻，是我人生的转折点。磅秤上显示着一个巨大的数字，可我此刻感觉就好像是一个零。我十分清楚地意识到，再不控制好自己，我就活不长了。想到我几个心爱的儿子，我可能看不到他们长大了，错过他们第一次拥抱，第一次头痛，还有参加中学舞会、拿到驾照、毕业典礼、婚礼等，我将永远没机会抱一抱我的孙子孙女了。那一刻，我明白我只有两个选择：要么好好活下去，要么可怜地死去。我的内心终于得到了解脱，有一个声音在拼命叫喊，"我要活下去，我应该要活下去！"

我的呐喊唤醒了一个全新的自我。那一天，我是多么想好好活着啊！内心感到一股从没有过的动力，我要竭尽全力来赢得这场战役，绝对不会再自暴自弃了。

内心这种强烈的求生欲望，其实也是一种爱的力量。这就是一直以来我对自己生命的珍爱。我平生第一次决定，我要用健康的方法来减肥。过去，如同我饮食无节制一样，我也无节制地节食。我曾经以绝食来减肥，结果是头发脱落，视力模糊。

这一次我想先定一些小目标，这样当我实现时就会有更多自信继续前进。我学会制作并享用一些低脂肪的健康食物，还找到了关于食物的一种自我对话方法。当食物"召唤"我时，不要说"吃吧，姑

*Who's going to know?*the new Teresa was firm.*No! I will not eat in private and guilty silence anymore.I will eat when I choose,not when food dictates.*How wonderful it felt when I made it through another day without cheating.

Toughest of all,I had to concentrate on the positives in my life.I had always been so good at encouraging others;now I realized the person who needed me most was me.I made myself wear make-up because it made me feel prouder of myself.Somedays that was just the little push I needed to get me through.As the weight came off and I got smaller,my confidence in myself grew and grew.

I remember the first time I went to the regular,not plus size,section of the local department store.I cried as I looked around at all the racks of clothes I knew I could wear.I grabbed twenty outfits and went to the dressing room.The attendant raised her eyebrows in surprise,saying,"All of these?"

I smiled broadly."*All of these,*" I answered proudly.

Zipping up a pair of jeans,I felt a wonderful sense of freedom.*I'm going to make it,*I thought.

In nine months,I lost 108 pounds,but then I hit a plateau.For years I had blamed my weight on a slow metabolism,and had always fought exercise like I fought losing weight.Now I knew I couldn't go any further without getting my body moving.I remember telling myself,*Girl, you weren't blessed with a great metabolism,but you were blessed with two legs,so get out there and do something about that slow metabolism.* So I did.

Parking my car near a wheat field by my home,I walked along the fence till I reached the end of the one-mile long field.If I wanted to get home,I had to get back to my car,so I had no choice but to walk the return mile.It was hard at first,but it got easier and easier as the weeks and months went by.

双语精华版·心灵鸡汤·

娘,谁知道？"焕然一新的特里萨是坚定不移的。不！我再也不会怀着内疚,背着家人乱吃东西了。现在我决定好了才吃,再不受食物的支配了。这样,不再欺瞒家人和自己,每天都过得精彩。

最不容易的是,我必须调动生活中的积极因素。我曾经特别能鼓励别人,现在我明白最需要我鼓励的恰恰是我自己。我逼着自己用起了化妆品,因为这让我对自己感觉更自豪。有时候就需要对自己狠一点才能闯过去。随着体重渐渐回落,身形渐渐苗条,我也变得越来越自信了。

记得在我们这儿的一家百货公司,我第一次走进常规尺码,而不是加大码的服装销售区。看着四周所有货架上的衣服我能穿上,我不禁泪流满面。我一下拽了20套衣服,直奔试衣间。售货员大吃一惊,皱着眉头说:"所有这些？"

我哈哈大笑。"所有这些。"我骄傲地回答。

轻松拉上牛仔裤拉链后,我觉得无比自由,无比开心。我会成功的,我想。

9个月内,我减掉了108磅,不过,接下来就停滞不前了。多年来我总认为是新陈代谢缓慢导致了我体重增长,所以我一直就像抵制减肥一样,也抵制运动。现在我意识到再不动起来,就不会有进步。我记得提醒自己,孩子,你天生新陈代谢不良,但你却享有两条长腿,所以,出去动起来吧,做点什么来解决新陈代谢缓慢的问题。

我把汽车停在离家不远的一块麦田附近,然后沿着篱笆走完1英里路,直到这块地的尽头。如果我想回家,必须要回到我的车上,所以别无选择,只有往回再走这1英里。开始很艰难,但是过了几周,几个月后,就越来越轻松了。

Within another eight months,I was at my target weight of 170 pounds.I had lost 130 pounds! At five feet,eleven inches,I am a size twelve.Best of all,I am alive not only in body but in spirit as well.

Now,my husband flirts with me,and our kids think we act weird because we're so happy together.Plus,I'm able to be the active mom with my sons the way I'd always dreamed.We fish,play ball or just hang out together,and amazingly,I have the energy to keep up.

Today,at age thirty-six,I'm blessed with a new career.Writing and publishing my low-fat cookbook has been one of the most exciting adventures I have ever been on.Because of the book and the motivational speaking I do to promote it,I've been given the opportunity to reach out to others who,like I once had,have all but given up hope of losing weight and gaining control of their lives.

For me,losing weight was about choosing life over and over and over again.I remember a day on one of my walks by the wheat field, when I reached over the fence and grabbed a stem of wheat to hold in my hand as I walked.I remembered from school that,to the ancient Greeks,wheat represented life.Whenever I felt like giving up that day,I looked at the wheat in my hand and it spurred me on to finish my two-mile hike.

I still have that piece of wheat.When I have a tough day,I look at it and it reminds me of a girl,and later a woman,who for years thought there was no hope,but through faith,courage and love,found her hope— and her life—again.It is,finally,my time to shine.

Teresa Collins

又过了8个月，我实现了目标体重——170磅。我居然减掉130磅了！虽然身高5英尺11英寸，我却能穿上12码的衣服了。最重要的是，我不仅身体充满活力，而且精神饱满。

现在，我丈夫经常和我开玩笑，连孩子们都觉得奇怪，因为我们太开心了。还有，我也能够像我梦想的那样积极地陪我的儿子们玩了。我们钓鱼、打球或者就是一起出去玩耍，令人惊讶的是，我精力充沛，丝毫不落后他们。

如今36岁时，我还找到了一个新的职业——编写出版低脂肪的减肥菜谱，这是我经历过的最刺激的冒险活动之一。因为菜谱的出版和我为了推广此书所做的激情演讲，我有机会接触更多的人，他们和我过去一样，都曾经对减肥和自我失去过信心。

对我来说，减肥就是一遍又一遍地选择自己的生活。我记得有一天，走在麦田边上时，我隔着篱笆伸过去抓了一根小麦放在手里。记得学校里学的：在古希腊小麦象征着生命。不论何时觉得快要放弃时，望着手里的小麦，我就会为之一振，继续完成两英里路的步行。

至今我还保留着那根小麦。当我遇到困难时，看着它就能让我回想起一个女孩，后来是一个女人，多少年来都觉得生活没有希望，但通过信念、勇气和爱，她最终找回了希望，获得了重生。最后，该是我光彩耀目的时刻了。

特里萨·柯林斯

Graduation Message

I'm a divorce lawyer.At times,I feel as if I've heard and seen it all. But ten years ago,a woman walked into my office with a whole new agenda,and neither my life nor my practice has been the same since.

Her name was Barbara,and as she was shown to my office,wearing a rather"plain Jane" outfit,I guessed her to be about nineteen and fairly innocent.

I was wrong.She was thirty-two,with four children between the ages of three and nine.I've heard many brutal stories,but the physical,mental abuse that Barbara had suffered at the hands of her husband made me sick to my stomach.

Yet she finished a description of her circumstances by saying,"Mr. Concolino,you know,it isn't all his fault.My children and I have remained in this situation by my choice;I take responsibility for that.I've known the end to my suffering would come only when I decided I'd suffered enough,and I've made that decision.I'm breaking the cycle."

I'd been practicing law for fifteen years at that point,and I've got to admit that in my head,I was getting great pleasure from thoughts of nailing that guy to the wall.

"Do you believe in forgiveness,Mr.Concolino?"she asked.

"Yes,of course," I said."I believe what goes around comes around, and if we try to do the right thing,good comes back to us.The clients of mine who have withheld forgiveness have withheld it only from themselves."

Those words were so common for me that they practically spoke themselves.And yet,if anyone had cause to be full of rage,Barbara did.

毕业感言

我是一名主办离婚的律师。有时,我感觉这些案子如同我亲身经历过似的。不过10年前的一天,当一位女士带着全新的待议事项走进我的办公室时,我的人生和律师生涯从此改变。

她的名字叫芭芭拉,穿着一套十分普通的衣服,她刚进来时,我就猜想她大概有19岁,有点不谙世事。

事实上我错了。她32岁,有4个孩子,3到9岁不等。我听过许多野蛮粗暴的叙述,但她丈夫对芭芭拉进行的身体、精神的虐待简直令人作呕。

然而她在描述悲惨遭遇的最后却说:"康科利诺先生,你知道,这也不能全怪他。我和孩子们现在的情形是我的选择,我也该为此负责。我知道,只有当我决定不再忍受时,我的苦难才能结束。我已经做了这个决定,我正在打破恶性暴力循环。"

我那时候已经有15年的法律工作经验,但我必须承认,当时脑子里只要一想到把那家伙狠狠揍一顿,心里就不知有多痛快。

"你相信宽恕吗,康科利诺先生?"她问我。

"当然,"我回答说,"我相信因果轮回,好人自有好报。我的当事人中也有些拒绝宽恕的,但其实那是不能宽恕他们自己。"

这些话对我来说再平常不过了,几乎是脱口而出。但如果有谁理直气壮地反对这些话,并且暴跳如雷的话,我想应该是芭芭拉。

"I believe in forgiveness,too," she said quietly. "I believe that if I hold on to anger at my husband,it will only fuel the fire of conflict,and my children are the ones who will get burned."

She gave a tremulous smile. "The problem is,kids are very smart. They can tell if I haven't truly forgiven their dad…if I am just saying words.So I have to really release my anger."

"And here is where I need a favor from you."

I leaned forward across my desk.

"I don't want this divorce to be bitter.I don't want all the blame put onto him.The thing I most want is to truly forgive him,and to have both you and me conduct ourselves accordingly." She paused and looked me in the eye. "And I want you to promise to hold me to this."

I've got to say,this request was against my best lawyerly business advice.But it fit my best human advice,hand in glove.

"I'll do my best," I said.

It wasn't easy.Barbara's husband had no interest in taking the high road.The next decade was marked with his ugly character assassinations of her and repeated periods of nonpayment of child support.There were even times she could have had him thrown in jail,but she never would.

After yet another court session that went in her favor,she caught me in a corridor. "You've kept your promise,Bob," she said,and she laughed. "I admit that there have been times I've wanted to curse you for making me stick to my beliefs.I still wonder sometimes if it's been worth it.But thanks."

I knew what she meant.In my opinion,her ex continued to violate normal standards of decency.Yet she had never responded in kind.

Barbara ultimately found and married the love of her life.Although matters were settled legally,I always enjoyed getting her Christmas card, hearing how the family was doing.

Then one day I received a call. "Bob,it's Barbara.I need to come in

双语精华版·心灵鸡汤·

"我也相信宽恕，"她平静地说，"我相信如果我老对丈夫发脾气，这将会火上浇油，引起更大的争吵，最后肯定会殃及孩子。"

她大笑一声，接着说："问题是，孩子们都很聪明。他们能看出来，我是真的没原谅他们的爸爸还是嘴上说说而已。所以，我真得好好地消消怒气。"

"这就要来找你帮忙了。"

我贴近写字台，身体往前探了探，继续倾听她的叙述。

"我不想把离婚弄得很痛苦。我不想把所有过错都归在他身上。我最想做的就是真心原谅他，所以希望你和我都相应调整处事方式。"她顿了一下，盯着我的眼睛。"我要你保证这么做。"

我要说的是，这项请求与我所信奉的律师职业准则完全不符，但与我的做人准则完全符合。

"我会尽力的。"我说。

但做起来并不容易。芭芭拉的丈夫根本不按我们的思路出牌。在接下来的10年里，他多次对芭芭拉进行了卑鄙的人格诋毁，再三拒绝支付孩子抚养费。甚至有几次恶劣至极，芭芭拉完全可以把他扔进监狱，但她从没这样做过。

又一次庭审结束，她的诉求仍然得到了支持。退庭后她在法院走廊上拦住了我。"你信守了你的诺言，鲍勃，"她笑着说，"我承认有好多次我都想诅咒你，因为你逼得我必须要坚守自己的信念。有时我也想知道，这么做是不是值得。但我还是要感谢你。"

我知道她的意思。在我看来，她的前夫不断在违反一般社会行为准则。但她从不以其人之道还治其人之身。

芭芭拉最后终于找到并嫁给了自己的真爱。虽然各项事务在法律上都得到了解决，但我一直很高兴每年都能收到她的圣诞贺卡，了解她家人的情况。

后来有一天我接到她的电话。"鲍勃，我是芭芭拉。我得上你这

and show you something."

"Of course," I said.

*Now what?*I thought.*How long is this guy going to keep at this? How long before she finally cracks?*

The woman who walked into my office was lovely and poised,full of so much more confidence than she had possessed ten years earlier. There even seemed to be a bounce to her step.

As I stood to greet her,she handed me a photo—an eight-by-ten taken during her oldest son's senior year in high school. John was wearing his football uniform;his father stood to his left rigidly and coldly. The boy himself was looking proudly at his mom,who stood close to him,a warm smile on her face.I knew from her Christmas letters that he had graduated from a very well-respected private high school.

"This was after he caught the winning touchdown in the championship game," she grinned."Did I mention that game gave their team the number-one ranking in America?"

"I think I heard something about it," I smiled.

"Read the back," she said.

I turned the photograph over to see what her son had written.

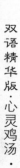

> *Mom:*
>
> *I want you to know that you have been the best mom and dad a boy could ever have.I know because of how Dad worked so hard to make our lives so miserable.Even when he refused to pay all he was supposed to pay for school, you worked extra just to make sure none of us missed out.I think the best thing you did was what you did not do.You never spoke bad about Dad.You never told me he had other "new" kids to support;he did.*
>
> *With all my love,I thank you for not raising us in a*

儿来一趟,给你看点东西。"

"当然可以,"我说。

现在她又要干什么了?我想。这家伙还打算这样坚持多久?还要多长时间她才能停下来啊?

她走进我的办公室,优雅可爱、泰然自若、充满自信,走起路来轻快有力,与10年前判若两人。

在我起身招呼她时,她递给我一张5寸左右的照片,那是她大儿子高中最后一年时照的。照片上的约翰穿着橄榄球服,母亲紧紧地靠着他,脸上带着温馨的笑容,他父亲则站在左边,紧绷着脸,面无表情。约翰自己倒是骄傲自豪地望着母亲。我从她的圣诞来信中得知,约翰已经从一所很有名气的私立高中毕业了。

"这是在橄榄球比赛中,他最后触地得分赢得冠军之后照的。"她开心笑着,"我有没有和你提过,这场比赛过后他们队在全美就排名第一了吗?"

"我想我听过一点。"我笑着回答。

"看看背面。"她说。

我把照片翻过来,看到了她儿子写给她的留言。

> 妈咪:
> 我想让你知道,你是天下孩子最好的母亲,也是最好的父亲。我知道这一切都是因为爸爸拼命想弄糟我们的生活。甚至在他逃脱义务,拒绝为我们支付学费时,你都毫无怨言,继续努力工作,确保我们都能受到良好教育。我想你做得最好的事情其实就是未做之事。你从不说爸爸的坏话,你从没告诉过我们他还有别的孩子要抚养,虽然他的确这样做了。
> 我要献上我所有的爱来感谢你,我有许多朋友都

home where the other parent was the bad one,like with my friends who went through divorces.Dad is and has been a jerk,I know it,not because of you,but because he chose to be.I love,respect and admire you more than anybody on the face of the earth.

   Love,
   John

Barbara beamed at me.And we both knew it had been worth it.

Robert A.Concolino

经历了父母离婚的破损家庭，而你却没有让我们在一个坏爸爸的阴影下成长，我知道爸爸过去一直、现在仍然是很可恶，但这不能怪你，完全是他自己的选择。我对你的爱、尊敬和钦佩超过对世界上的任何人。

   爱你的
   约翰

芭芭拉望着我眉开眼笑。我们俩心里都明白,当年她的努力终于有了回报。

罗伯特·A.康科利诺

女性系列／挥洒四季的芬芳

Judy's Birthday

I'm not sure exactly how or when Judy and I met.All I do know is that when she entered my life,a ray of sunshine broke through the clouds.At a time when my world was shrinking,Judy saw the opposite possibilities and gave me the spark I needed to create a new life…a life after multiple sclerosis.

In 1979,I was diagnosed with primary progressive MS.It wasn't long until I began retreating from all but essential family activities.My energy level was poor.Getting dressed required a two-hour nap.When I could no longer stand up on my own or move myself from place to place,I was devastated.The things I could do for myself were dwindling. My world shrank smaller and smaller by the day.By 1984,I was using a scooter full time because I had no use of my legs or dominant right hand and arm.

But all these changes in my life didn't scare Judy off,as it did some of my friends.She didn't care that I couldn't baby-sit her kids or take my turn driving carpool.She just cared about me and what I was going through.

One of the many things Judy did for me was to encourage me to write.Before raising her own children,she was an English teacher.After reading a couple of things I wrote,Judy saw something that I didn't see: that I could write.She mentored me and cajoled me through years of self-doubt.Her gentle prodding was always sensitive and understanding. She could see the toll MS was taking on my life.But she didn't give up on me.So many times she'd help lift me up when I was down.She gave me hope that there was still something important I could do.

朱迪的生日

我已经不清楚具体什么时间如何与朱迪认识的了，但我所记得的就是，她一走进我的生活，就像一缕阳光刺破乌云，照耀在我身上。曾几何时，我身患多发性硬化症，生活的世界渐渐萎缩，朱迪却看到了我仍有希望，于是她帮我再次燃起生命的火花。

1979年，我被诊断出早期多发性硬化症。不久，我开始生活无法自理，几乎所有主要的家庭生活都要依赖别人。我体力不支，就连穿好衣服也要睡上两个小时才能恢复。自己无法站立，也无法行走，这些情形让我痛不欲生。我自己能做的就是在那萎缩消亡。我的世界一天比一天缩小。到了1984年，我已经双腿无法动弹，主要的右手和胳膊也一样，只好整天坐在残疾摩托车上。

当我的一些朋友见状纷纷离我而去时，所有这些生活变故都没有把朱迪吓跑。她不介意我没法照看她的孩子，也不介意没法排我来开车送大家伙上班。她关心的就只是我，还有我所经受的痛苦。

在朱迪为我做的许多事情当中，有一件是鼓励我写作。她在开始养育自己孩子之前曾是一名英语教师。读过我写的几篇文章后，她看出来我有自己从未意识到的写作潜质。她主动给我指导，并慢慢地哄着打消我多年来的自我怀疑。她温和的激励总是那么善解人意。她能理解多发性硬化症长期给我带来的痛苦，但她从不放弃我，所以许多次当我情绪低落时，都是她来为我鼓劲加油。她给了我希望，让我看到还能做些有意义的事情。

It was not surprising that Judy had a wonderful circle of friends,and those friends also accepted me.When Judy was about to turn forty-five years old,her friends wanted to celebrate in a special way.They wanted to drive from our hometown of Madison,Wisconsin,to Milwaukee for lunch and meet two other friends who had recently moved to Milwaukee.The girls wanted me to join them.

My initial response was to say I couldn't go.Milwaukee was an hour and a half from Madison,and I could never be gone from home that long without using the rest room.No one besides my husband,David, had ever helped me in the rest room before.And who would lift me in and our of the passenger seat of our full-size,wheelchair-accessible van, and help me into my scooter?Only David had ever done that.What if the restaurant everyone wanted to go to wasn't accessible?And most important,would I be able to handle a whole day of activity without my daily nap?

I'm usually a positive,upbeat person,but this time,I was afraid the adventure would be too much for me.Then Judy called.Her lilting Oklahoma twang always made me smile.She said it wouldn't be a party without me.They had selected a restaurant that was wheelchair accessible,and it had an accessible rest room.The girls had talked and would do anything necessary to help me,including helping me in the rest room.Wouldn't please reconsider and come along?

For days,I vacillated between going and not going.Then,one by one, the girls called to talk to me about the birthday adventure.The more we talked,the more I began to believe that maybe I could do this.We had shared so much,the girls and I—births,deaths,marital problems,the challenges of raising children,and aging parents.For years,we had been each other's "family away from home". These women knew my limits and what they were offering.Why couldn't I accept it?Was my pride getting in the way?

没什么奇怪,朱迪这样热情的人有一大帮好朋友,而且她们都很接受我。当朱迪快到45岁时,她的朋友想用特殊的方法来庆祝她的生日。她们打算从我们住的威斯康星州首府麦迪逊出发,驱车前往密尔沃基吃午餐,还要和最近搬到那儿的另外两个朋友会面。这些女孩想让我也参加她们。

我的第一反应是想说我去不了。从密尔沃基到麦迪逊有一个半小时的车程,我没法这么长时间出门而不上卫生间。除了我丈夫大卫之外,以前从来没人帮我上厕所。每次出门我都用家里那辆方便轮椅进出的大型面包车,有谁愿意把我从座椅上搬进搬出,还要把我弄上残疾摩托车?只有大卫这样做过。如果大家想去的那家饭店不能进出轮椅怎么办?最重要的是,如果不能像往常那样白天睡上一觉,这一整天的活动我撑得下来吗?

我平常是一个积极乐观的人,不过这回,我害怕这样太冒险了。随后朱迪打来电话。她那欢快的俄克拉何马州特有的鼻音总是让我忍俊不禁。她说如果我不去,那就不能叫生日聚会了。她们已经挑了一家饭店,轮椅可以方便进出,而且还有同样适合轮椅进出的洗手间。这些女孩都商量过了,愿意帮我做一切必要的事情,包括上洗手间。能不能重新考虑和我们一起出去呢?

去还是不去,几天来我始终犹豫不定。于是这些女孩一个个打来电话和我交谈这次生日冒险活动。她们谈得越多,我越开始相信我也许能去。我和她们谈过许多事情,生与死,物质方面的困难,养儿育女的艰辛,还有年迈的父母,等等。这些年来,我们都已经成了对方的"亲人"。她们知道我的难处并提供了帮助。为什么我还不能接受呢?是我的盲目自尊在从中作梗吗?

For years I had been giving up pieces of my life.And once I gave something up,like working,driving,dressing myself,standing,it was gone forever.It never came back.Was this a chance to put something I had lost back in my life?

I think what tipped the balance was my love and respect for my friend Judy.This was something I could do for her.With everyone's help and encouragement,I was willing to take the risk and join in the celebration.

To prepare,I rested for days prior to the party.When the day arrived,Dave lifted me into the van passenger seat while the girls watched.Then he put the 110-pound Amigo scooter in the back storage area.We talked about how to get me out of the van in Milwaukee and then how to get me back in again for the ride home.Two or three of the women would help me with each of the transfers.Nobody was fazed. Their attitude was,"Tell us what we have to do,and we'll do it." We discussed how they would help me in the rest room.Two other women would help with that task.I was glad that everyone was sharing in helping me.I didn't ever want to be a burden to any one person.

With instructions given,my husband gave me a good-luck kiss,and we were off.

The trip to Milwaukee and the party were a huge success! We laughed,joked,reminisced and made new memories.I returned home tired but exhilarated.I'd had a wonderful time and that night cried tears of happiness because I had done something I *never thought* I'd be able to do.Giving myself permission to accept the help I needed was the single most important thing I could have done for myself.

It may have been Judy's birthday,but I was the one who received the greatest gift.

Shelley Peterman Schwarz

双语精华版·心灵鸡汤·

这些年来，我放弃了生活中方方面面，如工作、驾车、站立和自己穿衣等。而且一旦我放弃了就将永远失去，不再回来。这一次会是一个好机会让我找回生命中失去的东西吗？

我想我最终决定要去，还是出于对好朋友朱迪的爱和敬重。这是我唯一能为她做到的。有了大家的帮助和鼓励，我愿意冒这个险去参加她们的生日庆贺。

为了保证精力充沛，我在聚会前休息了好几天。到了那天，女孩们看着大卫把我抱上面包车，接着他又把110磅重的阿米戈残疾摩托车放在车后储物区。然后我们商谈了如何在密尔沃基把我弄下车，以及结束时再怎样弄上车回家。每一次上下都会有两三位女士来帮我，没有谁感到为难。她们的态度是，"告诉我们该做什么，我们就照做。"我们还讨论了如何帮我上厕所的事情，有另外两位女士愿意承担这项任务。我不愿自己成为某一个人的累赘，所以当大家都认真分工来帮忙时，我由衷地感到高兴。

所有的注意事项都再三嘱咐后，丈夫吻了我，祝我一路顺风，然后我们就开始上路了。

结果这次去密尔沃基的旅行和生日聚会非常成功！我们一路欢笑，逗乐打趣，聊天叙旧，同时也增添了许多新的美好回忆。回到家里，我又累又兴奋，因为我度过了一段美好时光。那天晚上，我激动地淌下了幸福的眼泪，因为我完成了一件我从没想过能做到的事情。让自己接受别人必要的帮助，是我能为自己做的最重要的一件事情。

虽然那一次是朱迪的生日，但我却收到了最珍贵的礼物。

谢利·彼得曼·施瓦茨

The Classified Ad

I noticed the woman by my desk immediately when I entered the newsroom.She wasn't sitting in my side chair,waiting;she was pacing back and forth,playing with her hands.When the secretary told me she wanted my help to write a classified ad,I was doubly intrigued.Our paper is small,but I'm a features writer;I don't usually sell ad space.And people who place ads to sell things like houses,cars or pianos usually do it over the phone.But as I was about to find out,people who place ads to sell themselves do it in person.

The ad that the woman wanted to place was to adopt a baby.It was very important to her that the wording be just right,so she had asked to speak to a writer.Of course,I'd seen ads in the big newspapers like the one she wanted to place,but our newspaper had not,as far as I knew, ever run one.Still,there are standard grab lines for these ads.I suggested several to her:*Wanted,Baby to Love;Please Give Us Hope;*or *Dear Birth Mother,Let Us Help You.*The ad would contain information about her and her husband—that they were stable,could afford to raise a child,and that they had a lot of love to give.We included a toll-free number that a birth mother could use at any hour of the day or night to contact the couple.What I tried to keep out of the copy was the desperation I could hear in this woman's voice.

I spent a lot of time with her.I could see how difficult this was for her.She looked to be about my age—in her early forties—and she kept twisting her wedding band nervously.When her eyes rested for a moment on the photo on my desk of my four daughters,she said,"You are so fortunate."

领养广告

　　我一走进新闻编辑办公室，就注意到有位女士在我办公桌旁。她并没有坐在我的靠背椅上等候，而是来回踱步，不停搓手。秘书告诉我她是来找我帮忙登一条分类广告，我听了一下来了精神，兴趣倍增。我们是家小报，但我是新闻特写作家，一般没什么广告业务，而那些要登广告卖房子、汽车或钢琴的，通常打来电话就可以办理了。当我正要出去联系业务时，登广告卖东西的人自己亲自找上门来了。

　　这位女士想要登一条收养孩子的广告。对她来说，广告措辞用语非常重要，所以她来找一位作家谈谈。当然，我在一些大报上也见过类似她要登的这种广告，但我们的报纸，据我所知，还没有登过。不过这些广告还是有一些吸引读者的标准广告词。我向她建议了好几条："诚领孩子回家疼爱"；"请给我们希望"；或者"亲爱的生母，让我们来帮你"。这条广告还要包括她和她丈夫的情况：家庭稳定，收入可观，有能力收养孩子，并且非常有爱心。我们还附上一个免费电话号码，让孩子的生母可以每天任何时候联系这对夫妇。我能从这位女士的声音里听出她的迫切渴望，但我在起草广告词时还是尽量避免表现出来。

　　我陪了她好长时间，明白了要一个孩子对她有多么艰难。她看上去跟我岁数差不多，40刚出头。和我聊天时，她一直在紧张地转着她的结婚戒指。突然，她的目光停在办公桌上我4个女儿的照片上，过了一会儿，她接着说："你太幸运了。"

"I know," I answered.And then,because I didn't know what else to say,I said,"Maybe you will be,too." But then something occurred to me: The major newspapers carried ads like these often and their circulations were hundreds of times what ours was.Why,I wondered,didn't this woman try those papers?

"I already have," she said."In fact,we've advertised everywhere and tried every imaginable avenue.My husband and I have really decided to stop trying.But I work close to here,and I decided on my way in this morning that one more ad wouldn't hurt.And who knows?" She smiled weakly,handed me a check to run the ad for three weeks and left.

I felt so sad for this woman.The news stories were always filled with adoption heartaches:People would go to foreign countries in search of adoptable children,only to meet with bureaucratic red tape.They would incur huge expenses,only to be duped by unscrupulous lawyers or baby brokers.Even if an adoption went well,through proper channels, there were court cases where the adoptive parents had to give up the baby when a birth parent changed his or her mind.

Yes,I was lucky.I glanced at the photo of my kids and went back to work.

A week later,the woman called."Please don't run the ad again," she said.Something in her tone of voice made me dare to ask if she had good news.

"Yes," she said."We've connected with a birth mother.The baby is due in a month!"

"That's great news!"I said."I hope it all goes well." Then,because I'm a features writer,I asked her if she would keep in touch if her adoption experience turned out to have a happy ending.She agreed.

A month later,the woman called to tell me that she and her husband had a son.All had gone smoothly,but the adoption would not be final for six months.At the end of that time,she would feel comfortable giving me the story.

"我知道。"我回答道。然后,我也不知道再说什么好了,只好说:"也许,你也会的。"但接下来我突然想到了一个问题:那些主流报纸经常刊登这样的广告,发行量也是我们的几百倍,我想知道为什么她不去试试那些报纸呢?

"我早就试过了。"她说。"实际上,我们到处张贴广告,跑遍了每一条大街。我和丈夫都已经决定放弃了。但我就在你们附近上班,所以今早路过时我想再登一则广告也无妨,于是就来了。谁知道会有什么结果?"她无力地笑了笑,递给我一张支票,要求刊登3周的广告,然后离开了。

我为这位女士感到非常难过。平时新闻报道里面总是充满了一些令人伤心的收养故事:人们常到国外去寻觅可以收养的孩子,结果却碰到官僚作风,程序复杂,拖沓冗长。他们支付了大笔开支,结果却碰到寡廉鲜耻的律师或贩卖儿童的罪犯,最终上当受骗。即便是通过正当渠道顺利收养了孩子,有时也不免官司缠身,因为当生身父母改变初衷时,法院经常判决养父母必须放弃收养。

是的,我是很幸运。瞥了一眼我孩子们的照片,我继续工作。

一周过后,那位女士打来电话,"请停掉广告吧。"她说。听她的语调,我感觉到了点什么,于是我斗胆问她是不是有好消息了。

"是的,"她说,"我们联系上了一位孩子母亲。孩子一个月以后就能来了。"

"真是个好消息!"我说,"我希望你们一切顺利。"随后,作为一名新闻特写作家,我敏感地问她,如果收养过程最后很顺利的话,她是否愿意保持联系。她同意了。

一个月后,这位女士打电话告诉我,她和她丈夫已经有了一个儿子。一切进展顺利,但6个月后收养工作才算最后决定。到那个时候,她会很乐意把这故事讲给我听。

I thought about that woman many times over the next six months, particularly when a news story came across my desk that had anything to do with a child.And there were plenty of stories during that time period:The world's first set of living septuplets was born in Iowa.A Wisconsin couple was indicted on child abuse charges;they had kept their seven-year-old daughter in an animal cage in a dark,cold basement.A newborn was kidnapped from the nursery of a county hospital but found unharmed and returned to his mother.

All of these stories evoked strong emotion in me.But I had a personal involvement in the drama of this woman's adoption experience.I think I identified with her in some way.I couldn't imagine what my life would be like if I had been childless.I didn't want to try.

One winter afternoon,as I was bundling up to leave for the day,my mind on carpools and dinner,my phone rang.I recognized her voice immediately.

"The adoption is final! " she said."I knew he was ours from the moment he was put into my arms,but now it's all legal and finished! Would you like to come and meet him?"

I was so happy to hear good news.I made an appointment with her for the next day.I also told her that I would bring a photographer with me and the newspaper would love to give her a free portrait.

When we arrived at her home,the baby was sleeping.The woman ushered us in and offered us refreshments.Everything in the house was lovely.The smell of cinnamon added to the coffee and the atmosphere. The fire crackled in the fireplace.

"His name is Ben," she said,as I started to take notes. "He slept through the night right from the start.Now he's smiling and starting to turn over.Of course,I'm not rushing him.I waited so long for this baby.If he's a little slow,it's okay with me." She paused. "Oh,I should tell you— Ben has Down's syndrome."

接下来的6个月里,我多次回想起这位女士,特别是只要有一些和孩子相关的新闻报道出现在我办公桌上时。那一阶段有大量这样的报道:世界上第一例成活的七胞胎在艾奥瓦州出生;威斯康星州一对夫妇被指控虐待儿童,他们把自己7岁的女儿关在动物笼子里,放在又暗又冷的地下室;一个新生儿在乡下医院的保育室里被拐走,后被找到,毫发无损地回到母亲身边。

这些报道都引起我强烈的情绪变化。但这位女士领养过程的戏剧性变化,我却是亲身参与。在某些方面我和她深有同感。我无法想象,没有孩子,我的生活将会怎样。我连想都不敢想。

一个冬日下午,我正收拾东西下班,脑子想着合伙开车回家和美味晚餐,这时,我的电话响了。我立即听出来是她的声音。

"收养终于定下来了!"她说,"从我抱他的那一刻起,我就知道他是我们的,但现在一切都合法了,终于定下来了!你愿意过来看看他吗?"

我很高兴听到了好消息。我和她约好第2天过去。我还告诉她,我会带摄影记者来,报社非常希望能给她拍照。

我们到她家时,孩子正在睡觉。她把我们领进屋里,拿出点心饮料招待我们。屋子里的摆设迷人可爱。桂皮的味道让咖啡的味道更加浓郁,屋里的氛围更加温馨。壁炉里的柴火烧得劈啪作响,一派喜庆场景。

"他的名字叫本,"她说,此时我也开始记录。"从来到我家起,他晚上睡得就特别香。现在他会笑了,也会翻身了。当然,我不是在催他。这么长时间,我才等到这个孩子,如果他学得有点慢,我是不会着急的。"她停了一下,继续说,"哦,我该告诉你,本患有唐氏综合症①。"

I stopped writing.I wasn't sure how to react.But the new mother smiled."Ben was meant for us,don't you see?I've got plenty of time to help him and he needs me even more than a normally developing child would."

At that moment,the baby monitor on the coffee table told us that Ben was up.His mother went to get him.I could hear her crooning softly to him as she picked him up and changed him.And I could hear his contented cooing in response.

She sat on the sofa,holding her son.Both of them smiled as the photographer took the picture."You wanted a story with a happy ending," said my new friend."You got it."

As I put on my coat,took a last look around that house and watched her kiss the top of her son's head softly,I knew,without a doubt,she was right.

Marsha Arons

听完我停下笔来，不知该如何反应。但这位孩子母亲笑着说："本天生就合适我们，你没看见吗？我有充足的时间来帮他，而他比任何一个正常孩子都需要我。"

就在那时，茶几上的婴儿监视器响了，告诉我们本已经起来了。他母亲赶快进屋去忙他了。我在外面，听见她一边轻声柔和地对他低吟，一边抱他起来换尿布，我还听见孩子舒服满意地咕咕作响来做回应。

她抱着她儿子出来坐在沙发上。摄影记者给她们照相时，两人都露出了灿烂的笑容。"你不是想要一个结局皆大欢喜的报道吗？"我的新朋友，孩子的妈妈说，"你已经有了。"

我穿上外套，最后看了看屋里，只见她温柔地亲她儿子的头顶。我知道，毫无疑问，她是对的。

玛莎·阿伦斯

注释：

① 一种先天性疾病，患者有轻至中度智障，身体矮小，脸扁平。

Love Can Last Forever

I can honestly say it was the best of times and the worst of times.I was joyfully expecting my first child at the same time that my once-energetic,zestful mother was losing her battle with a brain tumor.

For ten years,my fiercely independent and courageous mother had fought,but none of the surgeries or treatments had been successful.Still, she never lost her ability to smile.But now,finally,at only fifty-five,she became totally disabled—unable to speak,walk,eat or dress on her own.

As she grew closer and closer to death,my baby grew closer and closer to life inside me.My biggest fear was that their lives would never connect.I grieved not only for the upcoming loss of my mother,but also that she and my baby would never know each other.

My fear seemed well-founded.A few weeks before my due date, Mother lapsed into a deep coma.Her doctors did not hold any hope;they told us her time was up.It was useless to put in a feeding tube,they said; she would never awaken.

We brought Mother home to her own bed in her own house,and we insisted on care to keep her comfortable.As often as I could,I sat beside her and talked to her about the baby moving inside me.I hoped that somehow deep inside,she knew.

On February 3,1989,at about the same time my labor started,Mother opened her eyes.When they told me this at the hospital,I called her home and asked for the phone to be put to Mom's ear.

"Mom—Mom—listen.The baby is coming! You're going to have a new grandchild.Do you understand?"

"Yes! "

永恒的爱

老实说，那是我最幸福的时刻，却又是我最难过的时刻。我怀着第一个孩子，心情欢喜又激动，而那时曾经精力旺盛、热情积极的母亲却脑瘤加重，生命垂危。

10年来，自立勇敢的母亲一直在和病魔做顽强的抗争，不过，各种手术和治疗都没能成功。但是，她脸上始终没有失去笑容。然而现在，只有55岁的母亲最终完全不能动了——无法说话、行走、吃饭或自己穿衣。

在她离死亡越来越近时，我怀的孩子离出世也越来越近了。我最害怕的就是他们的生命永远无法相连了。我不但为即将失去母亲而悲伤，同时也为他们永远无法相认而难过。

我的害怕是有根据的。因为比我估计的提前了几周，母亲陷入了深度昏迷状态。医生已经不抱任何希望，他们告诉我们，她的大限将至。医生说，给她插上引食管已毫无意义，她不会再醒过来了。

我们伤心地把母亲接回家，回到她自己的房子里，自己的床上。我们坚持继续照看她，让她舒服些。一有时间我就坐在她身旁，跟她描述我肚子里动个不停的胎儿，我希望她在内心深处的某个地方能够感觉到。

1989年2月3日，几乎在同一时间，我开始了阵痛，母亲睁开了眼睛。当我在医院知悉后，我给她打了电话，让人把电话放到她耳边。

"妈——妈——听我说。孩子就快生了！你要当外婆了。你明白吗？"

"是！"

What a wonderful word! The first clear word she'd spoken in months!

When I called again an hour later,the nurse at her house told me the impossible:Mom was sitting up,her oxygen tubes removed.She was smiling.

"Mom,it's a boy! You have a new grandson! "

"Yes! Yes! I know! "

Four words.Four beautiful words.

By the time I brought Jacob home,Mom was sitting in her chair, dressed and ready to welcome him.Tears of joy blocked my vision as I laid my son in her arms and she clucked at him.They stared at each other.

They knew.

For two more weeks,Mother clucked,smiled and held Jacob.For two weeks she spoke to my father,her children and grandchildren in complete sentences.For two miracle weeks,she gave us joy.

Then she quietly slipped back into a coma and,after visits from all her children,was finally free of the pain and confines of a body that no longer did her will.

Memories of my son's birth will always be bittersweet for me,but it was at this time that I learned an important truth about living.For while both joy and sorrow are fleeting,and often intertwined,love has the power to overcome both.And love can last forever.

Deb Plouse Fulton

多么美妙的一个字啊！几个月来她说的第一个清楚的字！

一个小时后，当我再次打电话时，她家里的护士告诉我几乎不可能的事情：母亲坐了起来，氧气管也拔掉了。她正在微笑！

"妈，是个男孩！你添孙子了！"

"是！是！知道！"

4个字。4个漂亮的字。

到我把雅各布带回家时，母亲已经坐在她的椅子上，穿戴整齐，准备来迎接他。欢喜的泪水模糊了我的视线，当我把孩子放到她怀里，她冲着他咯咯地笑。他们互相盯着看。

他们认识。

随后的两周里，母亲抱着雅各布开心地笑。这两周里，她完整地跟我父亲，她的孩子，还有她的孙子说话。这奇迹般的两周里，她给我们带来了无尽的快乐。

然后，在所有的子女都来看望过后，她又悄悄地回到了昏迷状态，终于解除了痛苦，摆脱了那具不听她使唤的身体的束缚了。

关于我儿子出世的回忆，对我来说，永远是苦乐参半的，但是就是那一刻，我感悟到了生活的真谛。喜乐与忧愁时而转瞬即逝，时而又一起缠绕心头，但唯有爱的力量能够超越它们。爱能够持久永恒。

戴比·普劳斯·富尔顿

Highway Hero

A miracle cannot prove what is impossible；it is useful only to confirm what is possible…

Maimonides

During my third year as a speaker,giving seminars all over the country,I was driving into Wheeling,West Virginia,to teach a class on self-esteem to 150 women.

My background includes being raised by a mother and grandmother who took great pains to teach me that families take care of one another no matter what.I knew I could always count on them when I was in trouble,and they knew they could do the same.

I was driving faster than I should have been because I desperately wanted to make it to Wheeling before the severe rain that had been predicted began to fall.

As I saw the sign telling me Wheeling was eight miles away,I speeded up even a bit more,even though a few raindrops had just begun to fall.With no warning,I heard a boom—and too loud,but loud enough to know it wasn't a good sound.When I turned off the radio to further evaluate the sound,it became clear I had a tire problem:probably a flat.I slowed down,knowing from high school driver's education not to brake hard,but knowing still that I needed to get off the road for my safety.

On the side of the road,I looked around,saw nothing but rugged hills,a six-lane highway and very fast traffic.I locked the door,to be safe, and tried to figure out what to do.I did not have a cellular phone,as they were not that common many years ago.

双语精华版·心灵鸡汤·

公路英雄

奇迹不能证明什么是不可能的；奇迹只用来证明什么
是可能的……

迈蒙尼德

作为一名培训主讲人，我经常穿梭在全国各地举办研讨会。从事这行的第3年，我有一次驱车前往西弗吉尼亚的惠灵市，准备给一个自尊培训班的150位女士上课。

母亲和祖母养育我长大，她们总是教导我，不论发生什么，一家人都要互相照顾，相亲相爱。我知道，在困难时家人总让我有所依靠，而他们遇到麻烦时，我也不会让他们失望。

我以从未有过的速度一路飞车疾驰，因为天气预报说暴雨即将来临，我要拼命赶在大雨落下之前抵达惠灵市。

当我看见路边指示牌提示离惠灵市只有8英里时，虽然只有几滴雨水淅沥落下，我还是加大了油门，继续往前冲。

没有任何报警信号，我猛地听到轰隆一声——太响了，震得我立即明白大事不妙。我随即关掉收音机，进一步辨识这声响，这下弄清楚了，轮胎出问题了：可能是爆胎。高中驾驶知识教育让我当时还记得千万不能急刹车，要减速慢行，同时自己不要停路中央，确保安全。

我停在路边，四下张望，周围只有起伏的山丘，一条6车道的公路和风驰电掣的车辆。为了安全起见，我锁上车门，开始考虑该怎么办。我没有手机，再说那时候移动电话也并不常见。

Every story I had ever heard about women having bad experiences on the side of the road in strange cities ran through my mind like a movie reel,and I tried to decide if I would be safer staying with the car or walking to the next exit.It was beginning to get dark,and I truly was becoming afraid.

My grandmother taught me as a very little girl that things work out if you keep your head about you,and I was trying very hard to do just that.

At that very moment,a large semi passed very fast on my left, causing my car to shudder,and I saw that the directional light was on,indicating he was pulling over in front of me.I could hear his brakes squeal,as he was braking fast and hard.

I again thought,*Am I safer or in more danger?*I could see the truck as it slowly backed up on the shoulder of the road and decided that to be very safe,I would take a precaution I had seen in a movie.I took out a pad in my briefcase and wrote down the name of the trucking company and the Ohio license number,as they both were visible from my car.I put the pad with this information under the driver's seat just in case!

Even though it was now raining quite hard,the driver came running back from the truck to my car and said through my window that I had opened only three inches,that he had seen the tire blow and would be glad to change it.He asked for the car keys to get into the trunk;and although I knew I was about to lose all my safety precautions,it seemed to be my best choice.I gave him the keys.He changed the tire and gave me back the keys.I asked him through the three-inch opening in the window if I could pay him for his kindness.He said,"We drivers in Ohio believe in taking care of women in trouble on the highway."

I then asked him for the name of his boss so I could send him or her a letter relaying how wonderful he had been.He laughed a very odd laugh and gave me the name of his boss,a woman,and his card,which

双语精华版·心灵鸡汤·

这时我脑海里浮现了我听过的一个个故事,都是关于陌生城市公路边上妇女的恐怖经历,它们像放电影似的一幕幕闪过。于是我想决定哪一个方法更加安全,是待在车里,还是步行到下一个出口。天开始渐渐暗下来,我也越来越害怕。

很小的时候,祖母就教我说,保持镇静,不要慌张,问题就会迎刃而解。所以我当时正竭力使自己镇定下来。

就在那时,一辆大型拖挂卡车从我左边飞驰而过,把我的车子震得直抖,而且他的转向灯还亮着,这意味着他正要在我前面靠边停车。他猛地重重踩了一下刹车,吱嘎声顿时尖啸嘶鸣。

我又在考虑,我这样做是安全些,还是更加危险?我看见卡车慢慢地退后,安全地停在路肩上。这时想起一部电影里类似情况的防范措施,于是我也准备采用。我打开手提箱,拿出便笺本,记下了卡车公司的名字和一个俄亥俄州的车牌号码,因为我在车上恰好能看见。然后我把便笺本放在座椅底下以防万一。

尽管外面大雨如注,卡车司机还是下车朝后向我跑来,隔着我只开了3英寸的车窗对我说,他看见我的车胎爆了,很乐意为我换胎,并问我要车钥匙打开后背箱。虽然我知道这样做就失去所有的安全防范,但在当时看来,我别无他选。我给了他钥匙,他帮我换完车胎,又还给了我。我隔着只开了3英寸的车窗问他,我是否要付费给他。他说:"我们俄亥俄州的驾驶员,都乐于在公路上救助遇到麻烦的女士。"

我接着又问他公司老板的名字,好让我写信表扬他的助人事迹。他奇怪地笑了笑,给我他的公司女老板的名字,还有他自己的名

had the name of the trucking company,the address and the phone number.I thanked him again,and the now soaking-wet man ran back to the truck.Gratefully,I went on to Wheeling to present my seminar.

Upon returning to Florida,I had a T-shirt made for this man that showed an angel in a truck with the words printed across the picture, "Highway Hero", and sent it to the address on the card.

It came back,addressee unknown.

I called the number on the card and got a recording saying no such number existed.I called the city newspaper for that town,asked for the editor,explained the dilemma and asked that a letter to the editor be placed in the paper thanking the driver.The editor,who had lived there all his life,said there was no such company in that city.He further investigated and called me back and said there was no such business registered in Ohio.

The editor went one step further.He called the state motor vehicle bureau to ask about the license and was told no such plate had ever been issued.

The upshot is that this man,his truck and the company never existed,the"rescue" never happened and I must have been dreaming.

But I know I wasn't.

Carol A.Price-Lopata

片,上面印有这家卡车公司的名称、地址和电话号码。之后,我再次向他表示了感谢,而他则浑身湿透地跑回了卡车。我带着感激之情前往惠灵市开始我的研讨会讲演。

一回到佛罗里达,我就为那位司机定制了一件T恤衫,上面印着一个天使坐在卡车里面的图案,还衬着"公路英雄"的几个大字。并且,我按名片上的地址给他寄过去。

结果包裹给退了回来,说是查无此人。

我立刻拨打名片上的电话号码,却听到"您所拨打的号码是空号"。我拨通他所在城市的报社,找到了编辑,解释了我的窘境,希望在报上刊登我给那位司机的感谢信。编辑的回答让我大吃一惊,他说他在那住了一辈子也没听说有这样一家公司。后来经过调查他又给我来电话,说俄亥俄州境内找不到这家企业的注册情况。

这位编辑又进一步核实,他给州交通局打电话,查询我给他的车牌号,结果被告知从来就没有发过这样的车牌号码。

结果就是,这位司机、他的卡车和所属的公司根本不存在,那次"救援"也从没发生过,而我当时肯定是在梦游。

但是我很清楚,我当时不在梦游。

卡罗尔·A.普赖斯·洛帕塔

Never,Never Give Up

It was a very exciting day for us—the championship Little League game of the season.Two teams would be battling it out one more time for the championship.We were the only team all season to beat this "Paint Shop" team,and they were determined to win tonight's game.

We were a baseball family.Ben,my husband,had coached the Little League team for the past two years,but he had lost his battle to cancer two months earlier.Dying at the age of forty-three after a courageous struggle,he had left me and our two children,Jared,ten,and Lara,six.

He had coached while undergoing massive doses of chemotherapy and many stays in the hospital,along with daily trips to the hospital for tests.Despite being tired,worried and worn down,he had continued to coach.

How he delighted in Jared's accomplishments playing baseball,and how proud he would have been today of this team and Jared,the team leader and starting pitcher.

Ben was an English teacher by profession and had enjoyed coaching soccer and baseball for years.He taught the teams how to play the game and about good sportsmanship,fair play and physical fitness.He also taught his family and a caring community how to fight a terrible disease with faith,hope,courage and dignity.He gave us all the courage to hope when all hope was lost.

An avid reader,Ben jotted down quotes on index cards and left them here or there around the house.One quote he loved was by Winston Churchill during World War II : "Never,never,never,never give up." It seemed so appropriate for Ben,as those were the words he lived by,

永不言弃

这对我们来说,是非常激动人心的一天,因为本赛季的青少年棒球联盟冠军赛即将打响。两支强队为争夺冠军将又一次展开激烈厮杀。我们是整个赛季唯一击败过"油漆车间"队的一支球队,而今晚他们也将和我们决一死战。

我们是一个棒球家族。我丈夫本,在过去的两年里一直在青少年棒球联盟执教,不幸的是,两个月前他死于癌症。经过与病魔勇敢的抗争后,年仅43岁的他医治无效去世了,抛下我和两个孩子:10岁的贾里德和6岁的拉腊。

我丈夫生病期间,进行了大剂量化疗,经常住院,每天都要到医院做身体检查。在这样的情况下,他还在执教球队。尽管辛苦劳累,有时殚精竭虑,有时筋疲力尽,但他还是坚持不懈。

今天,如果他还活在世上,看到贾里德在棒球场上的出色表现,该多么高兴啊;看到现在这支优秀的球队,特别是贾里德身兼队长和首席投手,他该多么自豪啊!

本的职业是一名英语教师,但他多年来热衷于执教足球和棒球队。他不但教球员如何比赛,而且还培养他们积极的运动员精神、公平竞争意识和强健的体魄。他也教会家人和看护他的医疗人员,如何用信念、希望、勇气和尊严来与可怕的病魔斗争。当所有的希望都落空时,他把所有的勇气都给了我们,让我们重燃希望。

本很爱读书,每次都把一些名人名言摘抄在卡片上,丢在家里到处都是。他最钟爱的一句名言是英国前首相温斯顿·丘吉尔在二战期间说的,"永远,永远,永远,永远不要放弃。"这句话对本再适合不过了,正是他一生坚守的人生信条,尤其是在与癌症做斗争的那

fighting this disease for one-and-a-half years,up to his very last breath. Upon his death,we had those words inscribed on his tombstone.Those special words became a message to my children and me upon every visit to his grave.They were not something to be shared—they were just for us.Our secret message to each other from Dad.

The game was close,and Jared felt the pressure.

Because parents,family and friends on both teams had helped care for our children at a moment's notice during our nightmare and had felt much anguish upon Ben's death,every person at that field missed Ben that evening.

One enthusiastic father,whose son was new to the team,and who had not known our family circumstances over the past year,came to the game with twenty-five paper cups on which he had written different baseball expressions:"Get a base hit", "Catch that fly ball", "Pop-Up", "Bunt". What fun it would be for each player to read a message on his cup after quenching his thirst.

The score was close;it was a nerve-wracking game.In the fourth inning,Jared pulled a cup out randomly for his drink of water.Suddenly he ran from the bench over to me with the cup.Written on his cup were the words,"Never,never give up." The news spread fast.Ben was there,even if in spirit only.Needless to say,we won the game,and the cup now sits on a shelf next to Ben's picture to greet anyone who walks in our back door.

Diane Novinski

一年半时间里，他永不言弃，直到最后停止呼吸。他去世后，我们在他的墓碑上刻下了这句名言，作为他的墓志铭。每次我带孩子们来坟前祭拜时，这句话都能给我们以鼓励和启示。它的特殊意义只有我们能明白，无法与别人分享，因为这是孩子的父亲给我们的神秘留言。

当晚的比赛紧张激烈，势均力敌，贾里德感受到前所未有的压力。

在本去世后我们痛不欲生的日子里，当晚参赛双方球员的父母、亲人和朋友都立即来帮忙照看我们的孩子，对本的英年早逝感到无比悲痛，那天晚上球场上的每个人都十分怀念本。

有一位球员新近加入球队，他热心的父亲对我们家的遭遇并不知情。那天他带了25只纸杯来到比赛现场，上面写着各种棒球比赛用语："争取安打"，"接住腾空球"，"内野高飞球"，"短打"，等等。每一位球员在喝水解渴的同时，都能在杯子上看到一句鼓励，这真是相当有意思。

此时，比分仍然咬得很紧，比赛让人高度紧张。进入第4局时，贾里德随意拿了杯水一饮而尽，突然他拿着杯子从球员板凳上向我跑来。原来他拿的杯子上面写着："永远，永远不要放弃。"这个消息一下子在球场上传开了。尽管只能感受到他的精神，但是大家都说，本又回来了。不用说，我们赢了那场比赛。现在奖杯就放在架子上面，紧挨着本的遗像，进我们家的后门一眼就能看见。

黛安娜·诺文斯基

The Trellis

Why is this so hard,I wonder.All I have to do is tack together a few sticks of wood and daub them with white paint,but I feel as if I'm making a cross for my own execution.Already I've gone through a tablet full of designs and a forest of pine lath.I want this to be right.

"I'd like a white trellis," was your modest request."Something for a background at my wedding.Sara Parkes will cover it with ivy.It will be beautiful,Daddy,a symbol of life."

I was glad you asked me to make the trellis because I wanted to have a part in the wedding.Seems like men are mostly in the way at such occasions—like chess pieces standing around,waiting to be "positioned".The groom himself would never be missed if he didn't show. They would just stand a cardboard cutout in his place and no one would be the wiser.

Weddings are of women,by women and for women.But with this trellis,I can have a part of the action.

If I can ever get it made.

I've made far more difficult things for you,like that colonial cradle for your doll,and that two-story dollhouse with handmade furnishings. And your desk,with all the drawers.

But this trellis!

Kneeling one the patio,I carefully weave the pine slats into a crosshatch,and a design slowly emerges.As I work,I ponder the way your life has woven itself into mine,and I wonder what I will be like without Natalie around the house.

Can we unweave twenty-one years of sharing?Can a father give

婚礼花架

为什么这会如此艰难呢，我百思不得其解。我要做的不就是把一堆木条钉在一起，再上点白漆就大功告成了吗？可是我感觉就好像正在做一个十字架，用来把自己钉在上面。为了做这个花架，我设计图都画了厚厚一沓纸，几乎一片松树林的板条都给我浪费了。希望这一次，我能顺顺利利。

"我想要一个白色的拱形花架，"这是我女儿小小的要求，"用在我婚礼上当背景。萨拉·帕克斯会在上面架上常春藤，肯定很漂亮。爸爸，那是生命的象征。"

你能让我来做这个花架，我其实很高兴，因为我也想在婚礼上有所参与。在婚礼这种场合下，男人们好像总是碍手碍脚，如同棋子一样四处站着，无所事事，听候安排。新郎就不同了，他即使不出现，也不会被大家漏掉。在他的位置上，人们会立一个用硬纸板剪出的模拟他的人像，没人能够替代。

婚礼从来都是女人拥有、女人办理、女人享受。但做成这个花架，我也能在婚礼上露一手了。

我要努力地把它完工。

我曾经帮你做过比这更难的东西，如给玩具娃娃用的殖民地风格摇篮，带手工家具两层楼的玩具屋，你的书桌，还有里面所有的抽屉。

可就是这个花架，唉！

我跪在内院的地上，仔细地把松树板条搭成了十字交织形状，渐渐地一个图案呈现出来。我一边忙着，一边纳闷，你我的生活是如何织结在一起的，没有了纳塔利在家陪我，我的生活将会变成什么样子。

我们能从此忘却这21年来共同编织的美好时光吗？一个父亲怎

away his daughter without coming a little unraveled himself?

It's not that I don't want you to marry.I do.When your dreams come true,so do mine.Matt is such a good choice.A gentle,handsome man,as devoted to you as your parents."Nat and Matt" sounds right,like a little poem.

I can hardly see to drive these tiny nails.Allergies,probably.Or maybe it's the cool April breeze that keeps fogging my eyes.Or the smart scent of pine wood.

They will stand this trellis up on the stage at church.My job is to take you by the arm and gently lead you down the aisle to the trellis. Another man will help you up the next step of life.I'll sit there stoically with your mother,watching you embrace someone new.Your sister will sing your favorite songs.Your grandfathers will perform the ceremony. And God will come down to bless the union.Your mother has it all organized.

All I have to do is finish this simple trellis.

When the wedding is over,they will fold this ivy arbor and shove it into a dark storage room,where it will be forever forgotten.But memories of my little girl will vine themselves through the arbor of my heart for the rest of my years.

I stand the trellis up against the garage and slather it with bride-white paint—this fragrant veneer that covers the old,rugged tree with beauty and promise.

Painted,the trellis looks like two alabaster gates.Gates that lead to a future I may never see,if you move far away.Out there on the long road of daily living,who knows what will happen?There will be long days filled with sweet monotony.Bright moments of joy.And tedious hours of sorrow.I wish for you the full spectrum of life.

I rub the syrupy paint from my fingers with a rag that used to be your favorite T-shirt.Then I stand back to appraise my work.

能就这样送走女儿，竟无半点被拆散的心痛？

我并不是因为这个原因而不想让你结婚。我的确愿意。当你梦想成真时，我也备感欣慰。马特不愧是一位如意郎君，温文尔雅、英俊潇洒，对你情深意重，对我们也是体贴入微。"纳塔和马特"听起来就特别顺口，就像诗一样。

这些小小的钉子，我几乎看不见往哪下锤子。也许是有些过敏，也许是这4月清凉的微风眯了我的双眼，还有可能是松木浓烈的香味。

他们会负责把这个拱形花架立在教堂舞台上，我的任务就是手挽着你，沿着中央过道缓缓走向花架，那儿将有另一个男人带你进入新的人生。之后，我和你母亲将默默地坐在下面，看着你拥抱一个新人。你妹妹会演唱你最爱听的歌曲，爷爷和外公将为你主持婚礼，而上帝也将会来祝福你们百年好合。一切都由你母亲安排好了。

我要做的仅仅就是完成这个简单的花架。

婚礼结束时，他们会收起这个常春藤花架，然后扔进暗黑的储藏室里，然后就会被永远地遗忘。而我心头的拱形花架上，将爬满对我女儿的回忆，伴我度过余生。

我支起花架靠在车库上，开始给它厚厚涂上一层雪白的油漆，芬芳的饰面给这粗糙不平的老树枝铺上了美丽和希望。

上漆过后，花架看起来就像两扇雪花石膏制成的大门。随着你的生活渐行渐远，这大门将通往我可能无法看见的未来。在那平凡人生的漫漫长路上，天晓得将会发生什么事。漫长的日子里将充满甜蜜的单调，激动喜悦的片刻瞬间，还有乏味忧伤的分分秒秒。我祝福你生活丰富多彩，不错过任何一刻的精彩。

完工以后，我拿起抹布使劲擦去手指上粘粘的油漆，这抹布是你以前最喜欢的那件T恤衫改成的。接下来，我就朝后站了站，开始欣赏起我的作品。

Without the ivy it seems so empty and lonely.

It is,after all,just a simple trellis.

And it is finished.

But it's the hardest thing I've ever made.

Daniel Schantz

花架上面还没有缠上常春藤,看起来空荡荡,显得很孤单。

毕竟,这只是一个简单的花架。

它终于做好了。

但这是我做的难度最大的一样东西。

丹尼尔·尚茨

Emma's Bouquets

It was a hot June day when my mother and I crossed the Texas border and made our way to Minden,west of Shreveport,Louisiana.Although it wasn't far to the old George family farm,where my great-grandparents had homesteaded 100 years earlier,I had never been there before.

As we drew closer to the family homestead,through softly rolling hills of longleaf pine,sweet gum and red oak,I thought about what connects us with earlier generations of our family.Is it just a matter of eye color,height or blood type?Or are there other ties that bind us?If my great-grandmother Emma could find her way into the present,would she discover something familiar in my generation?

When my mom and I turned into the George property,we saw before us a real Southern farmhouse—mostly porch with a house attached. Although it was just a simple farmhouse,its front windows were graced with ornately carved dental moldings,and the steps from the porch— flanked by large brick pillars with granite plinths—were a palatial ten feet wide.The house bore a startling resemblance to the houses my brother and sister and I owned,even though none of us had ever seen this place.When I'd bought my old farmhouse in North Carolina,for example,the first thing I'd done was to add a replica of this porch.Similarly,my brother's and sister's Louisiana homes,although newly designed by architects,bore an uncanny resemblance to the old George homestead.

As my mother and I strolled through the garden,where roses,day lilies,iris,vitex and phlox still bloomed,my mother remarked,"Your great-grandmother Emma loved flowers." Wanting to keep a part of this,my heritage,I knelt down and dug out one of the iris pips.

Because I also wanted to preserve something from the inside of the house,before it crumbled and was lost to time,we gingerly explored the

埃玛的花束

那是6月炎热的一天,我和母亲从得克萨斯州出发,越过边界,一路劳顿,来到位于路易斯安那州什里夫波特市以西的明登市。乔治家族的老农场并不远,那儿是我曾祖父母一百年前的自耕农场,可是我以前却从没到过。

沿着微微起伏的山峦,穿行在茂盛的长叶松、枫香树和红橡木之间,离祖上的自耕农场越来越近,我慢慢地开始忖度,是什么在家族的先人和我们之间世代相传呢?难道仅仅是眼睛的颜色、身高或血型吗?还是有什么其他的纽带联系我们?如果我曾祖母埃玛能够穿越时空,来到现在,她会在我身上发现一些相似的地方吗?

当母亲和我进入乔治家族农场时,眼前映入一座真正的南方农场宅舍,外面带有典型的门廊。房子虽然很简单,但前窗上嵌有雕刻精美的齿形装饰线条,花岗岩基座上砖块砌起宽厚的支柱,支撑着漂亮的门廊,门廊前的台阶宽有10英寸,十分气派。这座古宅与我们姐弟几个的房子都有着惊人的相似,可我们谁也没来过这儿。例如,我在北卡罗来纳买了一座老农场房子后,做的第一件事就是加了一个和这儿一模一样的门廊。同样,我弟弟和妹妹在路易斯安那州的房子,虽然是由建筑师新近设计,但与这座乔治家族的古宅都有着不可思议的相似。

我和母亲漫步在花园里,只见那玫瑰、百合、蝴蝶花、淡紫花牡荆、福禄考仍在竞相开放。母亲说:"你曾祖母埃玛特别喜欢各种鲜花。"我听了过后,也想选一种花来承袭这一传统,于是我跪下来挖了一粒蝴蝶花种子。

因为害怕哪一天古宅就会轰然倒塌,最终随着时间而湮没,所以我还想到房子里面去看看,希望能保存一些东西。我们小心翼翼

interior,noting the twenty-inch-wide virgin pine boards,the hand-hewn beams and the handmade clay bricks,each marked with a G.Then,in the bedroom,I discovered Emma's 1890s wallpaper—a floral motif,naturally, with a repeating pattern of large bouquets of ivory and pink roses.It was peeling off the pine boards,but still lovely after all this time,just like my great-grandmother's garden.I knew this was the memento I wanted to take with me.With the tiny penknife on my key ring,I carved off two square-foot pieces,one for me and one for my younger sister,Cindy.

Before we headed for home,Mom and I stood on that familiar front porch for a moment of silent leave-taking.At that instant,I felt very connected to my ancestors,as though there were invisible wires running between us,anchoring each successive generation to the earlier ones.However,on the drive home,I began to wonder if I weren't making too much of this family ties thing.Perhaps a penchant for wide porches was just a coincidence.

The next day,eager to share the story of this trip with Cindy,I dropped by her house.I found her in the kitchen,happily perusing the materials she had bought on a recent trip to England in order to redecorate her home.We sat at the table together,and I told her about our great-grandparents' farmhouse with its verandah,floor-to-ceiling windows and high ceilings that had somehow found their way into the design of the homes of the Georges' great-grandchildren.We laughed about my muddying my dress in order to dig out a flower pip,and then I produced the little square of wallpaper I'd brought for her as a keepsake.

She appeared stunned,sitting stone-still and dead-quiet.I thought I had,in my big-sister way,offended her with my story.Then she reached into the box of her renovation materials and pulled out the rolls of newly purchased wallpaper from England.The design was exactly the same—the ivory-pink sprays and bouquets of roses were Emma's.

Emma's bouquets had found their way into the present.

Pamela George

地在屋里探寻，仔细看了20英寸宽的天然松木壁板，手工砍成的房梁，还有手工制成的黏土砖，每一块上都刻着一个大写字母"G"。接下来，我在卧室里发现了19世纪90年代曾祖母埃玛的墙纸，上面自然全是花纹，重复着乳白色和粉红色的大束玫瑰图形。虽然历经百年，墙纸已经从松木壁板上渐渐剥落，但依旧漂亮可爱，好像曾祖母的花园。我知道，这就是我想带走的纪念品。我用钥匙环上的小刀割了两小块，一块自己收藏，另一块送给我妹妹辛迪。

回来之前，我和母亲在那熟悉的前门廊下停留了片刻，默默地向这座古宅告别。那一刻，我深深地感受到与祖先紧密相连，好像有无形的铁丝将我们串联起来，每一个后代都与上一代牢牢地绑在一起。可是在驱车回家的路上，我开始问自己，我是不是将这家族血脉相连一事有些小题大做了。也许我们对宽大气派门廊的痴迷钟爱只是一种巧合。

第2天，我前往辛迪家，迫不及待地想要和她分享此次拜访家族古宅的趣事。她正在厨房，仔细地看着她最近从英格兰买来的原材料，准备重新装潢房子。我们一起在餐桌上坐下来，我开始和她讲起我们曾祖父母的农场古宅，像阳台、直达屋顶的落地大窗、高高的天花板等，都能在乔治的曾孙子女的房子设计上找到一些影子。说到为了挖一粒花籽而把我的连衣裙弄得满是泥泞时，我们都哈哈大笑。接着我拿出了那一小片墙纸，送给她留作纪念。

一看到墙纸，她突然目瞪口呆，坐在那一动不动，一声不吭。我心里想，是不是刚才我一直以老大姐自居在讲故事，说话不注意惹恼了她。接下来，她走到装修材料箱子跟前，抽出几卷从英格兰新买来的墙纸。我一看，图案设计竟然一模一样，就是曾祖母埃玛的那种乳白和粉红的花纹，还有一束一束的玫瑰花。

埃玛的花束已经超越时空，来到我们身边了。

帕梅拉·乔治

Between the Lines

Love is something that you can leave behind when you die.It's that powerful.

Jolik(Fire)Lame Deer Rosebud Lakota

After a moving memorial service for my beloved father,Walter Rist, our family gathered at our childhood home to be with Mother.Memories of Dad whirled in my mind.I could see his warm,brown eyes and contagious smile.I envisioned all six-foot-four of him in hat and coat,headed to teach his classes at the college.Quickly,a new scene flashed in my mind of Dad in a T-shirt,swinging a baseball bat,hitting long flies to us kids on the front lawn,years ago.

But special memories couldn't push away the dark shadows of separation from the man we loved.

Later in the evening,while looking for something in a closet,we found a paper sack marked,"Charlotte's Scrapbook".Curious,I opened it. There it was—my "Inspiration from Here and There"scrapbook I had kept as a teenager.I had forgotten all about it until this moment when I leafed through the pages of pasted pictures from magazines and church bulletins.They were punctuated with clippings of famous quotes,Bible verses and poetry.*This was me as a teenager,*I thought.*My heart's desires.*

Then I saw something I'd never seen before—my father's handwriting penciled on page after page! My throat tightened as I read the little notes Dad had slipped in to communicate with me.They were love

双语精华版·心灵鸡汤·

爱在字里行间

生命虽已消逝，爱却永世长存。这是多么伟大。

罗斯巴德·拉科塔

　　沉痛悼念过我深爱的父亲沃尔特·里斯特后，我们全家相聚在老家，陪在母亲身旁。父亲的音容笑貌又浮现在我眼前，一双褐色、慈祥的眼睛，极具感染力的笑容。我仿佛又看见了他6英尺4的高大身躯，穿上外衣，戴上帽子，去大学给学生上课。很快，又一幕情景在我脑海闪过，那是多年前，他穿着T恤衫，挥动棒球拍，远远地把球击到房前草坪上的我们这些小孩身边。

　　但特别的回忆也无法消散我们心头的阴影，心爱的父亲已和我们阴阳相隔了。

　　后来晚上，在壁橱里找东西时，我们突然找到一个纸袋，上面标着"夏洛特的剪贴本"。我好奇地打开来看，原来里面是我少女时期的剪贴本——"处处留心皆启示"。我早就把这忘得一干二净，当我翻看时才明白，这些都是从杂志和教会快讯上剪下来的图片，上面有一些加了标点的名人名言、圣经节选和诗歌。我想，这就是少女时候的我，还有我内心的渴望。

　　接着，我看到了上面我从没见过的内容：每一页上都有父亲的铅笔笔迹。读着父亲与我真情交流的只言片语，我开始喉咙哽咽发紧。这是爱的感言，智慧之语。我不清楚他是何时写的，所以现在正

女性系列／挥洒四季的芬芳

messages and words of wisdom.I had no idea when he had written these, but this was the day to find them!

On the first page,Dad wrote, "Life is never a burden if love prevails." My chin quivered.I trembled.I could hardly believe the time-liness of his words.I flipped the pages for more.

Under a picture of a bride being given away by her father,my dad wrote,"How proud I was to walk down the aisle with you,Charlotte! "

Near a copy of the Lord's Prayer,he had scrawled,"I have always found the strength I needed,but only with God's help." What a comfort!

I turned to a picture of a young boy sitting on the grass with a gen-tle collie resting its head on his lap.Beneath it were these words:"I had a collie like this one when I was a boy.She was run over by a streetcar and disappeared.Three weeks later she came home,limping with a bro-ken leg,her tail cut off.Her name was Queenie.She lived for many more years.I watched her give birth to seven puppies.I loved her very much. Dad."

My moist eyes blurred as I read another page. "Dear Charlotte,listen to your children! Let them talk.Never brush them aside.Never consider their words trivial.Hold Bob's hand whenever you can.Hold your chil-dren's hands.Much love will be transferred,much warmth to remember." What a treasure of guidance for me as a wife and mother! I clung to the words from my dad whose gentle big hand often had held mine.

In those moments of paging through the scrapbook,incredible com-fort was etched on the gray canvas of my life.On this,the day my father was buried,he had a loving "last word".Such a precious surprise,some-how allowed by God,cast victorious light on the shadows of my grief.I was able to walk on,covered by fresh beacons of strength.

Charlotte Adelsperger

是好好看看的时候。

翻开第一页，父亲写着，"如果人间充满爱，生活将不再是千斤重担。"我下巴抽搐，浑身微颤，几乎无法相信他在那时写下这些话。我继续往后翻看。

在一幅图片里，一位父亲在婚礼上将女儿交给了新郎，我父亲在下面写道，"夏洛特，陪你走过教堂过道，我将无比自豪！"

在我抄的主祷文边上，父亲潦草地写着，"只要有上帝的帮助，我一定能找到我需要的力量。"这是对我多好的慰藉啊！

我又翻到了一幅图片，一个小男孩坐在草地上，一只温顺的苏格兰牧羊犬头枕在他的大腿上。下面有这样一段话："我小时候也有一只这样的牧羊犬。它被电车撞倒后就消失了。3周后一瘸一拐地拖着一条断腿回到家里，尾巴也被碾断了。它的名字叫奎尼，后来又活了很多年，我看着它生了7只小狗。我非常爱它。爸爸。"

又读到一页时，我看着渐渐地泪眼模糊。"亲爱的夏洛特，倾听你的孩子吧！让他们倾诉，绝对不要对他们置之不理，绝对不要轻视他们的话。尽可能抓住鲍勃的手。抓住你孩子的手。许多爱将被传递过去，许多温暖将被永远记住。"这对我做一位好妻子和好母亲是多么宝贵的指导啊！过去父亲常常用那双有力的大手轻轻地抓住我的小手，如今我也牢记他的话语，抓紧孩子的手。

在一页页翻阅剪贴本的一个个瞬间里，我感受到灰暗的人生画布上铭刻了父亲给我的抚慰。就在父亲入土的这一天，他给了我们充满爱意的遗言。应该是上帝的安排，这样珍贵的惊奇体验在我悲痛的阴影上投射出胜利的灵光。我在这崭新的、充满力量的指路明灯的指引下得以继续前进。

夏洛特·阿德尔斯伯格

A Legacy in a Soup Pot

Have you ever noticed the busier your life seems to be,the more empty it appears to become?I remember staring at my date book early one Monday morning—scores of meetings,deadlines and projects leered back at me,assailing my senses and demanding my attention.I remember thinking for the umpteenth time,*What does all this really matter?*

And lately,with all this introspection,I had been remembering my beloved grandmother.Gram had a sixth-grade education,and abundance of kitchen-table wisdom and a wonderful sense of humor.Everyone who met her thought it was so appropriate that she had been born on April 1—the day of practical jokes,good laughs and hearty humor—and she certainly spent her lifetime buoying up everyone's spirits.

Cerebral she was not,but to a child,she was Disney World personified.Every activity with Gram became an event,an occasion to celebrate, a reason to laugh.Looking back,I realize it was a different time,a different sphere.Family,fun and food played an important role.

Meals were Gram's mainstay—occasions to be planned,savored and enjoyed.Hot,sit-down breakfasts were mandatory.The preparation of lunch began at 10:30 every morning,with homemade soup simmering, and dinner plans started at 3:30 P.M.,with a telephone call to the local butcher to make a delivery.Gram spent a lifetime meeting the most basic needs of her family.

Stopping to pick up yet another take-out meal for dinner,my mind traveled back to her kitchen.The old,oak kitchen table,with the single pedestal...the endless pots of soups,stews and gravies perpetually simmering on the stove top...the homey tablecloths stained with love from

双语精华版·心灵鸡汤·

218

汤罐里的遗产

不知你们注意到没有,好像生活越忙碌,日子就越来越空虚。记得先前一个星期一的早上,我盯着的记事本,上面写着一大堆会议安排、各项工作的截止日期,还有各种项目计划,都在不怀好意地看着我,烦扰我的思绪,抢占我的注意。我曾无数次地问自己,这些有什么要紧的?

经过一番反省,我不由得想起我亲爱的祖母。她只读到小学六年级,却有着丰富的厨艺智慧,极具幽默感。碰到她的人都说,她在4月1日出生实在是太合适了,因为愚人节这一天到处都是恶作剧、开心欢笑、真诚的幽默,不过祖母的确是一辈子都在鼓舞别人的士气。

她不是那种一本正经的人,对小孩来说,她就是迪斯尼乐园的化身。每次和祖母在一起都觉得是一次重大活动,一个值得庆祝的时刻,同样也是充满欢笑的一个理由。回首往事,我感到,那是一段完全不同的时光,一个完全不同的生活圈子。家庭、乐趣和美食占重要地位。

烧饭做菜是祖母生活的主要内容,包括了准备安排、品尝菜肴和享受美味。早餐是一定要坐下来趁热美美地吃一顿,午餐每天上午10点半开始准备,一定要亲自煨一罐美味浓汤,晚餐在下午3点半就要开始安排了,一定要给肉店打电话送来新鲜肉料。祖母一生都在努力满足家人最基本的饮食需要。

停下来照旧买了份外卖当晚餐,我的思绪又飘回了祖母的厨房。一张古老的橡木餐桌架在一个简单的底座上,炉上永远煨着无数罐鲜汤、炖肉和肉汁,每用完一餐,温馨的桌布都会沾上爱的印

a meal past.*My gosh*,I thought with a start.*I'm over forty,and I have yet to make a pot of soup or stew from scratch!*

Suddenly the cardboard take-out containers next to me looked almost obscene.I felt as if I had been blessed with a wonderful legacy,and for one reason or another,I had never quite gotten to the point of passing it on.

The following day,I rummaged through the attic searching for a cardboard box that had been stowed away.Twenty-five years ago,that box had been given to me when Gram decided to move from the old homestead.I vaguely remember going through my "inheritance" as a teen.Every granddaughter had received a pocketbook.Mine was a jeweled evening bag,circa 1920.I remembered I carried it at my college graduation.However,being a headstrong teen at the time of my "inheritance",I never really bothered with the rest of the contents.They remained sealed in that same box,buried somewhere in the attic.

It wasn't that difficult to locate the box,and it was even easier to open it.The tape was old and gave way easily.Lifting the top,I saw Gram had wrapped some items in old linen napkins—a butter dish,vase and at the bottom,one of her old soup pots.The lid was taped to the pot itself.I peeled back the tape and removed the lid.

At the bottom of the pot was a letter,penned in Gram's own hand:

> *My darling Barbara,*
>
> *I know you will find this one day many years from now.While you are reading this,please remember how much I loved you, for I'll be with the angels then, and I won't be able to tell you myself.*
>
> *You were always so headstrong,so quick,so much in a hurry to grow up.I often had wished that I could have kept you a baby forever.When you stop running,when it's time*

迹。天啊,我猛然一惊,都40多岁的人了,我还没从零开始学做过一罐浓汤或炖肉。

想到这,放在我旁边装外卖的纸板盒子,突然看起来几乎让人恶心。我感觉好像自己拥有一份令人羡慕的遗产,但因为这样或那样的原因,我却从来没想过要好好地发扬光大并继续传承下去。

第2天,我在阁楼上翻箱倒柜,寻找以前收起来的一只纸板箱。25年前,当祖母决定从以前的自耕农场搬离时,她给了我这只箱子。我依稀记得十几岁时,曾看过里面是传给我的什么宝贝。每一位孙女都收到一个手提包,我的是一个1920年左右饰有宝石的晚装包,我记得大学毕业典礼上我还带着它。但是,我当时还是一个倔强任性的少女,从没真正去看看剩下是些什么东西。它们至今还封存完好地放在这个箱子里,箱子也不知扔在阁楼的哪个拐角了。

找到箱子很不容易,但拆开却很轻松。密封胶带已经老化,很容易就撕下了。打开箱子,只见祖母用亚麻餐巾包着的几样东西:一个黄油碟,一个花瓶,最底下还有一只她的旧汤罐。汤罐的盖子被胶带封在罐上,我撕下胶带,打开了罐盖。

在罐底是祖母的一封亲笔信:

　　亲爱的芭芭拉:
　　我知道多年以后的某一天你将找到这封信的。当你读起这封信时,请记住我是多么爱你,因为到那时,我已经和天使们在一起了,没法亲口对你说了。
　　你一贯倔强任性,飞快地就匆忙长大了,而我经常希望你永远都是一个小女孩。当你停止飞奔时,当你该

for you to slow down,I want you to take out your Gram's old soup pot and make your house a home.I have enclosed the recipe for your favorite soup,the one I used to make for you when you were my baby.

Remember I love you,and love is forever.

Your Gram

I sat reading that note over and over that morning,sobbing that I had not appreciated her enough when I had her.*You were such a treasure,*I moaned inwardly.*Why didn't I even bother to look inside this pot while you were still alive!*

So that night,my briefcase remained locked,the answering machine continued to blink and the disasters of the outside world were put on hold.I had a pot of soup to make.

Barbara Davey

放慢脚步时,我想让你拿出我的旧汤罐,把你的房子变成一个真正的家。我给你附上了一个煨汤配方,这是你小时候我经常给你做的汤,也是你最爱喝的汤。

记得我爱你,永远爱你。

你的祖母

那天早上,我坐在那儿一遍遍地读着祖母的信,哭诉着她健在时我没有好好珍惜她。我内心在痛苦地呻吟,你对我是如此重要,而你还活着的时候,为什么我就没往汤罐里看一眼啊!

于是那天晚上,我把公文包扔在一边,任凭电话答录机①继续闪个不停,外面世界的一切灾难都暂停下来,我要好好地来煨一罐美味浓汤。

芭芭拉·戴维

女性系列／挥洒四季的芬芳

注释:

　①中国家庭并不常用电话答录机,但在北美家庭,几乎家家都用。外来电话拨入时,若该电话号码的主人不在,就会让拨入者听到一段留言,而后电话答录机就会不停闪烁来提示有未接电话。

The Odd-Shaped Vegetable

Don't sacrifice your life to work and ideals.The most important things in life are human relations.I found that out too late.

Katharine de Susannah Prichard,Australian author

The day had started as usual,busy and chaotic,and I was starting to feel exasperated when,for perhaps the hundredth time that morning,the voice over the intercom announced that I had a phone call.

"May I help you,"I asked in a hurried tone,thinking of all I still had to do.

"My mother works 3-D puzzles,"came the timid response. "Will you do a story on her?"

I hid my sigh behind a pause.I had been working for a community newspaper for about twelve years and found myself getting increasingly frustrated at what I referred to as the odd-shaped or large vegetable stories.A small town newspaper often has some unusual requests and,no matter how strange,each has to be handled diplomatically to avoid offending the paper's faithful readers.As I tried to form a tactful rejection, the woman continued.

"My mother has cancer,"was the introduction to her story.In between sobs,she explained that her terminally ill mother had started working 3-D puzzles and the new-found hobby had become her source of therapy.The daughter,feeling helpless as she watched her mother's battle,wanted her mother to feel special and hoped that a story might

"歪瓜瘪枣"

别因为埋头工作和追逐理想而忽略了生活。生活中最
重要的事情是与人交往。这一点我领悟得太迟了。

澳大利亚作家　凯瑟琳娜·德·苏珊娜·普利查德

这一天和往常一样，忙碌又混乱。对讲装置提醒我有电话。这差
不多是早上的第一百个了，我开始有些恼怒。

"有什么事？"我匆忙地问，满脑子里想的还是下面要做的事情。

"我母亲会玩三维拼图游戏，"电话那头一个腼腆的声音回答
道。"你们能为她写篇报道吗？"

我停顿了一下，克制住，没让自己叹气。我在一家社区报社干了
大约12年了，却对这类我称之为"歪瓜瘪枣"的题材越来越泄气。城
市里的小报社多半会接到些莫名其妙的请求。可是，再离谱的请求，
也得像对待外交事务一样谨慎处理，不能得罪了忠实的读者。我正
琢磨着怎样圆滑地拒绝，那位女士接着说：

"我母亲患上了癌症，"这是故事的开场白。她一边抽噎，一边解
释说她母亲已经处在癌症晚期，最近迷上了三维拼图游戏，就靠这
种新的爱好来减轻病痛。作为女儿，目睹着母亲与病魔的斗争，她感
到爱莫能助。她的愿望就是让母亲觉得自己了不起，于是想到报道

225

offer that to the dying woman.

She talked about her mother and by the time she finished,we were both sobbing.I could not even begin to imagine the pain she was experiencing as she watched her mother slipping away.Feeling sympathetic,I made an appointment to interview her mother.A few days later as I drove along the country road to the interview I tried to think about the questions and anticipate the answers,but I was filled with trepidation at meeting the dying woman.I dreaded the sadness that I knew awaited.I felt bound to do the story but struggled for an angle.All I really knew was that a woman was dying and she worked puzzles.To write of her impending death seemed much too intimate to intrude upon and the puzzle angle did not offer enough substance to capture the reader's attention.

Still pondering my dilemma,I arrived at my destination and was ushered in to meet the subject of the story.I'm not sure what I expected to find when the introductions were made,but it was not the woman who was presented to me.Mrs.Jones was not crying,nor did she show any signs of sorrow.Courteously she invited me to sit,offered me a cool drink and thanked me for coming.Then she told me there was not anything special about her life to warrant a newspaper story,but she consented to please her children.Even facing the most dramatic fight of her life,she wanted to make things easier for her family and consented to an intrusion into her last days and into the very private way in which she was coping with her disease.

Seated across from me with her husband and a grandchild close by, Mrs.Jones explained how she originally started working the puzzles because she needed something to keep her busy. Surprisingly she found that the hobby was therapeutic because the activity kept her mind occupied.Her life had always been busy and fulfilled as she reared her children,worked on the farm and dabbled in crafts.Her children were

也许可以帮她这个忙。

　　她讲述着母亲的故事。等她说完，我和她都已是泣不成声了。我不敢想象她眼睁睁地看着母亲即将离去内心会受到怎样的煎熬。出于同情，我和她约定了采访的日子。几天之后，我的车奔驰在乡间的路上。虽然我努力设计好要提的问题，也预计好了可能得到的答案，但是想到要会见的是一位即将离开人世的女人，我的心中充满惶恐。我害怕预料中迎接我的那份悲哀。这份报道我是一定会写的，但是从什么角度着手却令人煞费苦心。真正掌握的信息仅限于一位即将过世的女士，和她对拼图游戏的爱好这两点。要是从她不久就要离世的角度写，似乎过于冒犯了她的隐私，可是从拼图的角度来写又不能吸引读者。

　　还在犹疑不定当中，就已经到了目的地。进屋以后，我见到了故事的主人公。我不太记得主人在介绍我们认识时我心中有什么样的期待，但是我的采访对象和我期待的绝对不一样。琼斯太太没有流泪，也没有流露出悲伤的神情。她非常礼貌地请我坐下，给我端来一杯冷饮，感谢我的到来。然后她告诉我她的生活没有什么特别之处，不值得登报，但是为了满足孩子的愿望，她同意接受采访。即使是在生命危在旦夕的时刻，她也希望能够让家人活得轻松些，于是同意我闯进她最后的日子，探听她对付疾病的不为外人所知的方法。

　　琼斯太太坐在我对面，旁边是她的丈夫，和一个孙儿。琼斯太太告诉我，她玩拼图游戏的初衷是不让自己闲着，却意外地发现这种爱好让她大脑忙碌起来，反而有利于病情。以前生活总是在忙碌中充实地度过，带带孩子，干干农活，做做针线。现在孩子长大成人，屋

grown and the echoes of laughter that now filled the house were from the grandchildren she cherished.Her time was no longer spent knitting, sewing or cooking,so those hours were filled with the puzzles.She said there was nothing extraordinary about her or the puzzles she put toge- ther.Speaking in a voice void of selfpity,she said the hobby helped take her mind off the daily pain and her constant battle.By sharing her story, she hoped she might help others as they fought similar battles.Mrs.Jones explained that the puzzles allowed her to find peace at times when her thoughts might otherwise have been hard to bear,and gave her the ability to be strong to fight that daily battle with fear,doubt and weakness.

She didn't cry as she talked about her tragedy.Even though she knew that death was lingering closely in the shadows,she did not appear sorrowful or regretful.She spoke of her family and the joy they gave her. She beamed at a young granddaughter who wanted to brag on her grandmother's puzzle accomplishments.As she smiled at the child whom she would never see grow into a young woman,I saw the simplicity of life.This dying woman had never won a Pulitzer prize,nor flown to the moon.She had not touched the lives of multitudes,nor even saved the life of one.However,this quiet,dignified woman smiled contentedly as she talked about the love that had been bestowed upon her and did not lament the years she would never see.Even with limited time,her con- cern was to somehow help make the trip easier for her loved ones and for others who might travel the same road.

Several hours later as I climbed into my car my tears broke loose. During the drive to my office I thought of this woman I would never meet again and her story.The story became a labor of love as I tried to convey the message she wanted to send,while capturing in words her unselfish beauty.A few weeks later,Mrs.Jones's daughter stopped by my office to tell me her mother had passed away.She said the family would always treasure the story and,like her mother,they hoped that those last

里荡漾的是心爱的孙子孙女们的欢声笑语。因为不再需要编织、缝纫和烹饪了,时间就全都用在了拼图游戏上。她说她没有什么特别的,拼成的拼图也没有什么特别的。这个爱好使她忘却了每天常伴左右的疼痛,忘记了与疾病一刻不停的斗争。她说话的时候没有一点自怜的语气。她希望通过说出自己的故事,帮助与她一样在与病魔抗争的人。她说拼图游戏能够使她找到平静的感觉,使她抛开那些有可能压垮她的念头,使她能够坚强起来,战胜每天的恐惧、疑虑和软弱。

说起自己的不幸时,她没有哭。尽管清楚死亡已经在阴影里徘徊,她却没有显露出痛楚或者遗憾,相反她说起家庭以及家庭给她带来的快乐。年幼的小孙女想吹嘘一下祖母的拼图成就,就冲她笑了笑。她也许再也无法看到小女孩长成大姑娘的过程,可是我却从她的微笑里看到了生命的简单。这位将不久于人世的女士从来没有获得过普利策奖,没有登上过月球,没有对众多生灵的影响力,甚至未曾挽救过一条生命。可是她那么平静,庄重,知足。她微笑着谈起她享受到的爱,并不为无法亲历的岁月而悲哀。纵然已经来到生命的尽头,她在意的依然是深爱的家人,希望他们在她离去的路上不要太难过,也希望后来者走得轻松些。

几个小时以后,我回到车上,眼泪再也抑制不住地流淌下来。驾车回办公室的路上,我回想着这位我可能永远不能再谋面的女士,构思着关于她的故事。我心甘情愿为她写这份报道,替她传递她想传递的信息,用文字来捕捉她那无私的美丽。几个星期以后,琼斯太太的女儿路过我的办公室,告诉我她母亲已经离世了。她说,他们全家会永远珍视这份报道。他们与母亲有共同的愿望,希望母亲在生

words would help others with their battles with cancer or other terminal illnesses.I may never know if the story touched the life of a reader or helped another deal with impending death,but my life was changed forever.The tears that fell then were not for Mrs.Jones or her loved ones, but for me.I realized that God blessed me by bringing that dying woman into my life for a few hours.Not only did I realize my many blessings, but also her courageous selflessness and humility helped me understand the little things that are important during life's journey.

    I still work for a small community newspaper.Though I am now the news editor,I still write many of the stories each week and,almost daily, get calls about odd-shaped vegetables. Sometimes I feel the frustration building,but then I remember that if you listen with your heart,sometimes odd-shaped vegetables are inspirations in disguise.Mrs.Jones taught me to listen more closely so not to miss the stories that make differences on this road called life.

Rosalind Turner

命尽头的话语能够帮助癌症或者其它晚期重症患者更好地与疾病搏斗。这份报道能否影响到读者，能否影响到他们的生活，或者帮助他们勇敢地直面死亡，我也许永远无法得知，但是我的生活被永远地改变了。泪水不是为琼斯太太和她所爱的人而流，而是为我自己而流。我明白了，是上帝赐福与我，让我与这位女士相处了几个小时，让我重新审视我收获到的幸福。不仅如此，她的勇敢、无私和谦逊使我明白了人生道路上看似微乎其微，其实意义重大的事情。

　　至今我还在社区小报社工作。我已经是新闻编辑了，但是每周还是要撰写很多报道。几乎每一天，都会有人打电话，送来一些"歪瓜瘪枣"。每当沮丧感在积聚的时候，我就会想，只要你用心倾听，"歪瓜瘪枣"说不定是真正灵感的来源。琼斯太太教会我，更加细心地倾听，才能不错过那些影响我们人生道路的故事。

罗莎琳德·特纳

张洁　译